Readers love the B
by Don

The Zozobra Incident

"There are many likable secondary characters who play significant roles in the story. Combine that with the setting, beautifully detailed writing and a solid mystery makes this novel a must read for any mystery lover."

—Gay Book Reviews

The Bisti Business

"All the essential elements that made the first story so engrossing are there, with a fresh new mystery and more interesting characters."

—Michael Joseph Book Reviews

The City of Rocks

"Hands down, this is my favorite mystery series in a long time. Five stars!"

—The Novel Approach

The Lovely Pines

"There were no questions left unanswered, and by the end, I was hungry to read more of the BJ Vinson Mysteries."

—Love Bytes

Abaddon's Locusts

"*Abaddon's Locusts* is another smartly written installment in the BJ Vinson Mysteries. From the start the tension is thick and keeps the reader on edge…."

—QueeRomance Ink

By DON TRAVIS

BJ VINSON MYSTERIES
The Zozobra Incident
The Bisti Business
The City of Rocks
The Lovely Pines
Abaddon's Locusts
The Voxlightner Scandal

Published by DSP PUBLICATIONS
www.dsppublications.com

THE
CUTIE-PIE
MURDERS

DON TRAVIS

DSP PUBLICATIONS

Published by

DSP Publications

5032 Capital Circle SW, Suite 2, PMB# 279, Tallahassee, FL 32305-7886 USA
www.dsppublications.com

The Cutie-Pie Murders
© 2021 Don Travis

Cover Art
© 2021 Stef Kloibhofer
www.stefkloibhofer.com
Cover content is for illustrative purposes only and any person depicted on the cover is a model.

Trade Paperback ISBN: 978-1-64405-901-2
Digital ISBN: 978-1-64405-900-5
Trade Paperback published April 2021
First Edition
v. 1.0

Acknowledgments

MY THANKS to the people at the Albuquerque Police Department Criminalistics unit and to Eric Harrison, Public Information Officer, New Mexico Corrections Department, for their assistance getting the details right.

Prologue

Albuquerque, New Mexico, Monday, March 5, 2012

THE CURLY-HAIRED young man strode up Central, east of the university, slipping gracefully past fellow students, merchants, housewives, and giggling children. Intent on the coming assignation, he was oblivious to the admiring looks thrown his way. Had he noticed, he'd have ignored them. After eighteen years of being first cuddly cute and then staggeringly handsome, conspicuous attention failed to elicit a response from him. Not even the rumble of heavy traffic on Route 66—now reduced to an aging, neon-speckled Albuquerque city street—penetrated his awareness. Nor was he distracted by the tempting aromas wafting from a hot-dog joint a few doors away or the more pungent odor of a passing homeless man, the sole of his left shoe flapping in imitation of a muffled duck.

The recollection of what this venture had cost him triggered a misstep, but you only live once, and besides, he hoped to salvage that relationship without giving up his dream. A sudden image of his mother and father jarred him again. How would they look upon this venture? Cray, of course, but cripes, he was in pursuit of a *goal*. The script from rendezvous like this would finance the career he was born to pursue. One day soon a client would recognize his potential. Then he'd walk the runways—the big-time runways—turning heads, setting trends, and making the big bucks. He knew it. The bones of his body, the fibers of his being, incessantly crooned that lullaby.

The address he sought appeared to be one of the new apartments in the next block. Cool. Fancy digs meant easy money. He was new to the business, but he'd already learned a few things, and that was one of them. Prime start for an almost-spring Monday.

He dashed across the side street against the light and halted before a set of big double doors. After scanning the communications panel—and with a heart playing pitter-patter—he reached out a tremulous forefinger to push the proper red button. After a moment, a pleasant baritone reverberated through the speaker.

"Yes?"

He moistened dry lips and put some life into his speech. "Hi, this is your—"

"Fourth floor. Door's open. I'm getting in the shower but won't be a minute. Go down the hall to the bedroom on your right and make yourself comfortable."

Excited by the timbre of the voice, he couldn't resist. "How comfortable?"

"Surprise me."

Galvanized by the sound of a buzzer, he hastily pushed through the heavy doors into a vacant lobby, removed his aviator shades, and called up the elevator. His date was a man. He'd been left guessing because the message was simply signed "Anxious." This was only his third engagement of a personal sort since starting this new vocation. The first had been an attractive woman a bit older than he liked. Nonetheless, he'd played his part well enough to earn an encore in the near future.

The second was a good-looking middle-aged man who'd kept himself fit. In a critical review of the two trysts, he judged the second more enjoyable than the first. The man had begged for more and more, until there was no more to give. In all honesty, the second date had been less… heavy.

Now another man. And wow! If the dude matched the baritone on the intercom, it was full speed ahead.

As promised, the door to 4201 stood slightly ajar. He eased into the apartment and looked around. Nice! Black diamond floor tiles in the vestibule. A heavy mirror in a gilded frame hanging to the left of the door allowed him a quick inventory of himself. He approved of what he saw… a young man in his prime who belonged in a place like this. He pushed a wayward chocolate-brown curl into place and turned to examine the ritzy apartment.

How long before he'd be able to afford a place like this to moss around in? Probably about a bazillion years. He paused to take in a pleasant blend of bentwood contemporary couches and antiqued ball-and-claw-foot chairs, all lent a touch of elegance by ornate occasional tables and french ormolu lamps. His mind's eye saw friends sitting around sipping wine or guzzling beer and engaging in intelligent conversation as they looked down on the busy street. He smiled to himself as he imagined repairing a fractured relationship by nuzzling on the long sofa.

The only sour note to the *Better Homes and Gardens* atmosphere was the corner of what looked like a big canvas laundry cart visible in the kitchen area. Maybe his host was planning on messing up the sheets big-time. Go for it, dude!

The faint sensual scent of lavender teased his nostrils as he turned right and headed for the big bedroom at the end of the hall. From somewhere he heard a shower shut off. How much time did he have before the man with the voice showed? He closed the blond-oak bedroom door, wanting his client to open it and get a sudden, stunning glimpse of what he was buying.

Standing beside the king-size Tuscan bed, he ran a hand over the satiny yellow-and-cinnamon spread… or was this a duvet? Whatever, it felt dope against his fingertips. He eased off his loafers while debating over how comfortable to get. He'd heard some clients liked to undress their merchandise, but maybe he should go all the way and display what he had to offer. And without being smug about it, that was considerable.

He shrugged out of his windbreaker and tugged a polo shirt over his head, careful not to muss his shock of dark hair.

After hesitating briefly, he slipped out of his cargo shorts and lay back on the bed. A second later, he kicked off faux–leopard-skin briefs and lay naked except for socks. After plumping a pillow, he scanned his hairless torso to admire pecs and abs. How would he look to the guy about to come through the door any minute now? He nodded to himself. Probably hella bad. Everybody said he wore a pretty, girlish face on a toned man's body.

When the door opened, he threw up his hands and shouted, "Surprise!" The first sight of his date sent shivers down his back.

The man with the beautiful voice moved bedside, balancing two glasses of white wine in his hands. "Well, well, aren't you a cutie."

Chapter 1

New Mexico State Penitentiary, Santa Fe, Thursday, March 8, 2012

"B. J. VINSON, you're an idiot!" I told myself for the umpteenth time. Why in the hell was I about to drive up to the state penitentiary to see an inmate I remembered well and detested vehemently?

Why did José Zapata want to see me? The lawyer who called last week to make the arrangements claimed not to know, said he was merely passing on a request. Not sure I bought his answer. In order to gain access to a Level VI prisoner, I either had to be on Zapata's visitor list or work for his attorney, neither of which was true.

Zapata—better known by the tag of Zancón because of his long legs and lanky frame—had been the underboss of a vicious gang called the *Santos Morenos,* or Brown Saints. He'd played a prominent role in the case file I'd labeled the Zozobra Incident. José Zapata had kidnapped the human being I treasured most on this earth, my life companion, Paul Barton, and attempted to murder him before I literally dropped from the heavens to put a bullet in Zapata's gut.

Committed now, I sighed aloud and put the car in gear. When traveling from Albuquerque to Santa Fe, I normally drive straight up Interstate 25 for a pleasant trip of something under an hour, but the prison lay fourteen miles south of the state capital on the Madrid highway—better known as the Turquoise Trail—so I pointed my Impala's nose east on I-40 through Tijeras Canyon and picked up State 14 North. Two lanes instead of four; a twisting drive rather than one as straight as the proverbial arrow, but also more interesting.

For the first leg of the trip, I turned on the car's stereo to catch Kelly Clarkson warbling "Stronger"—or what I knew as "What Doesn't Kill You"—and a newscast dominated by speculation about whether oil restrictions would end Iran's nuclear weapons program. Wary of icy stretches of mountain road where the sun didn't reach—something unforeseen—I snapped off the radio to concentrate on driving.

I manfully resisted stopping in Madrid, a former coal-mining town now turned artist's enclave. Shortly thereafter I had to quell a desire to take a turn around the tiny square of yet another old western town called Cerrillos before eventually pulling into the visitor's parking area at the penitentiary.

Upon successfully maneuvering through the prison's metal detector, a piece of equipment no self-respecting airport would accept as adequate security, I addressed a corrections officer. "B. J. Vinson for Inmate José Zapata, Number 79805. His attorney arranged my appointment."

Although this was the new state penitentiary, iron bars threw the same ragged shadows as in the old one, as if emphasizing the blackness hiding in every man's soul, be he inmate or custodian. I mentally shook my head to clear photographic images of the riot at "Old Main" on Cerrillos Road I'd been required to study at the Albuquerque Police Academy.

Thirty-three inmates died and two hundred suffered injuries in February 1980 in the worst prison insurrection in US history. Endless streams of scholarly studies and airy articles and outright fiction vied to describe in minute detail the overcrowding, poor food, official incompetence, and lack of training that birthed the uprising. I'd gone to school with a kid whose father died in the bloodbath. The family subsequently moved out of town because of harassment. People can be real shits… even grade schoolers.

The officer I'd addressed scanned a list of names on a clipboard while metal doors clanged in the distance and voices echoed up and down the hallway. A prison was never silent.

The man made a check mark on a list he was holding before responding. "Yessir, I'll have him brought up." He nodded to a man standing nearby. "This officer will take you to the interview room."

I told him this wasn't my first time at bat before taking another look at the man's ID. "Simmons. Weren't you with APD a few years back?" I referred to the Albuquerque Police Department where I'd served for ten years.

"Yessir, it's Detective B. J. Vinson, isn't it?"

"Not since 2005."

The man loosened up a little. "I remember you getting plugged when you and the commander were apprehending a murder suspect."

"Gene Enriquez was a lowly detective just like me back then. And now you know why he's in charge of the Criminal Investigative Division and I'm not."

Simmons laughed. "Yeah, he let you take the bullet instead of him."

"Thanks for reminding me."

My escort, a young corrections officer named Pierce, took off down the hall, pulling me along in his wake. The absolute absence of odor in the stark hallway tempted me to believe the institution was pristine and sanitized... but I knew better. In the bowels of this concrete and metal beast, the intestines would stink. We reached the interview room a few minutes before Zapata.

When the inmate arrived in restraints and with his own escort, as was required for Level VI prisoners, I struggled to tamp down a surge of sudden anger. Not only had he manhandled Paul, his gang had killed a young man named Emilio Prada by hacking him to death in Santa Fe's Fort Marcy Park while thousands of people gathered there for the annual Burning of Zozobra ritual. Emilio had been a hustler, but he didn't deserve to die.

Now Zapata looked more like a sick old man than the fortysomething-year-old thug I knew him to be. My bullet apparently hadn't digested well. In the place of healthy—if malignant—swagger, I now detected decay.

After Zapata was seated, his guard checked his handcuffs, leg shackles, and belly chain to assure himself the prisoner was properly restrained. Then he and Pierce took up stations on the other side of the interview room door.

Zapata didn't wait for them to exit before speaking. "Vinson," he said in a gravelly voice—stronger than expected, given his appearance.

I settled into a chair on the other side of a bolted-down metal table and addressed him by his nickname out of habit. "Zancón."

"Thanks for coming."

"Surprised to get a call. Even more surprised it came from Brookings Ingles. Didn't know you went for the most expensive defense attorney in the state." Brookie was long rumored to be a mob lawyer.

Zancón waved a cuffed hand. "He wasn't my trial mouthpiece. I was a cooked goose then. But now he takes care of things a man can't take care of hisself. You know, when he's locked up like this." His black eyes looked filmed over with something: exhaustion, disease, hopelessness? "I got a brother with some coins, and he helps me out with the lawyer's bills."

I took that statement to mean Zancón had managed to hide some of his loot. The brother was merely managing the inmate's assets.

"I got a problem. At least my brother Juan has. But I figure you owe me, so I'm the dude putting the question to you."

"If you're referring to the slug I put in your gut, I owe you nothing. But if your brother has a legitimate problem, I'll listen to what he has to say."

Zancón flushed, showing a trace of the hood he was, before he relaxed and spread his hands over the table as far as his restraints would allow. "Fair enough. Everbody was shooting at everbody that night you'n the cops ambushed us, but I'm the one who can't eat or take a crap like everbody else because of the lead poisoning you give me."

"Now that's out of the way, what's your brother's problem?"

"Some son of a bitch offed his boy. And I want him to pay."

I leaned back in the hard chair. "A gang killing?"

He shook his head. "Naw. Kid wasn't into gangs. My bro ain't either. Stayed righteous while I was outlawing. He's got a car lot offa South Coors."

"So what happened?"

Zancón looked uncomfortable. "Juan'll give you the details. He's waiting for your call."

My antenna went up. "Look, if you're not straight with me, then I can't—"

"I'm telling it like it is. No gang stuff. Mateo wasn't in no gang."

"Mateo. He's your nephew?"

He nodded and seemed suddenly tired. The prematurely old man was ascendant now, but the gutter snipe was still in residence. "Yeah. Mostly went by Matt."

"How old was he?"

"Eighteen. Wasn't but eighteen."

"Give me some details." The warning look returned. "Okay, at least tell me where he was killed."

"Albuquerque."

It was my turn to spread hands over the table. "Hell, you don't need me. ADP will take care of it."

Zancón gave a sour smile. "Yeah, right. They'll see what you seen. Another gang member offed. Good riddance."

"That's not the way things work, and you know it. They'll give it their best shot."

He leaned forward and tapped the table with a long fingernail, determination back in his eyes again. "Maybe so. But I know you, Vinson. You're a damned good detective. And I want you to finish him." He dropped his voice. "You know, like with Puerco." He referred to the Saints' top man, whom I'd shot to death the night I wounded Zancón.

Now it was clear why this hood wanted me on the case. He wasn't interested in APD finding the killer. He was offering to hire me to settle with the murderer. Why did these guys always judge others by their own lights?

Zancón studied my face and must have assumed he was losing me. "Talk to my brother." He held my gaze for a long moment before dropping his eyes. "Please."

"All right. Do I work through Ingles?"

"Naw. All I wanted the lawyer for was to get you in to see me. Work with my brother. Juan's a straight-up guy."

From what he'd told me, Juan Zapata was a used car dealer, and I wasn't sure the two things held together. But maybe I painted with too broad a brush. We'd let time determine that factor.

"Do you know who killed your nephew?"

"Naw. One day he was doing good at the university, you know, UNM, and then the next he was dead."

"Okay. How do I contact your brother?"

Zancón lurched to his feet and cited a telephone number before shuffling to the door and tapping it with his knuckles.

The same clank of metal, the same hollow, echoing voices, the same ghosts from Old Main followed me all the way out of the prison. I took the quick way back to Albuquerque—Interstate 25.

"WHY WOULD you give that creep the time of day?" Paul asked later when I told him of my meeting. "Forget about him nearly shooting me, I damned near choked to death on the gag he stuffed down my craw."

When I'd found Paul that night almost six years ago, he'd been trussed up with a rag in his throat held in place by a handkerchief over his mouth. I grinned at the handsome hunk glaring at me with hands on hips, stance wide. "Maybe Zancón is right. Maybe I do owe him."

Paul's mouth fell open, and he dropped into an easy chair in our den. "Huh?"

I reached out and tousled his dark brown hair. He batted my hand away. "If he hadn't kidnapped you, I couldn't have ridden in on my white horse and saved you, earning your everlasting love and gratitude."

"Ha! Ha! I was scared, Vince." Paul calls me Vince. Most of the rest of the known world addresses me as BJ.

"As I recall, you were spitting mad."

"That too. But why do Zancón a favor?"

"Not a favor. A job. Remember, there's an eighteen-year-old kid lying on a slab somewhere. I don't like killers, particularly those who kill youngsters before they've had a chance to try their wings. Believe me, I've seen more than my share of adolescent corpses."

My lover gave me an uncertain smile. "Can't cure the world, Vince."

"No, but maybe I can catch whoever did this one killing. See he doesn't do it again. Regardless who pays for my time, it's Mateo Zapata I'm doing it for... providing I take the case."

"Mateo, huh? I remember him as a little guy." Paul was a South Valley kid who'd avoided joining a gang and, like most of the neighborhood, grew up to be a decent, law-abiding citizen. "Matt was nine or ten years younger than I was. Cute kid. Smart."

"How about his father? Did you know him?"

Paul brushed a stray lock from his brow. "Juan? I remember him as a solid citizen. He's about ten years on the other side of me."

"Was he close to his brother? To Zancón?"

"Yeah." He thought over his answer. "In some ways. Always got the feeling he stayed away from the Brown Saints. Skirted the gang stuff as much as he could."

"And now he's a used car dealer."

"Last I heard. Who knows? Maybe he got his start peddling cars the Brown Saints stole."

Chapter 2

HAZEL HARRIS Weeks stuck her head through the door of my downtown private office. "Fellow here by the name of Juan Zapata. Says he has an appointment." My office manager's voice held a note of censure. One more thing I'd neglected to tell her.

I swung my feet off the corner of the desk and sat up straight. "Called him on the way back from Santa Fe yesterday."

Hazel frowned. "Any relation to Zancón Zapata?" Hazel had taught alongside my parents in the Albuquerque public school system and had been my mom's best friend. When I lost my parents to a car wreck, she'd appropriated the job of surrogate mother. Fortunately, her late-life marriage to my business partner Charlie Weeks eased that burden. Even though Hazel didn't totally understand my "lifestyle," she'd grown as protective of Paul as she was of me, and she knew every detail of what the Saints had done to him.

"Somebody killed Juan Zapata's boy. He's entitled to the same respect as any other paying customer." The word *paying* would get to her faster than any other explanation. She nodded and disappeared.

A moment later, she ushered a younger, healthier version of Zancón into my inner office. The man's overcoat was damp from scattered snowflakes falling outside. Thank goodness my trip to Santa Fe had happened yesterday. Today's snowfall didn't amount to much in the city, but if it was flurrying here, it was likely heavier in the mountains. I stood and gripped the man's outstretched hand.

"I'm Juan Zapata. I understand my brother filled you in on my problem yesterday."

"B. J. Vinson. Everyone calls me BJ. Zancón told me about your son's death but gave me no details. Said you'd explain it."

Juan flushed and took the seat I indicated. "Sounds like something he'd do. My son was gay, Mr.... uh, BJ. And that's something Zancón can't deal with."

"Why don't you fill me in?"

The man on the other side of my desk blew through his nostrils in exasperation. "I don't know a hell of a lot. I misspoke saying Matt was gay. He was probably bisexual. He's had a couple of girlfriends over the years, but I suspect he's had a few boyfriends as well."

Score another one for Zancón. He not only wanted me to kill his gay nephew's murderer, but he'd come to a gay investigator with the request. Probably figured it took one to know one. Some things never change.

"Let's start with the basics," I said. "Tell me about Mateo. I understand he was eighteen. Was he still in school? Live at home? Have his own place? Show me the young man before you tell me about his murder."

Juan took me literally, dragging out his billfold and handing over a snapshot. The kid almost took my breath away. Beautiful eyes the color of rich humus. Curly hair so dark it was barely short of black. Thin nose, broad sensual lips. This guy was movie-star handsome, with enough irregularity to his features to render him sexy.

Juan sighed before starting down the road of his son's short life. "Mateo... Matt... finished high school last year, a year ahead of most of his classmates, and enrolled at the University of New Mexico. He wanted to be a commercial photographer. But I think that was just so he understood the camera. His real ambition was to be a professional model."

"He had the looks for it. Did he live on campus?"

Juan shook his head. "Had a small one-bedroom apartment on Princeton. Half a block south of Central. Easy walk to his classes."

I learned a lot about Matt Zapata while his father worked around to something obviously difficult to face, the thing Zancón hadn't wanted to discuss yesterday. Matt was a swimmer. A tennis player. A whiz at poker. Popular with girls and guys alike. Played a mean guitar and had a decent singing voice. Finally Juan hesitated. He'd arrived at his destination.

"Although I provided for his needs, Matt was always independent. He'd recently taken a job. I discouraged the idea, saying he ought to enjoy these college years, but he wouldn't listen."

He was dragging his feet again, so I cut straight to the chase. "What kind of job?"

Juan averted his eyes. "He never actually told me, but from what I can gather, he was an escort. He... ah, he was an amazing kid. He fit in any social circle you could imagine. And when he dressed up in a suit or tux, he was really something."

"Who did he work for?"

Juan tapped the arm of his chair, a nervous gesture. "Best I can figure, he was freelance. He booked his calls through a phone service. He was new to it. Only had a few assignments before... before...."

"Did he die on one of those assignments?"

Juan Zapata dropped his head to his chest. "I don't know. He... he was found on the West Mesa."

He swallowed hard, but I could see he had more to say. "And?"

"My son was naked. At least that's what they tell me. And...."

I spared him the agony of continuing. "Let me get a copy of the police report and talk to a couple of people, then we'll discuss this again."

"So you'll take the case?"

"At the moment, I don't see why not. Is there a question in your mind about it?"

He lifted anguished eyes. "My brother is someone you shot and put behind bars. My son might have been a call boy. So—"

"Mr. Zapata—Juan—was Matt a good man?"

"To me he was."

"And his life was taken from him. Tell me, are you looking for justice for your son or revenge?"

A startled look passed over his face before understanding dawned. "I am seeking justice, BJ. Find the bastard who killed Matt and get him tried, convicted, and locked up for the rest of his life."

I thought for a moment. "Locked up in Santa Fe where Zancón is waiting."

"Send him somewhere else. I don't care. Just so he can't slaughter someone else's son."

"The police can do that for you."

Juan dry-washed his face. "Zancón and I agree on one thing. The cops will take one look and consider it simply as some gang killing a queer. I want someone fighting for me. For Matt."

"I need to clear this with a couple of people first, but who your brother is and what you think your son might have been will have nothing to do with my answer. I should be able to call you by Monday afternoon."

"You haven't mentioned your fees. Please rest assured I'm willing to meet them. And the funds will be mine, not Zancón's." He reached in his shirt pocket and pulled out a folded piece of paper. "I've taken the liberty of writing a retainer check. Please let me know if it's adequate."

I glanced at the amount. "This will do just fine."

After he took his leave, I talked to the two people who had to be consulted, Charlie and Hazel Weeks, the retired cop who happened to be my partner in Vinson and Weeks, Confidential

Investigations, and my office manager. They expressed no reservations about the case. Hazel even smiled when I laid the retainer in front of her.

THAT AFTERNOON I sat across the desk from Don Carson at APD headquarters. Gene Enriquez, my old riding partner, would have been my preference, but Lieutenant Carson might resent my going over his head since Gene was now head of the department. When my buddy made commander and took over the Criminal Investigative Division, he named Don to fill his old position.

Don cocked an eye at me and rubbed his nose. "Let me understand this. The guy you shot and put in prison for the rest of his life reached out and asked you for a favor. Didn't he think the APD would take his nephew's murder seriously enough?"

Don had been around long enough to figure things out for himself, so I kept my mouth shut and allowed him to do just that.

He nodded. "My guess is he wanted to hire himself a hitman."

"My conclusion as well. Plus, he thought you guys would look at the murder as a gang killing and stop trying so hard. His opinion, not mine," I added when Don gave me a hard look.

"So why are you here?"

"I never take on an active APD case without clearing it with you guys first. You oughta know that."

Don sighed and leaned back in his chair. "Yeah, I know."

"So do you have a problem with me poking into the killing?"

"Not unless the OIC objects."

I knew OIC to be officer-in-charge. "Who is it?"

"Friend of yours. Detective Roy Guerra… and his partner, Detective Glenann Hastings."

"I see you got smart and made Glenann a detective. Great. You mind if I talk to them?"

"No problem."

"Do you know the Mateo Zapata case, Don?"

"Know about it. Too early to get much feedback. All I can tell you is the kid was found naked on the West Mesa, Albuquerque's favorite body dump. I take it he was strangled and spread out in all his glory on a broken-down old sofa somebody abandoned." He speared me with his eyes. "Fair warning, he wasn't the first."

"What do you mean?"

"The detectives can fill you in, but I gather the kid was covered in dried semen."

"His own or someone else's?"

"Have to ask Guerra."

A cue if I'd ever heard one. It seemed like a good time to go in search of the detectives, so I said my goodbyes and left Don's office.

DETECTIVE ROY Guerra still looked like the South Valley boy he was. Last year, as a brand-new detective, he'd gladly accepted Paul's and my help in what I called the Voxlightner Scandal case. In all candor, I don't believe he would have solved the case on his own, but he'd learned a lot and was now seasoned by a year. Word around the station was he'd turned into a capable investigator. When he heard what I wanted, he readily agreed, had second thoughts, and called over his partner, Glenann Hastings. I'd met her a year before I ran into Guerra when then-Officer Hastings helped on the Abaddon's Locusts case. She was still the pretty, sassy cop I remembered.

"Congrats," I said when she ignored my hand and gave me a hug. "*Detective* sits well on you."

She beamed and pointed to Guerra. "Thanks, but it means I have to put up with this guy. The shield's worth it, I guess. What gives?"

I related the details leading to my interest in the Mateo Zapata killing, and both agreed to work with me... within limits.

"Mateo Zapata isn't the first pretty-boy killing we've had," Glenann volunteered, explaining Don Carson's enigmatic comment. "He's the third in the last year. We've had some rumblings Zapata was a call boy."

"If he was a call boy," Roy cautioned, "he was new to it. According to the medical examiner there were signs of sexual penetration, but it wasn't recent and didn't appear to be habitual. And he hadn't shown up on our radar screen yet."

"Who were the other two victims?"

Roy searched the corner of his desk and pulled out a couple of files. "The first was an eighteen-year-old street kid named Dustin Greene, also found on the West Mesa naked. That was on September 5 of last year. Medical examiner figures he died twenty-four to forty-eight hours earlier."

"What day was he found?" I asked.

"Let's see." Roy flipped through the file. "Monday. Miracle he laid there through the weekend without being spotted."

"Cause of death?"

"There was some animal damage, but the doc determined it was death by strangulation."

"Manual?"

Roy nodded. "Probably by somebody's hands."

"Drugs?" I asked.

"According to the Office of the Medical Investigator, an olio. Not surprising. He was a street kid."

"Signs of a struggle?"

"OMI says some bruising. Nothing serious. And there was no evidence of recent penetration. But there was dried semen on the kid."

"His or the killer's?"

"Hard to say. It had deteriorated some. But the medic figures it came from both."

"So you have DNA," I said.

He shrugged. "No sperm in the semen. Maybe the killer had a vasectomy or an injury."

"So no DNA, huh?"

"Victim's, yes. Perp's, no. But we'll get some. The crime scene boys found a stray hair or two. Don't know yet if they're Greene's or the killer's."

"You have a picture of the victim?"

"Living and dead. As I said, he was in our system. Petty stuff. Street fights, theft, that kind of thing."

Even in a mug shot at age seventeen, the kid looked good. Dark blond locks, blue eyes. But he appeared to be husky enough to take care of himself. His death photo, presumably little more than a year later, was harder to take. As Roy had said, predators had worked on the kid some. The photo revealed how street life had hardened him. Even so he was still good-looking.

Glenann handed me a second folio. "Meet Charles Hubbard…. Chuck to his friends. Found off Highway 14 on December first of 2011. Also naked even though it was winter. Also strangled."

"By hand?"

She nodded.

The photo showed a good-looking Black kid. "Our perp's an equal opportunity killer. Highway 14 is in the county. They give it to you?"

"Seems like a related case, so it's ours," Glenann said. "There's also semen on this one. His own and someone else's. Still no DNA."

"Semen in the body cavity?"

She shook her head. "External. Copious amounts. Mostly in groin and stomach areas. Ejaculation took place on the victims, not in them. Apparently the killer isn't into anal sex."

"Saliva?" I asked.

"No. It wasn't oral."

"So the killer did it the little boy way. Not what you usually find in sex cases. Drugs?"

"Zopiclone."

"A sleeping pill?"

"Several sleeping pills. It's quick, and it's hypnotic. Apparently it worked well."

"Ingested?"

"In beer."

The victim's photo, likely a family snapshot, showed a cute, apparently healthy young man with short dark hair and black eyes smiling out at the world without a clue of what lay in his future.

"He in the system?"

Glenann shook her head. "Clean. On holiday break from classes at UNM."

"So two of the vics were UNM students. How about Greene?"

"High school dropout."

I scratched my head. "Still, a street guy his age might hang out at the U. That would give us a connection."

"Could be, but no evidence of it. Also no evidence the two college boys knew one another. But it's something to look at," Roy said.

"Now tell me about Mateo Zapata."

"The first two were good-looking, but Zapata's the real cutie of the trio," Glenann said. "You already know the circumstances of his death. Again, no penetration but plenty of semen. Zapata's and the unknown donor's."

"Let me guess, the anonymous donor matches the semen on Hubbard and Greene."

"You got it. It ties the three cases together. Three killings by one sicko." She indicated the photos of the three victims lying on Roy's desk. "We're calling them the cutie-pie killings."

I rolled my eyes. "Wait until the press gets ahold of that."

"They already have," Glenann said. "If there's another killing, that'll be the headline."

"Any reason to believe all three victims were call boys?"

Roy sighed. "Greene was on the streets, so he probably sold himself now and then. Hubbard was living at home while at the university. His folks can pretty well account for his time, so I'd say no. He was visiting a college friend in Edgewood and was headed back home when his car broke down in Tijeras Pass. Instead of using his cell to call home for help, he must have hitched."

"And accepted a ride from the wrong person."

"Right," Roy said. "As for Mateo Zapata, reason says he wasn't a call boy. The family has plenty of money, and they weren't stingy with the boy. But reason's not always right. My folks knew his folks. Hell, I know them. Even knew Matt to say hello to. Good kid. Didn't take after his Uncle Zancón."

"But…?" I said into his sudden silence.

"But Matt was an independent cuss. He wanted to do things on his own, not ride his dad's coattails. And he was in a hurry."

"And," Glenann put in, "he was sexy as hell. Played both sides of the street. The guy was made for the business."

I claimed a seat at a nearby vacant desk and steepled my fingers to think a minute. "If Zapata was working in the sex trade, he had to have a contact. Someone and somewhere to make his dates. You find it?"

Glenann snickered before answering. "Ernestine Flanagan."

I felt my eyebrows climb. "Ma Flanagan?"

"The same."

Ernestine Flanagan, a seventysomething, prim, gray-haired lady of sweet nature and hardheaded business acumen, started a telephone answering service in Albuquerque years before telephones had their own voicemail systems. Many professional firms still used the Telephone Me Call Center she operated out of her home in the near-downtown area.

"You think she's…?"

"A madam?" Roy shook his head. "No, her service is merely handy for a lot of people who don't want to give out their own telephone number… for whatever reason. Some of them aren't as legitimate as others."

"Have you talked to her?"

"Oh yeah. She remembers Matt, as she calls him, well. He set up his account himself. Every time you mention his name, her immediate response is 'what a fine young man he is.' He told her he hired himself out as a laborer and as an escort for dances and weddings and such."

"Laborer?"

Glenann brightened the room with a smile. "Oh yes. We contacted some of his callers and found he did yard work, acted as an escort to weddings, hired out as a dance partner, did some plumbing work—which was likely illegal, no license—and tutored a couple of kids in Spanish."

"And these checked out?"

"Matt was the real thing to the people we've been able to contact."

"The others?" I asked.

Glenann smoothed ash blonde hair back on her head. "Moved away or didn't answer. One contact we talked to was a woman of a certain age who said Matt posed as her nephew and escorted her to a wedding and a country club dance. Two of them were burner cell phones. Untraceable."

Roy spoke up. "All the contacts were voice calls except for three. They were texts. You want to guess which three?"

"The woman looking for an escort and the two burner phones."

"Right."

"You buy the lady's claim he was merely an escort?"

"I'm sure he did all of that for the lady and more. It's the more she won't admit to."

"So get her down here and grill her."

"Uh-uh," Roy said. "The woman's connected to some people who wouldn't want her embarrassed."

"The burner phones?"

"Dead end. They seemed to have been used once to text Ma's answering service. She logged them in as requests for yard work and babysitting, respectively."

"You have copies of the text messages?"

Roy handed over three pieces of paper from Matt's file. The first was signed "Ruth" and asked for a presentable young man to escort her to a wedding. The second, sent by "Bob," requested a hardworking young man who was not afraid to shuck his shirt for some yard work and personal work. The third, signed "Anxious," requested a babysitter, preferably a handsome young man of a pleasing and amenable manner. It also mentioned "personal work."

"The babysitting call came the day before he died," Glenann said when I looked up from reading the messages.

"Which was?"

"Don't have autopsy results yet, but the doc on the scene estimated the kid died sometime between noon and 4:00 p.m. on Monday the fifth. He was found by some lovebirds parking out on the West Mesa later that night. I gather the discovery scared the young lady right out of her romantic mood."

"No doubt. Let's see, Zancón's lawyer got in touch with me yesterday morning, and I visited the pen the same afternoon. Zancón's moving fast."

Roy agreed and provided a reason. "Yeah, he wants you to find the boy's killer before we do. Why, I wonder?"

"Because he wants the killer dead, not arrested," I said. "I put a bullet in Zancón's gut a few years back, so he figures I owe him. Nonsense, of course, but the question is why is he so bent on revenge?"

Glenann shrugged. "Maybe he knows who killed Matt and that makes it personal."

Roy disagreed. "If he thought he was simply hiring a hitman, he'd have given BJ a name and where to find the bastard."

"True. I asked him, and he said he had no clue."

She sighed. "Maybe he does know but *doesn't* want it to get around his nephew was in the sex trade."

"I'm sure the last part's true," I acknowledged. "He wouldn't even tell me the kid had been found naked. He left those details to his brother."

"Maybe the boy's dead because of something Zancón's doing up in the pen," Glenann speculated.

"Always possible. Or maybe he figures he can't afford to let violence against family members go unpunished. A con's mentality."

"Did he offer a sum certain for finding the killer?" Roy asked.

I shook my head. "No, my usual fees, which he said his brother would pay. When Juan confirmed that, I got the feeling Matt's father wants justice, not retribution."

I took my leave and tromped back to my office through a swirl of tiny flakes. The snow melted the moment it struck the ground, but mother nature was making a real effort. Given the leaden clouds overhead, she'd keep trying the rest of the day.

As I hugged my too light jacket around me, I wondered at the fact so many of my major cases in the last few years had involved homosexuality. Was it because of my orientation, or just the breaks of the game? I could name a gay character in many of my major cases. Was that because I was so aware of the brotherhood? I snorted a laugh into the cold air. Likely they were involved in *most* cases; we simply didn't notice them. Wouldn't it be great if sexual orientation were something no one paid any attention to? Sorry we aren't there yet. Maybe someday.

MA FLANAGAN gave me a motherly look through her rimless granny glasses, and for a moment I thought she was going to say "tsk-tsk." We sat in the tiny office of her small house on Roma NW. So far as I knew, she'd lived there for most of her seventy years.

"Now, BJ, you know I can't divulge such information. My business is built on confidentiality... as is yours, I'm sure. My goodness, I can't get over how much you look like your mother. She was a beautiful soul, as well as an attractive woman."

"That she was, Ma." Ernestine Flanagan insisted everyone call her Ma. "But the owner of the account I'm asking about is dead. Brutally murdered, and I'm trying to find out who killed him."

"Like those two delightful APD detectives I talked to. They made an attractive couple."

"You do realize they're a professional couple, not a romantic one."

"Are they married? To other people, I mean?"

"Not so far as I know."

"Well, you just wait. They'll wake up to the fact they're compatible... quite compatible."

"Maybe, but I need—"

"Yes, I know. You always were such an impatient young man. Always in a hurry. Take it from someone who knows, one day you'll discover how much you missed in your rush through life."

"Yes, ma'am, I probably will." *Like the time I'm wasting now.* "But at the moment, I'm trying to catch a killer. Someone who's murdered three young men and deprived them of the rest of their lives."

A hand flew to her chest. "Three? Oh my goodness. That's why the nice detective couple asked if I had accounts for those other two names."

"Did you?"

She hesitated a beat before revealing how sharp she really was. "No, just for young Mr. Zapata. I had nothing for Mr. Greene or Mr. Hubbard."

"So explain to me how Mr. Zapata's account worked. Let's say I wanted to leave a message for him. Would I need to give you my name?"

"Perhaps. Perhaps not. Most people identify themselves, but not all. Some merely leave a message for Mr. Zapata to return a call to a certain phone number. So my operators take down the number and leave a message on the client's personal voicemail or forward a text to Mr. Zapata's telephone."

"Is it always a request for a phone number?"

"Sometimes it's to confirm a meeting time and place."

"So I could merely call and leave a certain hour and a specific address."

She nodded her head without dislodging a single strand of gray hair held in a bun by a huge tortoiseshell comb. "Exactly."

"But would I have to leave my name and phone number?"

"Most do, but sometimes prior arrangements have been made, and the pertinent information is all that is given." She smiled and shook her head. "And I can see your father in you too. Robert was as handsome as Frances was beautiful. You have good genes, BJ."

"Thank you. Do you—"

"What a tragedy. How long have they been gone now?"

"January 2003. Do—"

"Nine years now. Seems like yesterday I heard the news about their automobile accident."

"Ma, I'm taking up too much of your valuable time. I have a couple more questions and then—"

"Oh pshaw. My operators handle most of the calls. Did you know I have a male operator now? Can you believe it? First time in forty years, but you can't discriminate, you know. Name's Robert, like your father. Such a nice young man."

My skin crawled, but I kept at it, refusing to believe Ernestine Flanagan was going dotty. This was her way of evading my questions.

"Ernestine, cut out the old lady act, and let's get down to business."

"Why, Burleigh J. Vinson, I can't believe you were so rude to me." The words were prim, but there was a smile hiding in the pastel-blue eyes. "Your mother would give you a smack on the back of the hand."

"You may do so in her stead, but, Ma, this is serious. *Someone* is murdering handsome young men after—" I fought for an acceptable word. "—debauching them."

"Well, why didn't you say so? What do you want to know?"

"Are there recordings of the calls?"

"Goodness, no!" She apparently rethought her vehement answer. "It's not like in the old days, BJ. Now you can call me on my cell and leave me a message. When I opened this business, there was no such convenience. And when it came along, I had to adjust my way of doing things to stay in business. Most of my clients are medics or medical services who need a human to discern what is an emergency and what is not." She paused again. "In order to survive, I had to accept other customers. I'm certain some of my clients arrange trysts, for example."

"Why not use email or Skype or something similar?"

"Do you know what I believe it comes down to?"

I shook my head.

"The authorities are watching for that sort of thing on the internet because it's become so prevalent. My clients want to be a bit more discreet."

"Okay, you don't record the calls. Do you log them?"

"Oh yes. Otherwise I couldn't bill my clients. You see, they get a certain amount of traffic for a blanket fee, but—"

I held up a hand. "I understand. May I have a copy of the log for Mateo Zapata's account? And the three text messages?" I saw her internal battle and added, "The police already have them."

She surrendered gracefully. "Do you want a copy of the calls and texts that came in after the young man died?"

My eyes widened involuntarily. "Absolutely. How many were there?"

"If memory serves, three more phone calls and one text message. I see no reason why you shouldn't have the information." Her eyes sharpened. "Providing you can tell me who engaged your services."

She probably thought she had me over a barrel, but I fooled her. "The family engaged me, Ma. They want me to help APD catch their son's killer. And I've okayed this with Homicide and the two detectives you mentioned."

I knew how much I'd been played when she picked up a slender file folder from her desk and handed it over. "Here are your copies."

Chapter 3

I RETURNED to the Vinson and Weeks, Confidential Investigations, suite in a five-story downtown office building at Fifth and Tijeras NW and stood for a moment on the third-floor landing to glance down into the open atrium. That never failed to provoke a tortured memory of a thug attacking me with a knife some years back. After a brief tussle, he'd ended up flying over the banister and dropping to the hard tile floor. Come to think of it, the tragedy was a part of the Zozobra Incident case in which Zancón played such a prominent role.

After returning a few phone calls, I gave Hazel the assignment of running down the telephone numbers on Matt's client list and asked my partner, Charlie, to see what he could dig up on young Mr. Zapata's background.

I took a seat at the small conference table in my private office to concentrate on the new text message.

Had a great recommendation from Bob, who said you do fabulous yard work. Wonder if you're available for some of the same? I pay better than the going rates for such personal service. Especially if you become my regular lawn boy. How about the morning of Saturday the 10th at the Range Café on Wyoming & Montgomery NE? I'll be there at 10:30 sharp; the salt-and-pepper guy with a green turquoise bolo. Until then. Desi

To my eyes, Desi looked to be a made-up name. Perhaps short for "Desire?" Someone wanted to advertise without being too blatant about it. None of the usual text abbreviations. Complete sentences. It read more like a business letter than a request for a tête-à-tête. Did that mean anything? Not necessarily, except that "Desi" was meticulous and not at ease with this type of communication.

I glanced at my watch calendar and pulled out my cell. Roy and Glenann were out, but dispatch put me through.

"Roy, it's BJ. Ma Flanagan gave me a new text message setting up a date with Matt Zapata tomorrow. I think we should keep the date."

"How'll we know him?"

"He ID'd himself. Salt-and-pepper hair with a green turquoise bolo. Signed the text message with the handle 'Desi.'"

Roy agreed it was a date that should be kept, although he wondered aloud if Desi hadn't seen the newspaper story about Matt's murder.

"Even if he did, he may not have recognized his date was the victim. After all, the text makes it clear they haven't met before."

Roy agreed, and we made arrangements for the next morning. He and Glenann would arrive as a couple while I went solo to approach the mark and solicit his cooperation.

Our plans complete, I headed home, salivating over Paul's announcement that morning he intended to fix a pot of his delicious green chili stew for our dinner. The love of my life was there and still seated before his computer in our shared office, but the savory aroma of the promised repast hung heavy in the air.

He rose to give me a smile and a hug after I plopped my attaché case on my desk. "Hungry?" he asked.

"In more ways than one." My first glimpse of him after a day's absence always rocked me on my heels, reminding me how fortunate I was to have such a handsome and hunky mate to share my life. His lopsided grin went straight to my heart. His right eyebrow rose slightly.

"We'll take your appetites in order."

I showered and changed to casual clothes while he finished an article on the Albuquerque Isotopes baseball team.

Paul was a freelance journalist, and his articles on last year's Voxlightner Scandal case had been well received, giving his career a boost. Although I made no financial demands on him, he insisted on carrying his share of the household expenses. What he couldn't contribute in dollars, he supplemented with sweat labor. The redbrick, cross-gabled house I'd inherited from my folks at 5229 Post Oak Drive in northwest Albuquerque hadn't looked so spiffy—inside and out—since my mom took care of the interior and my dad puttered around the outside.

I emerged from the bedroom as Paul hit a key and gave a satisfied "Done." I took that to mean he'd emailed his article to the target magazine.

We ate at the kitchenette table where, as usual, Paul's tasty, piquant stew slaked one craving while his bronzed arms and admirable pecs excited another.

He brought me back to the moment by asking about the Zapata murder.

"The case has a name now. Matt was the third young man killed and discarded naked in some public place. The police are calling them the cutie-pie murders."

"Cutie-pie? Who came up with such a lame name? Nobody's used 'cutie-pie' in ages."

I went for my attaché case and brought back three photographs.

"Wow!" he said after looking at them. "They are hotties. Cutie-pie fits, I guess. Any leads to who killed them?"

"Someone who's not afraid to leave clues. All three of the victims were covered in semen. Their own and someone else's. And the someone else doesn't happen to have sperm in his semen."

"So no DNA, huh? But if the vic's own cum was on him, he must have been a willing partner."

"Not a valid assumption," I said. "Sexual excitement can be stimulated even when you don't particularly want to participate. But at this point, there's no reason to assume the three victims didn't voluntarily participate."

"Any connection between the three dead guys?"

"Matt and Hubbard were both students at UNM."

"Hubbard?"

"The Black youngster. But they were in different disciplines, so there's no apparent connection. I suspect the fact they were both students is coincidental since Greene, the other one, was a street kid."

"Were they call boys like we believe Matt was?"

I shook my head. "As I say, Dustin Greene lived on the streets—literally. Last known address was a downtown alley. It wouldn't surprise me if he occasionally covered his meals offering himself to some guy. I'm willing to bet Hubbard wasn't."

"Do you think Hubbard was gay?"

"No indication of it."

"So Matt was the only gay guy in the bunch."

"And I think he was more of a bi. Or maybe a pansexual."

"Since they had cum on them, it probably wasn't robbery," Paul said.

"Given the semen and the fact they were found naked, this was likely purely sexual. But I think it's a psychological thing." I described the circumstances surrounding all three deaths.

"Some loony doesn't like pretty boys," Paul suggested.

"Then why become sexually active with them?"

He shrugged. "Maybe he wants it, but when he gets it, he's disgusted by what he's done. We've both known guys like that."

"True. But they're usually disgusted with themselves."

Paul wagged his head from side to side. "For the most part. But sometimes they take it out on their partners."

"Also true. Until society at large comes to accept gay sex isn't a criminal or disgusting act, that's one of the dangers we face." I sighed. "Now I need to get into the killer's mind."

Paul reached across the table and touched my hand. "Just so long as that's all you get into with him."

"I don't think this is someone I want to socialize with."

Paul stretched his back and rose. "Me neither. But I want in on the case. I think this is my next featured article. A couple of mags I know will jump through hoops for this one."

Whenever Paul and I retired to the bedroom for anything other than sleep, there's a third presence in the room. My mate has a small tattoo on his left pec, an inked depiction of a shy dragon he calls Pedro, living on his chest with one claw clutching a nipple. Pedro's peaceful appearance notwithstanding, anytime Paul calls him out to play, the little beast gets fiercely aggressive. I dearly love to watch Pedro romp. And romp he did. I believe even the dragon was exhausted by the time it was over.

Chapter 4

PAUL INSISTED on accompanying me to the Range Café the next morning. It wasn't a bad idea since Desi had exhibited an interest in handsome young men, and my lifemate certainly qualified. Roy and Glenann were already in the parking lot behind the café when we arrived. Paul favored Roy with a handshake and Glenann with a hug. The two detectives entered the café first in order to get between our quarry and the restaurant's customers, while Paul and I followed to block escape through the entrance.

Paul entered slightly before me and walked straight to a well-built man of about sixty sitting on a painted wooden bench provided for waiting customers. His close-cropped salt-and-pepper hair and a turquoise bolo weren't hard to spot.

Paul held out his hand. "Desi?"

The man stood, his eyes lighting at his first sight of Paul.

"Matt? My word, Bob wasn't exaggerating. You're something!"

"Thank you, sir, but my name's Paul." He half turned to indicate me. "This is BJ Vinson. We need to talk to you."

Desi closed down immediately. "Sorry, there must be some mistake. Excuse me, I have to leave."

Roy, standing only a few feet away, stepped over and held out his shield. "Detective Roy Guerra, APD. As the man said, we need to speak to you. I suggest we go to the parking lot to sort things out."

With Paul leading the way, Roy and Glenann on either side of the unhappy mark, and me bringing up the rear, we exited the café without exciting too much attention. Paul halted to lean against the fender of my white Impala.

"What's this all about?" Desi asked, addressing Paul, who had obviously caught his attention.

"It's about the murder of a young man named Mateo Zapata, sir," Glenann said. "Will you please identify yourself?"

"Not until you explain why you accosted me. I didn't kill anyone."

Roy took over. "And we're not accusing you of doing so. But you made a date with the young man via a text message, and we need to understand how you learned about him."

Anger disappeared from the man's face. "Mateo. Matt. I see. I learned about him—"

Glenann poked his chest with a manicured finger. "We'll need those details, but first, who are you? May I see your identification?"

With obvious reluctance, Desi drew out a wallet and handed over his driver's license.

"Bixby Morton," Glenann read, citing a posh address in the Midtown/University area.

"And who is Bixby Morton?" Roy asked.

"I'm the owner of Morton Roofing. And I'm not comfortable standing out here talking to police officers. Look, I'm married and have children—"

I intervened. "How about we go to my offices on Fifth and Tijeras. Or we can go to police headquarters if you prefer."

"And who are you?"

"B. J. Vinson of Vinson and Weeks, Confidential Investigations."

"I've heard of you. Let's go to your office. I'll follow you."

"Detective Hastings will ride with you, sir," Roy put in. "She knows the way."

ONCE SEATED in the conference room at my downtown office, we wasted ten minutes convincing Morton that Roy and

Glenann weren't the sex police. Then the information came tumbling out.

His friend "Bob," who turned out to be an architect named Richard Wright, shared a "common interest," as Morton put it. They didn't get together with one another but took pleasure in sharing their experiences verbally. I knew "Bob," or rather Dick Wright, slightly, and remembered him as a man a little older than the pack who hung out on the edges of the gay scene back when I was in college. Dick had never approached me, but I wouldn't have been surprised if he had.

Morton denied knowing how Dick stumbled onto Matt, but the architect had sung the young man's praises so loudly and graphically Morton decided to text the contact number Dick provided him. From the glances he kept shooting Paul's way, the roofing contractor was disappointed my mate wasn't the legendary Matt.

Paul took advantage of one such adoring look to ask how Morton knew Matt didn't show up expecting to mow the lawn or clean out the garage.

"Dick made it clear I had to include the words 'personal service' in the text."

"You didn't expect an answer from him before showing up for the rendezvous?" Paul pressed.

"Dick said the guy never acknowledged anything. You went in blind."

Once we were satisfied Morton had told us all he knew, we sent him on his way and stayed at the conference table to plan our next move. Then Paul and I, ignoring the still intermittent snowflakes, bundled up and headed for the North Valley Country Club for a chilly round of golf. I took scant satisfaction in noting we weren't the only idiots braving the elements. Paul took five dollars from me. It would have been more, but I reached the green in two on the five-par eighteenth hole and two-putted for a birdie. I wasn't that good, but I was cold and miserable and wanted to get this game over with so I could warm my frozen carcass in the comfort of the clubhouse.

ROY GUERRA gave Richard Wright the option of meeting with him and Glenann at the police station or in my office. Monday morning, Hazel ushered all three of them into our conference room, where Charlie and I joined them. "Bob"—whom I remembered as a cool customer—showed signs of nervousness. We got the introductions and small talk out of the way before Roy opened the real conversation.

"We understand you had an assignation with a young man named Matt Zapata late last month."

Dick Wright's jaw sagged. "Matt's last name is Zapata? Oh my word. I know the family!" He recovered. "At least I know *a* family named Zapata. Not necessarily the same one."

"If it's Juan Zapata of Zapata's Pre-Owned Cars on Bridge SW, then you do."

The architect's pale features went even paler. "That's ghastly!"

"Murder usually is," Roy said.

Dick lost even more color, making him closely resemble a corpse. "Murder! Heavens, all I did was—" He clamped his mouth shut. "Maybe I should have a lawyer present."

"If you had anything to do with the death, an attorney's a good idea," I said. "If not, then all we're interested in is understanding how you learned about Matt and how to contact him."

"I-I don't want to incriminate myself."

Glenann sailed in to play good cop. "Discreet consenting sexual contact between adults is not a crime, Mr. Wright. Detective Guerra and I are Homicide, not SVU."

He gulped air. "All right. Yes, I arranged a meeting with Matt. Heard about him from a woman I know. He'd escorted her to a wedding or a funeral or something, and they'd had a delightful time afterward. She said he asked her to recommend him to some friends."

"Recommend him to *male* friends?" Glenann asked.

"Apparently, the young man made it clear he didn't discriminate."

"And who was this woman?" she pressed.

"I-I don't think I should say."

"You don't need to. It was Hilda Thornton, wasn't it?" I named the sender of the first text message Ma Flanagan had given us. The police had determined she was Mrs. James Thornton, the wealthy widow of a real estate broker.

"How did you know?"

"I'm a detective, remember?"

"Oh. You're right. Hilda told me about him and gave me the number I was to call or text. I chose to text."

Glenann moved in again. "Signing yourself as Bob."

"I didn't want to use my real name."

"Understood. I'm not asking for intimate details, but please tell us about your date."

Dick went from cadaver gray to russet red in an instant. "We... we met at the Range Café. He was a delightful young man. Not just movie-star handsome, but personable as well."

"Did you have dinner at the Range?" Roy asked.

Dick nodded. "Yes, and he showed his consideration. Most people—on the make, so to speak—would have ordered the most expensive thing on the menu. He had a salad and a glass of red wine. Very considerate."

"Where did you go after that?"

"To my office. We sat on the couch and talked for hours. I almost hated to interrupt the conversation for... well, you know. And he was considerate there as well. Like I say, a totally delightful companion."

"And how much did you pay him for his companionship?" Roy asked.

"Is that relevant?"

"I'm afraid so."

"Five hundred dollars."

"Did you go to the office in one car?"

"Yes, and I took him back to the Range to pick up his Jeep Wrangler."

Dick had a dreamy look on his face by the time we completed our interview. Instead of considering it a violation of his privacy, I believe we'd allowed him to relive his magical night. But none of us were inclined to make light of his mood. After all, the likable young man he fantasized over was dead. Murdered.

"Where was Zapata's Wrangler the day he died?" I asked the detectives after Dick's departure.

"A patrolman found it in the parking lot south of Organic Books in Nob Hill a day or so after the body was discovered," Glenann replied.

"I assume you surveyed the neighborhood?"

"Talked to everyone we could find. Zapata apparently frequented a couple of restaurants in the neighborhood and was known at the bookstore in the center. But nobody can remember if he was around on the Monday he died."

MRS. JAMES Thornton did not come easily into my web. Calls from Hazel, Charlie, and me went unheeded, so Roy and Glenann went to her home in a luxury high-rise in Midtown to invite her to the police station. She claimed the need for a lawyer and asked if she could meet them in my office the next day instead.

Despite the fact it had quit snowing and spring was only a few days from springing, she showed up at 10:00 a.m. with a mink stole around her shoulders. An attorney named Henry Walken trailed along behind her. Even though Albuquerque was a "small-town" type of city, I knew neither of them, although

I had met her dead husband a time or two at Kiwanis Club meetings. During the introductions, Roy and Glenann arrived. Charlie joined us for the confab in our conference room.

"Am I to understand that delightful young man who escorted me to my cousin's wedding last month is dead?" She waved a hand toward her lawyer. "His daughter's wedding, as a matter of fact."

"You're related?" Glenann asked.

"Yes, Henry's my father's brother's son."

That meaningless detail out of the way, we started on the interview and learned little new. Except how Hilda got in touch with Matt. A friend of hers had used the young man for a routine job of cleaning out her garage and had been taken with his manners and efficiency—and apparently his looks.

The friend mentioned him to Hilda. She, in turn, contacted the young man through Ma Flanagan's telephone service and had him clean out her storage area in the apartment building's basement. With something more in mind, she suggested she might ask him to escort her to a function the following week. Apparently receptive to vibes or pheromones or something, Matt told her to contact him when she was ready, but to include the words "personal services" in the message. While Hilda termed it as escorting her to a family wedding, it developed Matt also took her to a dance the same evening. After that, she was a bit vague on what happened, but not vague enough for us to misunderstand.

As they left the office at the end of the interview, Cousin Henry cautioned Hilda she "had to stop picking up young men." Cousin Hilda merely sniffed.

After they were gone, Hazel joined us at the conference table and took a seat where she could keep an eye on the front door through the room's glass wall. She handed around copies of all the notes and interviews she'd transcribed thus far—minus the recently concluded conference, which she'd add later from my recording of the event.

The room was quiet—except for the shuffling of paper—for a few minutes before I spoke.

"Roy, have you found any more murders with a similar MO?"

He shook his head. "Nothing. And I checked every jurisdiction in the state, including the feds. Nothing remotely close. Not even anything that could have evolved into these three killings."

"So Dustin Greene, who died on Monday, September 5 of last year, was the first."

Glenann raised a finger. "He was *found* on the fifth but killed days earlier."

"The killer likely picked Greene up off the street," Roy said, restating the theory I'd outlined to Paul earlier. "The kid sacked out in a downtown alley with some other homeless guys. During the day, he scrounged for a living, probably including exchanging sex with men for money."

"You say Greene was found on Monday, September 5. I believe Zapata was killed Monday, March 5. Any significance there?" I asked.

Glenann shook her head. "Don't think so. Greene was killed a couple of days before he was found. And Hubbard was found December the first of last year."

"What day was that?"

"Thursday, I believe," she said, "which breaks the pattern."

"More or less three months between each killing," Charlie said. "Indicates to me the killing satisfies some perverse urge. Takes a little time to build up to it again."

I pursued my line of thought. "Makes sense, but something must have happened during the first rendezvous with Greene to set our killer off on the road to murder. Something traumatic. Any signs of excessive violence on Greene—or any of them, for that matter?"

Roy shook his head. "You have copies of the autopsies. A little more trauma with Greene than with the other two. But he was a rough street kid. No telling if his bruises were sex related or gathered on the street."

I dug around in the reports Hazel had given us until I found the summary of Greene's jacket. "Street fighting, petty theft. You hadn't tossed him for any sex crimes before?"

"Nope."

I tapped the table with a forefinger. "What did this kid do to turn a sexual assignation into murder?"

"You're assuming the vic brought it on himself?" Glenann asked.

"I'm assuming something happened during the encounter to *change* one of the participants from seeking a sexual encounter into feeling the need to kill."

"Given Greene's record," she said, "maybe he tried to rob his mark."

"Or maybe," Charlie said, "the perp wanted the kid to do something he wasn't willing to do."

"Like submit to anal sex, for example," Roy said.

"That's a possibility. But if so, then do we assume the next two victims died because they wouldn't engage in the same activity? It's possible, of course, but somehow it doesn't fit. Something happened in that first encounter with Greene to cause this man to kill. And he found the killing as important as the sex in subsequent trysts."

Glenann frowned. "That assumes the perp goes for three months at a time without sex. Then he does the deed and kills afterward."

"Not necessarily," Hazel put in. "Maybe he has a wife or a girlfriend but has a latent desire for crossing the street, so to speak. And that's what causes him to kill his partners. Because he considers they've led him off the proper path."

"Makes sense to me," Glenann said. "We're looking for a heterosexual fighting against his homosexual side."

I shook my head, mostly to myself. "Paul suggested the same thing to me the other day. And it could be true. But I'm not willing to make that particular jump yet."

We examined a few more ideas before I worked around to what made sense to me. "Roy, you said you couldn't find any killings that might have evolved into this perp's modus, right?"

He nodded.

"What about other types of incidents? Reports of being propositioned. Someone trying to force himself on a guy."

"No, and I looked. I found two reports of unsolicited advances. Neither fit. One was a best friend getting drunk and overly friendly. The other was a family member taking liberties."

"Did you take a look at the accused?"

"Interviewed both of them. The drunk guy was a kid not even old enough to drink. He's more likely to end up a victim than a killer. The other one was a middle-aged uncle who's since left town to escape the outrage of his own family."

"Of course," Charlie said, "it's possible this is someone new to the area. He might have killed somewhere else."

"True," Roy acknowledged. "But I cast as broad a net as I could."

I intervened. "Let's assume for the moment he's not new to the area. He's been here all along."

"You're back to thinking Greene did something to set him off," Glenann said.

I gave her a thumbs-up. "And Hubbard and Zapata merely fed whatever went wrong with the first assignation. Which means...."

Glenann sagged back in her chair. "There will be more killings."

"Until we find him and stop him," I said.

"The same's probably true under Hazel's theory that he's fighting his homosexual tendencies as well," Charlie said.

Roy summed it up for all of us. "Oh crap!"

Chapter 5

PRINCETON DRIVE for a block or so south of Central is mostly commercial, with shops of various kinds catering principally to University of New Mexico students and staff. The buildings were aging adobe residences now converted to commercial use. Matt's apartment at 134 wasn't an apartment at all; it was a small house set well back from the street.

Matt's rent was paid through the end of the month, so his father provided a key for Paul and me to look through the place. It wasn't the murder scene, and because Roy and Glenann had ceded the Zapata case to us, APD hadn't gone through it. In fact, Matt's father claimed the place was untouched since his son's death as neither he nor his wife had been able to muster the emotional courage to pass through the doorway. After parking on the street, Paul and I trod the twin strips of concrete doing double duty as walkway and driveway to the pink stucco sitting at the back of the lot, almost behind its neighbors.

Like most edifices in the area, the structure was old, its electric-green wooden door cracked and most likely glued together by countless coats of paint. But once we stepped over the threshold, Matt Zapata's personality shone through. The place was extraordinarily neat for the pad of a teenager. The furniture was piecemeal, but good. Walnut stood next to blond oak, but somehow it worked. The spring lock clicked behind us as I closed the door.

As you would expect of a young man majoring in photography, scads of photos adorned his walls. Landscapes mostly, with a few portraits thrown in the mix. They were good but not yet professional. But he would have gotten there.

Surprisingly few images of Matt adorned the walls, but a large—probably half-size—black ink drawing of him hung to the right of a small hogan-style fireplace. The artist had caught the essence of the well-formed, handsome young college student in a tastefully done nude. Matt stood—hip sprung—facing away from us, looking over his left shoulder. The image caught and held my eye, not simply because of its powerful sexuality, but also because it portrayed a young man I would have liked to have called a friend. The broad shoulders, narrow waist, and firm buttocks were as provocative as the casual, unassuming look on the model's features. A color photograph of him in dungarees and a brown leather jacket, hanging on the other side of the hearth, was as sultry as any I'd ever seen. The camera loved this kid.

"Keep an eye out for his cell phone in case he didn't take it with him on his final date."

"Fat chance," Paul said. "Kid that age was married to his phone. But I can try to find out if it's been used since he died."

"Roy already did. No activity at all."

"We'll probably never find it."

Paul headed straight for a laptop computer with an external monitor and keyboard sitting on a desk in the corner of the combination living and kitchen area. "Neat setup." A moment later, he called, "Password protected. I can probably get in, but it'll take some time."

"Okay, we'll take it with us."

He shut the machine down before gravitating to a checkbook lying on a glass-topped coffee table. I pulled my attention from the drawing and walked to the desk Paul had just abandoned. The first thing I found in the upper right drawer was a Lenovo notebook. Surprisingly, it opened without calling for a password to reveal the boy's personal journal. Intrigued, I settled down and relived the last few months of Matt's life, discovering the mental process of how he became a call boy.

Everything he wrote, virtually every notation, screamed both ambition and impatience. He was going to influence the fashion world one day... one day soon. He wasn't willing to wait. It had to be now. And the way wasn't cheap. There were skills to be learned, photo shoots to undergo, and it all cost money. Big money if you wanted the best. The best charm schools, gymnasiums to tone the body, personal trainers, and especially the best photographers.

Paul's voice pulled my head out of the notebook. "This guy moved some dough through his account the last few months. Maybe I oughta consider opening an escort service."

"Can I be your first customer?" I paused meaningfully. "And your last. What did he spend his money on?"

"Clothes mostly. Paid his bills, you know, rent and utilities, like clockwork. Building a decent savings account. Had at least two credit cards and paid them down to zero regularly. He was organized."

I returned to the notebook and learned something about the young man's morals. He had no trouble accepting pay for work performed... no matter the nature of the work. But he wanted no part of his father's money, especially when he couldn't discern if it was Juan's or Zancón's. Older entries revealed a fondness between nephew and uncle had died a slow, tortured death as the youngster grew to understand his uncle's business and with Zancón's dawning understanding of his nephew's nature. A couple of entries lent some credence to Paul's question of whether Juan's used car business might not be tied to some of his brother's activities.

This kicked off another thought process in my mind. Could Matt have paid the piper for Juan Zapata's crossing swords with the wrong people? Or could Zancón be involved in something up in Santa Fe that cost his nephew his life? He wouldn't have been the first inmate to direct criminal enterprises from a prison cell. I paused my reading long enough to phone Charlie and ask him to get someone to look into the family situation. Since we would need bank and financial information, I suggested he call on Roy and Glenann for help. I returned to an examination of the journal upon closing the call.

I held no truck with male whores, but neither did I look down on them. They, like their female counterparts, earned their money in a way unacceptable to me. But they were human beings first and foremost, and by this point in the scanning of Matt Zapata's electronic journal, I concluded he was at heart a decent human being. And a real man existed within that arresting physique and pretty face.

Paul got up from the chair he'd been using and mumbled he was going to "toss the bedroom." Too many TV detective shows.

In early January, a new name began appearing in Matt's journal. He apparently met Barkley Pierson at a New Year's Eve party thrown by some friends. Casual mentions became more frequent and more intense. A friendship was building between these two university students. Barkley—or Bark, as he soon became—was an Easterner. A Connecticut Yankee. An artist, apparently.

I got up to examine the nude sketch again. In the bottom right corner was a discreet signature, Barkley Pierson '12. A later entry in the journal described the circumstances surrounding the sketch. A growing friendship was evident. The depth of it came in mid-February when posing for the drawing led to their first physical encounter. And it was meaningful, at least to Matt. He rhapsodized about their coupling, their lovemaking. From the entries, it became obvious Pierson was older than Matt by a couple of years.

I roamed the room, examining the images of the portrait photos Matt had taken, looking for one I thought might be Barkley Pierson. A couple of his models almost matched Matt's own good looks, but I instinctively rejected each one as this new friend who so caught his attention. I failed to find a photo I could accept as Barkley Pierson until I opened the bottom right desk drawer and pulled out a small, framed photograph of a young man, slightly built but rangy. There was nothing on the photo or the frame to identify the subject, but there was not a doubt in my mind this was Pierson.

Behind gold-framed eyeglasses, a young man stared out through eyes with irises that reminded me of the browned biscuits my mother used to bake for Sunday dinners. The eyes were the most arresting thing about him. He wasn't plain, but neither was he handsome, not in the spectacular way Matt Zapata had been. Once again, Zancón's nephew rose in my estimation. Despite his own breathtaking beauty, Matt didn't judge his fellow man solely by appearance. He had liked this young man for other reasons.

I sat at the desk and frowned. Then why did Pierson disappear from the most recent notations in the notebook? Why was his picture facedown in the bottom drawer of Matt's desk? I picked up the Lenovo and read again, finding the answer to my questions just days before Matt's death. Bark had objected to Matt's new line of work, putting up with it through the first "date" with Hilda Thornton but drawing the line when he found the next client was "Bob."

Matt's internal struggle to choose between what he believed was a fast road to the fulfillment of his ambition and a man he clearly cared for spread anguish over the last few notations. *Would they have reconciled had Matt lived?*

Then the hardened—perhaps callous—investigator showed up and made me consider if Matt selling sexual favors to other men might have caused this Bark Pierson to go off the deep end and kill the object of his affections. Insane jealousy has murdered more than its share of lovers.

Paul came out of the bedroom and caught me staring at Pierson's photograph. "Who's that?"

"Name's Barkley Pierson. He's the artist who did the nude sketch and was Matt Zapata's lover until recently."

"How recently?"

"Until Matt opted to be a call boy."

"Jilted lover, huh? Makes him look good for doing in Matt."

I shook my head. "At first glance, maybe."

"But?" Paul asked. "Oh, I get it. Greene's and Hubbard's killings. They took place first, and the same killer murdered them all. But maybe Matt's death was a copycat."

"Hard to see how. The circumstances were the same in all the killings. And not everything was reported in the press. The semen, for example. How would a copycat know about that?" I shook my head. "The foreign semen was identical in all three cases. Unless this fellow Pierson killed them all, it doesn't wash."

"Maybe he did."

"Anything's possible, but I don't buy it. Even so, we'll have to find him and get the answers to some questions."

"Where do we start looking?"

"At UNM. According to Matt's notebook, he's a student there."

"And you're sure he did the nudie of Matt?" Paul asked.

I led him to the picture and pointed out the artist's signature. "And Matt's notes confirm it. Did you find anything in the bedroom?"

"Nothing. He lived alone. Only one toothbrush, and that sort of thing. Some nice threads in the closet."

"Drugs?"

"Aspirin. But he's got more skin conditioners than I knew existed."

"Took care of his appearance."

"Big-time. Found a supply of condoms. He didn't go cheap there either."

"Prudent, I'd say. He didn't want to compromise his health. Anything else?"

"Nope."

"Okay, let's collect the computer and notebook and go."

A sound at the door startled us both.

"Someone's keying the lock," I said. "Bedroom, quick."

With Paul observing over my shoulder, we watched a lanky, brown-haired young man in gold-framed glasses enter. Barkley Pierson closed the door behind him and walked straight to the nude sketch of Matt Zapata. He flinched when we moved into the room.

"Who—"

"Mr. Pierson, my name is B. J. Vinson. I'm a confidential investigator looking into Mateo Zapata's killing. This is my associate, Paul Barton."

"H-how do you know my name? Look, I wasn't breaking in. Matt gave me a key, and I-I was just coming for the sketch I did of him."

"A very good one, I might add."

"Th-thanks. I want it to remember him by."

"I'm sure there will be no problem, but first we need to talk. Why don't we all have a seat at the kitchen table?"

"I guess. But I don't know anything about who killed him."

Paul plopped down at the dinette table. "Maybe you know more than you think."

Pierson more or less fell into the chair I pulled out for him. I took a digital recorder from my belt. "You okay with me recording our conversation?"

He didn't reply, but that wasn't an objection, so I clicked it on and laid it on the table, taking a moment to identify the participants for the record.

Pierson didn't even wait for a question. He snatched off his glasses and swiped at his eyes. "I begged him not to go on those dates."

"Yeah, I can see your problem," Paul said.

Pierson jerked back and looked at him through myopic eyes. "Not like that. I... I mean...."

I nodded. "We understand. I read Matt's notebook. We know you were lovers."

Pierson put his glasses back on and looked less helpless. "Not for long. I only met him recently. But... but it was great. Could have been great."

"Matt's journal documented the struggle he had choosing between you and his life's ambition."

Pierson threw a hand at the sketch on the wall. "Look at him. No way he wasn't gonna make it. But he was in such a damned big hurry."

"Do you know why?"

The man blinked. Those biscuit eyes fascinated me. "Nature of the beast. Matt had everything. It came to him easy. Because of his looks, people would give him anything to be around him. He recognized it and used it, but it made him less... I don't know, less respectful of them, I guess. It didn't work with me. Probably why we got along so well." He flipped a hand in front of his face. "Look at me. Certainly not in his class in the looks department, but we could talk. Frank talk. And he liked that. And he appreciated my drawings, my paintings."

"Was the nude your idea or his?" I asked.

"His. He stripped naked one night, turned his back, and told me to draw him. So I did."

"That was the first night you made love," I said. It wasn't a question.

Pierson nodded. "Yes, and...." He gulped as his eyes flooded. He swiped the tears away. "It was like nothing I'd ever experienced. He-he felt the same way."

"And things were fine until Matt decided to go into the escort business," I said.

He nodded.

"And you objected."

"Strenuously." He blinked twice and turned to look at me. "But not because of *that*. I wasn't jealous of the sex."

Paul swiped the table with a hand. "Matt had sex with the others, but you two made love."

"Yes."

"Then why did you object?" I asked.

"Because of exactly what happened to him! I was afraid of it. Making dates with strangers and getting intimate with people you don't even know seemed dangerous to me."

"You're sure there wasn't a little bit of jealousy there?"

"Sure, there was some. It hurt imagining what he was doing with them, but mostly it was fear… for him."

"And maybe some disease he might bring home to you," Paul suggested.

"He was careful about protection."

"Are you sure? There was semen all over him when he was found."

Pierson closed his eyes. "Oh God. Why wouldn't he listen?"

We talked to Bark Pierson for over an hour as his feelings and emotions whipsawed between anger and sadness. He was angry, at times with Matt and at times with his lover's killer. He was saddened by the loss of a friend more than the loss of a lover, or so it seemed. And he had an alibi for the afternoon and night of Monday, March 5. Because he knew his lover was meeting a client, Pierson went to a bar directly from class with a couple of friends and got blotto. In fact, he was probably still in class when Matt died.

Even so, I told him to expect a call from a couple of APD detectives named Guerra and Hastings.

After he left, bearing the sketch he valued so dearly, I removed Pierson's photograph from its frame and slipped it into my pocket. Then I phoned Hazel and asked her to do a background check on Barkley Pierson using the contact information he'd provided for both here and back in Connecticut. Then Paul and I left, taking the laptop and notebook with us.

I gave Hazel the notebook to transcribe for me. I wanted to be able to read it as a continuing story without pushing buttons to see if I'd missed anything of significance in my quick scan. Absent Matt's cell phone, this was as close as we'd get to his thinking, unless there was something on the laptop when Paul finally figured out the password.

THE CASE dried up. Bark Pierson came out clean. Not even a parking ticket, either here or back East. His alibi checked. In fact, one of the guys drinking with him that night bunked over.

Nothing else we tried brought results. We spent the rest of the week looking into the backgrounds of everyone who'd ever called Matt's contact number with Ma Flanagan's telephone service. We talked to people who had *never* called Ma but who'd been told about Matt by satisfied customers. Interviews with friends and classmates confirmed Matt was an easygoing, popular guy who nonetheless excited envy with his comeliness.

The transcript of Matt's notebook added nothing to our store of knowledge, merely intensified the feeling of loss. The laptop, when Paul finally opened it with APD's help, gave us access to his website, which filled in a few blanks and provided new leads that led nowhere.

We talked to Charles Hubbard's parents, friends, fellow students, and found the murdered youth was shy and cautious. He'd never have accepted a ride from a stranger—except in the circumstance he found himself, stranded with a broken-down car.

We roused Dustin Greene's homeless neighbors in the downtown alley and found a slew of petty complaints and bitches but decided they were generated by envy. The guy had it easier than most of the others by playing on his good looks.

The APD forensics team and lab found plenty of footprints, tire tracks, and the like on the West Mesa dump sites, but it was impossible to figure out which ones—if any—were connected to the two murders. Any such prints at the Tijeras Canyon location had been carefully erased. Of course, Locard's Exchange Principle came into play, giving us pubic hair and skin cells, so we finally had DNA. But DNA was useless for identifying a perp whose info wasn't on file, and the two APD detectives had searched every database existent. Nothing. When we caught the bastard, such data would be key, but at the moment it was worthless.

We did garner one bit of useful information. Matt's toxicology report indicated a substantial amount of zopiclone was found in his system. Roy had told me Greene's results showed an "olio" of drugs, but the tox results showed that zopiclone was one of them. Hubbard, who seemed squeaky clean for a teenager these days, had the same drug in his system. For me, at any rate, this explained how a buffed guy like Matt was killed following a sex act without incurring defensive scratches or bruising. It was also enough for me to add the use of zopiclone to the killer's MO.

Paul and I spent the weekend playing golf and tennis at the country club in between dips in the indoor pool. I swam more or less regularly as therapy for the bullet wound in my thigh, which—even eight years later—still tended to stiffen. My forty-year-old body felt battered by the end of the weekend. Of course, some of that might have been caused by watching Pedro play on Paul's chest at night.

The telephone woke me around 6:00 a.m. Monday morning. Paul was already awake, but I was still recovering from last night's lovemaking. He poked me and handed over the phone.

"It's Roy. They found another body."

WHEN PAUL and I arrived at the entrance to the Petroglyph National Monument off west Paseo del Norte thirty minutes later, a cluster of city and county cars and an OMI wagon clogged the area. Although the criminalistics team wouldn't permit us access to the actual site, OMI allowed us a good look at the body after Roy and Glenann intervened. The young man lying on the gurney appeared a bit older than the previous victims, but he obviously had been attractive before he'd been strangled to death. No ID, since the corpse was naked.

"Anything different about this one?" I asked.

"Older, Asian," Glenann said, agreeing with my assessment. "He must be in his midtwenties. He was shoved out of a vehicle right in front of the locked gate to the park. Plain view of anyone on the highway. The killer intended this one to be found fast. The park attendant got a shock when he came to open up this morning."

She drew a breath. "You could argue the others weren't hidden either. But even the kid found in the canyon was off the road and out of sight. This one was obvious to anyone driving down the access road."

I glanced around the wide-open space. Except for the remnants of one of the dead volcanos dotting Albuquerque's west side, there wasn't even a fold in the landscape, just gently rolling hills like swells on a placid ocean.

I turned to Roy. "Technically, this is still the West Mesa. Even so, the Double Eagle Airport is north of here, and the monument gets good traffic. This is a well-traveled area. The guy took a chance dumping a body here. Tire tracks?"

"Nope. Stayed on the pavement."

"Is the county going to give you this one too?" I asked.

Roy nodded. "Looks like it. Sheriff was here a little earlier making the proper noises. He'll let Don Carson know."

"Anyone recognize the vic?" I asked.

"Nope. Have to jump through hoops to ID this one, unless he's in the system."

"He wasn't a street kid," Glenann said. "He's slender but muscled. He didn't miss many meals."

I glanced at an obviously shaken Paul. "What's the matter?"

"I-I know this guy. He was in a couple of my journalism courses at the U."

"What's his name?" Roy asked.

Paul tapped his left temple. "Lee or Lieu. That's it, Lieu. Yeah, John Lieu. Have to confirm it by looking in my annual, but I'm pretty sure that's right."

"What can you tell us about him?" Glenann asked, nodding for the OMI techs to zip up the body bag and load it in the wagon.

"Not much. We nodded in passing. He made a point of speaking to me a couple of times. You know, 'How you doing?' That kind of thing."

"Was he gay?" she asked.

Paul shrugged. "Wouldn't surprise me. But I don't know for sure."

"I thought you guys had a built-in alarm system." Judging by the wry smile on Glenann's lips, she was yanking my partner's chain.

"Okay, he pinged on my gaydar, but I don't go around proclaiming somebody's gay because of a feeling."

"And that's a good thing," I put in. "But now your opinion matters."

"Yeah. I think he was gay."

"The kind of gay who'd hang out on the streets looking for a pickup?"

Paul shook his head. "No way, but it might have been a chance pickup. You know, a meet in the cafeteria or in the head. Or somebody he already knew."

"Would he surf the web looking for a date?" I asked.

"I didn't know him well, but yeah, I could see him doing that."

Visions of Jazz Penrod flashed into my head. My young friend had gone on the internet and got caught up in a sex-trafficking ring. But Jazz was lucky; we'd managed to get him out in time. Our four victims fared far worse.

"Roy," I said, "have there been body fluids at any of the drop sites? Besides the semen?"

"Nope, they were all killed someplace else and dropped at the sites."

"Okay, I'm going to concentrate on Zapata's killing the old-fashioned way. Shoe leather. His car was found in the parking lot behind Nob Hill, and the center is east of the university. Probably not a mile from his apartment. I'm going to walk the area again. Reinterview people. You want to help, Paul, or would you rather stay on your friend's case?"

"I'll go with you. We can cover more ground that way."

THE PEOPLE at the Organic Bookstore knew Matt Zapata as a regular customer and a friendly guy but could add nothing beyond the fact he favored reading memoirs and biographies. A few people in other places in the shopping center recognized his photo. Once again, they could contribute little. One cashier believed she had seen him make a pickup in her restaurant, but it had been several days prior to his murder. The pickup was a regular customer, whose name she reluctantly provided.

From there we started up East Central, Paul taking the north side of the street; me, the opposite. It was drudge work, and I didn't really expect results. At the end of each block, Paul and I met on the median and compared notes. He found more than I did. A record shop recognized Matt as a regular, and one clerk there finally admitted he'd had a one-time relationship with him a couple of years back. He did nothing but sing Matt's praises. Beyond that… zilch.

Four blocks up the street from the shopping center, I hesitated in front of a new four-story apartment building with a small, discreet sign announcing it as Park House. Rather than attempting to contact each of the occupants, I rang the buzzer marked Manager. It was the only black button; the rest of them were red.

The voice answering the ring didn't match my mental image of a typical building super. It was young and cultured and obviously reluctant to take me at face value. A moment later a college-age man admitted me into the lobby. He listened as I repeated my explanation for disturbing his day. When I handed over the photo of Matt Zapata, he shook his head.

"Nope, never seen him. Murdered, you say? Shame." The man frowned. "When did you say this happened?"

"March 5. The fifth was a Monday."

His forehead puckered into a deeper frown. "Never seen him, but something odd happened that day. Or right around then. I'd have to check my calendar to make sure."

"What was it?"

"We keep one of our apartments vacant to show prospective tenants. A company apartment, we call it. Right about that time, someone gained unauthorized access to the show unit. Nothing taken except a duvet from one bedroom. Only other sign of an intruder was someone took a shower and used the linens."

"Did you report it to the police?"

"No, but I let the management company I work for know about it. It was an expensive duvet. Hundred bucks or so."

"Is the apartment still vacant?"

"You bet."

"May I see it?"

"Sure." He started for the elevator and then lurched to a halt. "Wait a minute. You don't think somebody was killed there, do you?"

"I don't know, but the victim's car was found at Nob Hill. He could have picked up someone and walked the four blocks."

"You think a woman killed him?"

"No. He was an equal opportunity escort."

"Oh."

Neither of us spoke during the elevator ride to the fourth floor. I followed the manager down the hallway to an apartment marked 4201 and waited as he opened the door.

"If-if this is a crime scene, do I need to stay outside? Oh crap! It's been cleaned since then. My staff cleans the apartment regularly, you know, vacuum and dust."

"How many times has it been shown since the fifth?"

He shrugged. "God, I don't know. Half a dozen times, probably."

"It's okay. Come in and show me the bedroom."

He took a right down the hallway and stood aside for me to enter the room. He obviously didn't like being at the scene of what might have been a violent death.

I glanced at the bed, now sporting a replacement duvet. "What did the stolen duvet look like?"

"Like that one. We have several identical ones."

Although convinced I'd found Zapata's murder scene, there was little to see. The bedroom was spotless. As was the bathroom when the manager showed me the shower the intruder had used. The housecleaning crew was still on the premises, and he located the woman who'd alerted him to the situation. She remembered there had been a spot on the floor, but she'd worked hard to get it clean, so there would likely be little for the crime scene crew.

I dialed Roy's cell phone and reported what I'd found. He promised to come straight over, so I decided to collect Paul and wait for the detectives.

The manager, who belatedly introduced himself as Quinton James, remained with us in the small entryway.

"Who has access to the apartments?" I asked when we were seated on small couches in the lobby area. East Central traffic rumbled continuously outside the street-side windows.

"I do. The housekeeping staff and my boss at the management company. Oh, and the maintenance guy. He's off today."

"I assume you questioned everyone when the intrusion was discovered."

Quint—as he said we should call him—nodded. "Quizzed them at length. Everyone denied stealing the duvet. And you know what? I believe them. If they'd wanted to steal one, they'd have taken an unused spread we have in storage. The theft might not have been discovered for months."

Roy and Glenann arrived to take over the questioning. We learned little more. They debated between themselves over whether to call in the crime scene unit at this late date, but finally decided to do so. After all, suspecting this was where Zapata died was one thing. Knowing it was another.

Quint, decidedly less confident now, hauled out his records and gave us a list of all the tenants, including personal data. I was surprised he didn't require a subpoena before opening his files, but he was obviously a freshwater fish floundering in seawater. Awe of the police probably overwhelmed his cautious nature.

The Park House had been open for something over a year. The manager's apartment and office, mailboxes, and a small reception area occupied the front of the ground floor; a combination maintenance and housekeeping space plus laundry facilities lay behind those. And the rear of the first floor was taken up by storage lockers for tenants, along with a secure undercover parking facility. The other three floors held six apartments apiece. Fifteen of the units were leased, three—including 4201—were vacant. Two elevators served the apartment building, one for tenants and guests, and the other a freight elevator for housekeeping and maintenance.

By the time Roy and Glenann finished making copies of all the information they wanted, it was getting late. We decided to convene at nine the next morning in my conference room to plan a strategy. Although it was past office hours, Paul and I swung by to see what Hazel had left for me to deal with. As usual, she had a pile of things for me to sign. As I sat dealing with the mess on the desk, Paul took the chair opposite me.

"Those are bitching apartments," he said. "But how can they make a go of it with only eighteen for rent?"

"Gives you some idea of what they charge, right?"

"An arm and a leg and your left nut, I imagine."

"Maybe both of them."

"Oh Lord. What if you only have one?"

"Then you don't live at Park House."

As I returned the pile to Hazel's desk in the outer office, I turned to look at him. "Are you all right?"

He glanced at me. "Why?"

"You lost a friend."

"More like an acquaintance, but yeah, it hurts some. Hurts to see anybody killed like that. A little more if you knew him."

"Would a good steak dinner make you feel better?"

He looked vacantly into the distance a moment. "I've got some green chili stew in the fridge. Think I'd rather have that. Okay?"

"I'll settle for your stew any day of the week. Let's go."

Chapter 6

GLENANN'S PREDICTION proved true. The next morning's *Albuquerque Journal*'s below-the-fold headline detailed the fourth "cutie-pie murder" in laborious detail. Unfortunately, a lot of people would be caught up in the sensationalism and fail to see Greene and Hubbard and Zapata and Lieu as flesh-and-blood young men, would view them merely as the by-product of this mysterious—and let's face it, romanticized—killer. Human tragedies transformed from horrid to torrid. Of course, it also sold newspapers.

I'd always considered myself a fair man, giving equal weight to every human being's basic worth, even as I readily admitted some contributed to society more than others. Even so, each of us has the same right to occupy our own tiny space on this planet as the next individual. As my father used to say, "Everyone contributes something... even if it is only to serve as a horrible example." During my years as a Marine MP, APD cop, and now as a confidential investigator, that belief had been tested many times but always held fast in the end.

Then why did the murders of four handsome young men haunt my dreams so? I'd seen more than my share of corpses, both young and attractive, and old and ugly, over the last twenty years, but none claimed my dreams more than the cutie-pie victims. Could someone have sought them out and killed them simply *because* they were young and attractive? I was coming to believe that was precisely the case.

Although we didn't discuss it—unusual because we talked almost everything to death—I understood Paul was as haunted as I was. He touched me more than usual, as though seeking confirmation I was still here. More, that *he* was still here.

By the time we gathered in my conference room Tuesday morning, Roy and Glenann knew a little more about John Lieu. The man had been twenty-four, a native of Albuquerque, and as previously believed, employed in his family's business. Single, he had been a gay halfway out of the closet. The detectives located only a sealed juvie jacket, which probably meant Lieu got caught drinking underage or in a compromising situation with someone. Back in the day, APD hadn't been above setting up stings for pursuing "deviants." In retrospect, it was amazing they had put up with me during some of those years. For that I could thank my partner, Gene Enriquez. For an aggressive overt heterosexual, he'd been amazingly tolerant—and protective—of me. Why? That's something I'd never completely understood. Perhaps I needed look no further than Glenda, his wife and mother of his five children, who welcomed me into her home as a brother. Even the kids looked upon me as either a pesky or a nurturing uncle, depending upon whether they'd reached their teens.

All in all, everything the detectives had learned about Lieu painted him as a solid citizen making his own way through this wild world of ours.

The two detectives shared CSI's belief that apartment 4201 at Park House was where Matt Zapata had died. Despite all the housekeepers' efforts, the forensics people had identified the spot on the floor beside the bed was body fluid from Matt.

After reconfirming that Charlie, Paul, and I would concentrate on the Park House tenants and staff, Roy and Glenann left to pursue the latest killing.

HAZEL WENT to work on the computer, checking out the current list of tenants and staff of Park House, while Charlie,

Paul, and I spent a couple of days chasing each of them down and interviewing everyone. Thursday afternoon while I was interviewing the custodian on the ground floor of the apartment house, Paul rang my cell and asked me to come to the fourth floor.

I terminated my interview and took the service elevator, which happened to be closer, to the fourth level. Paul was waiting for me in the doorway to apartment number 4202.

"Find something?" I asked.

"Maybe. Like to introduce you to a couple of guys."

A moment later, I met Willow Schmidlin and Wally Cauldwell, both definitely males despite one being called Willow.

Schmidlin—tall, thin, and rapidly losing his good looks to gauntness—either saw my confusion or was accustomed to explaining his name. "Willow's a nickname. My birth name's William."

His partner picked up the tale. "But when he was a kid, he walked around looking sad all the time."

"So they called me Willow."

Cauldwell finished up what was obviously a practiced piece. "You know, like a weeping willow?"

I flashed an obligatory smile and turned to Paul.

"They didn't see anything that particular Monday, but they knew the guy who once rented 4201."

"Oh yes," Willow put in. "Burton Neville. Wonderful man. We've known him forever. Lived in the same apartment complex on Montgomery he did before we came to Park House. Actually, he came first and sang its praises so much we followed. We're one of the first tenants… along with Burton, of course. He was one of the brotherhood, you know. Single, but he had friends stay with him on occasion. Sometimes for a protracted while."

Cauldwell, whom I'd taken to be the more reserved of the two, proved me wrong. "One was an especially wonderful man. Very handsome… much like your friend here."

"Why did Mr. Neville change partners so often?" I asked.

The question earned me two pairs of fluttering eyes. "Way he was, I guess. The one Wally was talking about—" Willow shot a look at Paul. "—the real dish, might have proved a keeper, but he came down with some kind of sickness. Something serious, I think. Never did quite find out what it was. Guess I never will because Burton— nobody ever called him Burt, he didn't permit it—got a transfer and moved away about six months back. He was a scientist on the base." He turned and smiled at his partner. "Like my Wally is."

"I'm a chemical engineer at Sandia Labs," Wally explained.

Willow felt obligated to ID himself. "And I'm a personal financial advisor. A good one too, if either of you gentlemen is interested."

"Thank you," I said. "Do you recall the names of his roommates?"

Willow cackled. "Roommates! What a polite way of putting it. No, just the special one. Spectacular young man. Early twenties. Bluest eyes you've ever seen. Hair the color of honey. Jules, I believe it was. But I don't have a last name for you. Beautiful, beautiful Jules."

I immediately thought of Jules McClintock, a kid I'd known back in my University of New Mexico days. Strikingly handsome, popular, a good basketball guard, and a closet gay. I hadn't attended UNM until after I completed my Marine Corps enlistment and was serving with APD, so I was older than most of the guys. The Jules I knew had been about eight or nine years younger than I was at the time. And the bit about the former roommate falling ill rang a bell as well. Jules McClintock had been struck down by some kind of muscular ailment and had to drop out of school.

I mentally shook my head. The timing was all wrong. The Jules I knew fell ill twelve years or so ago, not six months.

"How long since you've seen this Jules?" I asked.

"Oh, ages. Simply ages," Willow said. "But I couldn't tell you exactly when."

Ages? I put the term down to Willow's flair for the dramatic and continued. "Mr. Cauldwell, have you seen him?"

"Mercy. Not since Burton said he fell ill. I guess it was awful. Put him in a wheelchair. Jules, not Burton. He was fit as a fiddle the last time we saw him."

"You say Mr. Neville was transferred?"

"Not transferred, actually. He got a new job at the Livermore plant out in California."

"Can you tell me how to contact him?" I asked.

"Heavens, no," Willow said. "He hasn't called or written since he left. He's far too busy for that. But he promised to keep in touch, so we'll hear from him sooner or later."

"Or maybe we'll take a trip out there and surprise him," Wally suggested.

I felt my brows knit in confusion.

Willow must have caught my look because he spoke up. "Silly, we can't do that until we hear from him."

"I know that. I was just—"

"If you knew that, why didn't you say so?"

It was time to leave.

"What caught your attention about those two?" I asked as Paul and I waited for the elevator in the hallway. The crime scene tape had not yet been removed from 4201.

"Lived on the same floor. Both gay. Let me know the former roommate at the crime scene was gay, and Matt was killed while on a gay date."

"I'll call Hazel and ask her to track down Neville at the Livermore Labs and see what she can learn about him and his beautiful Jules. In the meantime, let's see if we can finish interviewing the tenants."

A LITTLE before five, we met Charlie in the small reception area on the first floor of the apartment house. He'd been stuck with one of the tenants on the third floor for the last half hour. At first he thought the middle-aged widow who answered his ring might have some information. By the time she pressed the second cup of tea on him, he was convinced she was merely lonely and willing to make up stories to keep him seated on the couch in her living room. She'd claimed to have seen a stranger in the service elevator on the afternoon of the fifth. But when pressed, Charlie decided she'd merely heard someone descending in the elevator.

I immediately flashed on the big laundry carts I'd seen on the first floor, which prompted me to look up Hector Valdez, an attractive man something shy of fifty who'd been Park House's maintenance man since the place opened. Had he been twenty years younger, I'm certain Willow or Wally—or both—would have been calling him for imaginary leaks and malfunctioning light sockets on a regular basis. Hector kept himself fit.

"Sometimes tenants use the laundry trucks to move heavy stuff—you know, groceries and the like—from cars to apartments and vice versa."

The term he used, "laundry trucks," was probably more appropriate than carts, as they were essentially big canvas baskets mounted on wheels.

"If they're doing the vice versa thing, taking something heavy from apartment to vehicle, do they leave the cart… uh, truck in the parking area?" I asked.

"Some do, some don't." He wrinkled his nose, giving the impression of disapproval. "Most do. I'm always dragging them back to the laundry area."

"Do you recall one in the garage the afternoon of the fifth? That was a Monday."

"Coulda been, but I don't remember one way or the other."

"How do tenants gain access to parking?" Paul asked.

"Key card. It lets you go about anywhere."

His answer was no surprise. The killer had to have a key to gain access to the apartment where he'd killed Matt.

"Do you recall seeing any strange vehicles in the parking garage around that time?" I asked.

Hector shook his head. "Don't recollect nothing. Course, I don't check the place regular like, but I do keep an eye on it. On everything." He looked startled at where his own thought process was taking him. "Don't rightly see how a stranger coulda got inside this place without me or someone taking notice." His brow cleared. "Course, sometimes I get Mondays off if Mr. Quint has me do weekend work. And I done some weekend chores along about the first week in March. Mr. Quint can tell you for sure, but like as not I wasn't even here that Monday."

Although forensics had no evidence to indicate a body in any of Park House's laundry trucks, I was nonetheless convinced Matt, wrapped in the missing duvet, had been removed from the premises in precisely that manner.

OUR INTERVIEW of the tenants finally complete, we gathered around the small conference table in my private office to compare notes. Hazel joined us and confessed she'd not been able to locate Burton Neville at Livermore Labs.

"It's a big outfit, and I got the runaround. Finally located someone in Human Resources interested enough to give me some help. The woman I talked to called back not half an hour ago and said she'd discovered Neville had notified HR he'd taken other employment and never showed up."

"She know where this other employment was?"

Hazel shook her head. "No idea. No notation in the file. She contacted the man who was to be his immediate supervisor, but he'd simply been notified by HR his new employee had gone elsewhere."

"She find who'd taken Neville's call?"

"Lawrence Livermore National Laboratory has upward of 5,000 employees, but she eventually found the right one. His notes didn't give us any more than what we already knew. Neville was going somewhere else. Period. And before you ask, the call wasn't recorded."

"So anyone could have called and left that message," I said. "I assume you undertook a search for Mr. Neville."

She nodded. "Dead end. Last reference to the man I could find was right after he left Albuquerque. I called a friend at APD, and she was able to locate one credit card. American Express. He used it at a gas station in Gallup six months ago. Then he vanished."

"Did you find a car registration?"

"A black 2010 Jaguar convertible. No sign of vehicle registration transfer."

"No other credit card charges?"

"Just the one at the gas station in Gallup. Nothing since then on the Amex. Of course, he may have had other cards we haven't located."

"Looks like he was on the way to Livermore."

"Presumably," she said. "I checked APD for a missing person's report. Nothing."

I sighed. "Okay, pull a credit report on him. That might give us more credit cards to run down. In the meantime, it's back to Willow and Wally to see if they had an emergency contact for Neville. Paul, it looks like your instincts were good about those two."

"I'll give them a call," he volunteered. "Do I share Neville's disappearance with them?"

"Not yet. I'd prefer to be standing in front of them when we reveal that information. Oh, and see if they know what credit cards he carried."

"Awkward if I can't tell them he's disappeared."

"There's a difference between 'haven't located him yet' and 'he's vanished.'"

Paul took out his cell phone and headed for the outer office. We had Roy Guerra on the speakerphone when he returned.

"You're doing better than we are," Roy said. "Greene was a street kid, Hubbard a stranded motorist, and Zapata a call boy. So far as we can tell, Lieu wasn't any of those things. Worked at his family's food store in the International District. We're running down his contacts to see if any of them overlap with the other three. So far, nada."

"Hold on a minute," I said. "Paul, what did you find out?"

"Willow checked his address book. The only contact he had was an estranged sister in Illinois. I gave her a quick call, but she hasn't heard from her brother. Didn't seem too broken up when I told her he was missing. She promised to let me know if she hears from him."

"Okay, so that's a dead end. What about the credit cards?"

"Besides the Amex, they knew of a CITI Mastercard and a Chase Visa."

To spare Hazel from having to tap her contact at APD again, I asked Roy to check into the card activity.

"Do you want us to contact his coworkers at Sandia?" Roy asked.

"We'll cover it. You keep on with what you're doing. If we run into a problem, I'll give you a ring."

BEFORE THE day was out, the police department was busy answering questions about a fatal police shooting. According to news reports, a longtime APD officer answered a call about a man fencing stolen stereo equipment in a Heights apartment-house parking lot. When the alleged fence was confronted, he tried to run down the officer with his automobile and was shot for his efforts. Well, that would put the barm on the brew, as my granddad used to say. Rumors had been floating for a year the Department of Justice was preparing to investigate the APD. There had been far too many police shootings recently. Gene Enriquez had hesitated before accepting his promotion last year because he was concerned over being drawn into the middle of the investigation. I would have put down a sizable hunk of change betting Justice would be on the scene before the year was out. Man, was I glad I turned down an appointment to the Police Oversight Board.

THE NEXT morning, winter reminded us spring had not arrived quite yet. Puffy gray clouds clinging to Sandia Peak didn't deliver snow to the town—although wind gusts blew a few errant flakes down on us—but when those clouds cleared away, the mountain would be dusted white. Paul and I donned heavier jackets before heading to the office. We took Paul's 2009 black Dodge Charger because he claimed the beast needed exercising.

"You finished with the article you're working on?" I asked, watching him skillfully maneuver freeway traffic.

"Submitted it last night."

"That was quick."

As usual his grin sent my hormones on a binge. "Different slant on the article I sent last week. That's what I like about writing for magazines. You can sell the same story—well, essentially the same story—to more than one editor."

"What's the next project?"

"Short piece for *Sports Illustrated*, but you and me are working on my next major project right now. I like Glenann's name for the case. The cutie-pie murders. That makes a hell of a title, doesn't it?"

He parked in my reserved spot in the Sixth Street lot behind my office building, and we took the stairs to the third level.

Hazel was already at work at the computer when we entered. Charlie fiddled with the automatic coffee machine nearby.

"Morning, crew. Anything new?"

"Still haven't located Neville. Glenann called to say no more activity on his credit cards."

"No sign of his car," Charlie said. "Neither the license tag nor the VIN showed up anywhere."

"Leading us to believe…?"

"I think he's dead," Hazel answered.

"That's a bold prediction. What leads you to that conclusion?"

"Hard to vanish without leaving a trace, short of spending a lot of time and effort preparing for it. But one way is to be in the ground."

"All the more reason to talk to his friends and coworkers."

By the time the clouds cleared from Sandia—leaving the crest with a snow cape and the setting sun creating a kaleidoscope of interesting colors—we'd talked to a dozen of Burton Neville's friends and fellow workers and learned precisely nothing. He had been in touch with none of them since his departure for California. Some thought it odd; others thought it typical of the man.

I began to take Hazel's conclusion more seriously.

Chapter 7

SATURDAY MORNING Paul wanted to drive up Sandia, supposedly to see how much snow fell on the mountain yesterday, although I suspected he had an ulterior motive. Remote mountain roads made my companion horny, and as pleasurable as that could be, the temperature at the top of the mountain was bound to be somewhere between slightly below uncomfortable to a smidgen above unbearable.

We didn't encounter road ice until three-quarters of the way up the mountain. The snow was always thicker than it appeared from downtown, which was logical. It had to be a reasonable cover to be apparent from the valley. Upon reaching the crest, we discovered we were the only ones dumb enough to brave the icy wind gusts. Even the gift shop was closed. I'd long since discovered windburn and chilblains sat better on Paul's half-Hispanic skin than they did on my Anglo flesh. He looked sexy; I appeared what I was—cold and uncomfortable. But as they say, we do countless things in the name of love. Here I was on a blustery, snow-encrusted mountaintop instead of back home in a sweater and thick socks, sitting before a blazing fireplace, sipping a hot toddy, and reading a book. Even stranger, I'd rather be here with Paul, freezing my fanny, than comfy at home alone.

What was I bitching about? The snow would be gone by morning. Water was already rushing down the barrow ditches on either side of the road. But maybe it was even too chilly for my mate because he waited until we were back at the house before demonstrating his hot Latin blood. Pedro and I had a ball. Paul probably did too, but he had to do all the work.

MONDAY MORNING brought a surprising new development that might bear fruit. Paul and I had no sooner arrived downtown than Charlie breezed through the door to my private office.

"Alan had a call from the pen this morning."

Alan Mendoza was one of two retired APD cops who worked part-time for us when Charlie and I had more than we could handle. Or, as Hazel would put it, when I took on hopeless cases that ate up our resources. Alan had been a detective in Homicide prior to putting in his papers. He liked to take work from us occasionally because it got him out of the house and out of his wife's way.

"And?" I prompted.

"I gave him the job of checking on Zancón's activities up at the pen. I used him because he has a brother-in-law who's a corrections officer up there."

I motioned Charlie to a chair and took a seat behind my desk. Paul settled in the client's chair next to Charlie.

"Brother-in-law says Zancón's pretty much a con serving out his time. Health's not good, and he doesn't have many visitors. His brother, Juan, a few times a year, and that's about it. He's built a circle around him in the prison, but Alan figures that's more for protection than anything else. Everyone's convinced Zancón's got some assets the authorities didn't find."

"That matches my impression when I visited him up in Santa Fe," I said. "His brother probably manages them for Zancón."

"Which explains why Matt didn't like taking his dad's money," Paul added. "He couldn't tell whether it was his dad's or his uncle's."

"Are we at the end of this story?" I asked Charlie.

He ran a hand over his bald dome. "Nope. Zancón got in a beef with an Albuquerque hood named Garson Debbins."

"Who's he?" Paul asked.

"Owns South Broadway Junkyard. Got in trouble when he bought some cars caught in a south Texas flood and retitled them without noting the fact. He got caught and spent five years in Santa Fe. Just released in January of this year after serving every last day of his sentence."

"Five years is stiff for that sort of crime. And to serve it all? Something's missing from this picture."

"Wasn't the first time he got caught. Rolled speedometers back and sold junk for quality. Did a year for that."

"Still…," I said.

"His beef with Zancón killed the good time he'd banked. Way Alan got it is, it wasn't anything more than an argument over the last piece of cake or pie or something sweet. Anyway, they got into a brawl over it in the dining hall, and it ended up in a food fight. Zancón's a lifer, so the dustup didn't cost him. But they took away all Debbins's good time."

"I wonder if Mr. Debbins carries grudges?" Paul asked.

I carried his thought down the road. "And if he takes them out on relatives when he can't get to the primary target? I think we need to have a talk with Mr. Garson Debbins. Who's up for a trip to the South Valley?" I asked.

Paul wanted to go, so Charlie stayed behind to do some records checking for other contacts between the Zapatas and the Debbins clans.

ON THE way to the junkyard, Paul turned to me. "You don't really think Debbins killed Greene and Hubbard before he got in a beef with Zancón and killed his nephew, do you? Doesn't make any sense."

"You're using logic, my friend. Normally, that's a good thing. But investigators need to keep open minds and eliminate any possibilities. Besides, I want to try something."

"What?"

"You'll see."

My first look at Garson Debbins convinced me we should have brought Charlie along with us, and possibly Alan Mendoza as well. The man behind a rough, oil-stained counter must have stood at least six two, weighed something over 280, and looked like he was considering punishing the world for wrongs real and perceived. His voice and demeanor did nothing to alleviate the impression.

"Yeah, whaddya want?"

"Need to ask you some questions, Mr. Debbins," I said in my most courteous and correct form.

"I don't talk to fuzz without my lawyer present."

"We're private, not official."

"What's the difference?" His curiosity must have gotten the upper hand because he added, "Questions about what?"

"About Zancón Zapata."

I only thought he'd been scowling. *Now* he scowled. "I don' wanna talk about that scumbag less'n you're here to tell me he's bought the farm."

"Afraid not. So far as I know, he's still wheezing away in the penitentiary."

"Well, come back when he stops wheezing."

"You're going to answer the questions, Mr. Debbins, either to me or to two APD detectives named Guerra and Hastings. And I ask them nicer."

He tilted his head and fixed me with a stare. "Whadda I know about Zancón you don't?"

"Who killed his nephew, Mateo Zapata, for instance."

Debbins surprised both Paul and me by breaking out in a genuine laugh that rattled the rafters and set the ballpoint on his counter to dancing. He stopped just as abruptly.

"And you figure I done it? Let me tell you something, I was gonna kill somebody, it'd be a nasty bag o' bones up there in Santa Fe. I don't even know who his nephew is." His eyes opened fractionally wider. "Wait a minute. His nephew? You talking about Juan's kid?" The laugh made the pen jump again. "That's rich. Juan finally getting some justice coming his way."

"Explain that, please," I said.

"How the hell you think Juan got his business started? Offa cars them Muddy Saints, or whatever they called themselves, stole. He shoulda been locked up there in Santa Fe with his brother."

"You have proof of that?" I asked.

"All the proof I need," he said. "And that's all I care about. Now get offa my property."

As we walked back to my Impala, Paul asked what I thought.

"If those two yardbirds had a beef, it didn't kill Matt Zapata."

"That's what I said on the way down here. Why are you so sure after one talk with the guy?"

"Because of you."

Paul halted midstep. "Me?"

"Yep. Debbins didn't pay one bit of attention to you. He wasn't attracted by your looks or youth or…." I let my voice trail off.

"*That's what you wanted to try?* Using me for a guinea pig?"

"As you correctly pointed out, if Debbins didn't kill the first two victims, he didn't kill Matt. All three were sex killings. So if Debbins isn't interested in young men, he's not our killer. What did your gaydar say?"

Paul grimaced as he started walking again. "It crashed."

"Basic lesson in detecting—and journalism too, I'd guess—you always follow every lead, no matter how improbable."

Paul slammed the car door behind him. "So we're back to square one."

"You can look at it that way, or you can consider we chased one more lead into the ground."

"What about what Debbins said about Juan's used car business?"

"My first reaction is to consider the source. Crooks are convinced everyone else is crooked too. Still, it bears looking into. But I'll reserve judgment until that's done."

"Me too. I like the guy," Paul said. "Well, back when I knew him, that is."

"Don't let rumors infect the way you think about the man. Wait until the facts are in."

WE GOT back to the office in time to take a call from Roy about another body on the West Mesa escarpment, not far from the eastern entrance to Petroglyph Park. We immediately got back in the Impala and headed west.

A patrolman stopped us short of where four cars sat in a tight cluster. Roy and Glenann walked out to meet us.

"OMI hasn't arrived yet, so we're all waiting," Roy said.

"What can you tell us?"

"Young, good-looking," Glenann answered.

"Naked?"

"And naked."

"How'd he die?"

"Strangled. But he put up a fight. He's got cuts and abrasions."

"ID him yet?" I asked.

"Yep. The guy's clothes were scattered all over the place by the wind. We found a billfold with ID. Name's Patricio Aragon. Twenty years old."

"Drugged?" Paul asked.

Glenann looked like she'd been sucking on persimmons. "Have to wait for OMI to tell us that."

Roy lifted his official APD field cap and ran a hand through his dark hair. "This guy's really accelerated his timetable. Like you pointed out the other day, there were three months between each of the first three murders. Then Lieu was killed thirteen days after Zapata. Now eight days later… Aragon."

"If it's the same killer. Was there semen on the body?"

"No visible sign of it."

"Then the signature's wrong on at least three accounts," I said. "There's never been any signs the victim fought back, the killer never left the victim's clothes behind, and there's no semen on the body."

"BJ's right," Glenann said. "Let's wait for OMI to finish his examination before we add this one to our list."

"Fair enough," Roy said.

My mind went back to the last confirmed cutie-pie killing. "Have you determined how the killer got in touch with Lieu?"

"Friends say Lieu was clubbing at Viewers, got in an argument in the game room, and left in a huff. He rode to the club with a friend, so he was hoofing it home. Like Hubbard, he hitched a ride with the wrong guy."

"Viewers. That's in the Mountain Run Shopping Center, isn't it?" Paul asked.

"Yep. Popular place. They were crowded that night."

"So he was probably killed Sunday night?" I asked. "If it is the cutie-pie killer, why do we think the killings have accelerated?"

"Target of opportunity," Glenann said. "Hadn't worked up the need to kill again, but here was this cute guy stomping down the street and catching his eye."

"Have you profiled the killer yet?" Paul asked.

Glenann screwed her face into a frown. "Not much to go on. The only crime scene we have to study is the one you and BJ found at Park House. From that we know the killer's organized. Power assertive. Male. Probably white and between 30 and 40. Strong enough to lift a deadweight of at least 160 pounds. And he chooses extremely handsome young men."

I considered her words. "How did you come up with the age estimate?"

"Has to be young enough to interest a young person and not too old to be able to carry dead bodies. It's nothing but a guess."

"Zapata, and probably Greene, were in it for the money, so age might not be a factor. The other two hitched rides and so weren't necessarily attracted to their killer."

"They stayed with him long enough to be drugged into submission."

"True, but maybe he's a sympathetic ear."

"Possible. You have any better ideas?"

"Nope," I admitted. "When the crime lab comes up with DNA from hair or skin cells, they don't test for ethnicity. If you'll get me a sample, I'll take it to K-Y Labs and have an ancestry test run. That'll confirm your theory about him being white... or disprove it."

"See what we can do," Roy said. "You finished ripping our profile to shreds?"

"You say the killer's probably power assertive. Have you ever thought he might be anger assertive, or even anger excited?"

Roy pursed his lips and nodded. "Could be, I suppose. Might be why he kills after he has sex with them. Like somebody who won't admit he's gay but can't keep away from good-looking boys. So he's mad at himself but takes it out on them."

"Possibly. Self-loathing's killed more than one individual. And let's examine that statement about strength. He dopes his victims. Logical way to get what you want with someone who's not gay. But what if it's connected to the killer's strength? It takes time and considerable effort to strangle a man into unconsciousness and death. Either way, the victim would struggle, but a hell of a lot less if he was heavily sedated."

Roy shook his head. "Now you're questioning the killer's strength? You do agree he's male, don't you?"

"I'd say the semen proves that, DNA or no DNA."

"I dunno, BJ. Takes some muscle to deadweight 160 pounds. And Zapata was every bit of that."

"Just thinking aloud."

"Something to consider," Roy agreed.

"You intend to use K-Y Lab for the DNA ancestry test?" Glenann asked.

"When I can't get the city or state to do it for me, that's who I use."

ZAPATA'S PRE-OWNED Cars occupied a full block on Bridge Boulevard near Old Coors Drive SW. The background of a large sign fronting Bridge featured the sole of a huge shoe, reminding me Zapata meant shoe in Spanish. A quick glance at the lot showed Juan covered the gamut of his local clients. A bright pink 2008 Cadillac lowrider sat beside a faded brown 1998 Ford Taurus. The showroom was big and airy and full of hungry salesmen anxious to part me from my Impala and put me into... anything. Possibly even the lowrider. They lost interest the moment I asked for Juan Zapata.

When he greeted Paul and me in a commodious office with a glass wall looking out into the showroom, Juan showed he was only a cut above the others. "Hello, BJ. Aren't you tired of your four-year-old Chevrolet? I can put you in a 2012 with only 9,800 miles on it. Loaded."

"Thanks, I'm happy with my wheels."

He turned to my companion. "*¡Orale!* Do my eyes deceive me? Is this little Pauly Barton standing here?" He clasped Paul's hand. "You've grown up. How long's it been?"

If Paul had been unduly influenced by Garson Debbins's opinion of Juan Zapata, he didn't show it. "*Buenas tardes.* A lot of years, Mr. Zapata. Sorry about Mateo. He was a good kid."

Sadness claimed Juan's features. "That he was. Had you seen him recently?"

"Ran into him at Zimmerman Library not long back and said hello. Talk about growing up! He'd really done some growing since I saw him last."

"Ah, yes. Zimmerman Library at UNM. He liked to do his homework there."

"If it helps any, Matt… uh, Mateo—"

"Matt. He liked to be called Matt."

"Right. Matt was a happy, contented guy. Comfortable with who he was."

Juan indicated chairs and took a seat behind his desk. "He accepted who he was better than some of the family. Not his mother or me, of course. We loved him exactly as he was."

It wasn't hard to figure Zancón as "some of the family." He hadn't even been comfortable discussing the details of how Matt died.

"Juan," I said, "Paul's working the case with me."

"I'm a freelance journalist, Mr. Zapata," Paul said.

"Juan. Please call me Juan."

"Yessir. If it's okay with you, I intend to write an article on Matt and his murder. I know the whole thing's painful for you and Mrs. Zapata, and seeing Matt in print is going to hurt. But someone's going to do it. I think it oughta be me. I knew him, and I liked him. Respected him." Paul shrugged. "And I share some of his traits. It oughta be me who writes his story."

Juan's eyes softened as he studied my companion. After a lengthy silence, he nodded. "Yes, it should be you. You will deal with my son with respect and understanding. You have my blessing."

"Thank you, sir."

Juan shifted his attention to me. "What can you tell me?"

"I can tell you Matt was the third victim of a single killer. And the murderer's fourth victim was found eight days ago out near Shooting Range Park."

"They were all the same? Violated and… and strangled and left naked?"

"Exactly the same. Another strangled body was found near the escarpment on the West Mesa, but in my opinion, it was a copycat. Too many details varied from the other four killings. Nonetheless, I'd like to ask if you know a young man by the name of Patricio Aragon?"

"I know some Aragons, and a couple of them have sons or grandsons named Patricio."

"But they weren't familiars of yours or Matt's?"

Juan expressed his frustration with a shrug. "Not mine. And not Matt's… that I know of. He moved in different circles of late. I-I don't know all of his friends." He put both hands to his temples and ran them through his hair. "What is happening to this world?"

"What's been happening to it for millennia," I said. "But we only become intensely aware of it when it strikes home." I handed over the live-shot photos of the other three cutie-pie victims. "Do you recognize any of these young men?"

He devoted a minute to studying the pictures intently before shaking his head. "No. Who are they?"

"The other three victims of your son's killer."

Juan looked as if he'd taken a body blow. "They… they're all like Matt."

"Handsome, you mean."

He nodded. "What kind of monster is this man? Killing off our youth."

I pulled out the photo of Bark Pierson. "How about this man? Do you know him?"

Juan accepted the photo and studied it intently. "No. I've not seen him before. Who is he? Is this the man who murdered Matt? And the others?"

I shook my head. "I don't believe so, but we are checking into his background. This is a photo of a young man named Barkley Pierson. He was a good friend of your son's. Since the beginning of this year, he and Matt were lovers, until Pierson was unable to talk Matt out of becoming an escort."

"So he was jealous?"

Paul spoke up. "No, sir. He was afraid for Matt. If you ask me, Pierson still had strong feelings for Matt, but he hoped by breaking it off, he could make your son recognize how dangerous it was to do what he was doing."

Juan looked to me for confirmation.

"I agree. There was genuine feeling between those two young men. Matt not only put his life in jeopardy when he started accepting clients, he also put an important relationship to a test."

Juan blinked, and I could see him clutching at straws. "But you're going to investigate this Pierson fellow, right?"

"It started when I asked if you knew him."

"What will you do next?"

"Hazel, my office manager and a heck of an investigator in her own right, is starting a record check here and back East where Pierson comes from. But the most important thing is to establish a connection to the Park House."

"What is that?"

"A high-end apartment building in the 4200 block of East Central."

"Why is it important?"

"We'll get into that in a moment, but I have a few more questions first."

Juan's sigh seemed to come from his soul. "Will this ever end?"

"The investigation, yes. Your loss, no. But it'll grow more bearable with time. Just a few more questions, please. Don't take offense at them. Most are pro forma and need to be asked in every case. Did Matt take drugs?"

Juan straightened, his face animated. "No! Never." He slumped back in his chair. "Hell, BJ, the truth is I don't know. When they go out on their own, who knows what they do? But I never saw evidence of drugs. We talked about it when he was younger, and he swore he'd never subject his system to such abuse. But of course he drank alcohol. In moderation, but he drank."

"Do you or your son have any connection with that new apartment house I mentioned? The Park House."

"I have some real estate holdings, but none on East Central. I'm also in a real estate investment trust, but so far as I know, Park House isn't one of our properties. In fact, I've never heard of the place. As far as my son is concerned, perhaps he knew someone who lived there. Otherwise no."

"How about your brother?"

"Zancón has a few pieces of real estate left, but I manage them and can assure you Park House is not one of them. Why are you so interested in this apartment building?"

"Because that's where Matt died. It's the only crime scene we've found for the four killings. All of the bodies were simply dumped where they were found."

"And this is important how?"

"It grounds us. Lets the APD forensics lab study the crime scene and compare it to others, looking for leads. Gives us a place to start searching for who had access to the site."

"I understand. But if you know Matt died there, you must have an apartment number. Simply arrest the tenant."

"No one's lived in 4201 for six months. It's now used as a show unit."

Juan buried his face in his hands momentarily. "I see. I'll ask Zancón if the name or address means anything to him. I'll also ask Matt's mother and some of his friends."

"Which brings us to the next item. We need a list of those friends. We need to talk to them to establish a pattern to your son's life."

"His mother and I will compile a list of those we know with contact information and email it to you this evening. Will that be satisfactory?"

I nodded. "Now some more hard questions. Again, they have to be asked." I cleared my throat and started down a road I didn't want to travel. "Matt and your brother were close at one time, right?"

"When Matt was smaller, yes."

"Why did the situation change?"

"Who says it did?"

"Juan, I tell every client they can lie to me once, but not twice. In some of Matt's notes we found in his rental, he makes it clear his relationship with Zancón went south."

Juan fell back in his chair. "Sometimes it's hard to know when to wear a face and when to put it aside. You also probably know why he was fighting so hard to make his own way."

"He didn't trust the source of your money," I said.

It all came out then. How Juan tried to stay clear of his brother's Brown Saints connection. He had a hard time starting his business, and in the early days Juan had bought some vehicles at a below-market price from his brother. Not many, he insisted, and not for long, but that helped him over the hump. Thereafter he refused any more vehicles from them, even though he was threatened and even roughed up once or twice. But when Zancón became convinced his brother meant it, he had the gang back off.

Juan finished up by self-justifying. "Since that time, I've not accepted any help from or provided any help to the *Santos Morenos.* Or my brother. He went his way, and I went mine. But we continued to be brothers. And I've done what I could to atone. Prayers. Donations. Even giving cars to deserving families who wouldn't be able to afford one otherwise."

"Okay," I said when he finished. "We now understand why Matt wouldn't let you support him. Up to a point. Why did he let you pay his college expenses?"

"Something I've pondered for a long time, BJ. Best explanation I can come up with has to do with family. Matt figured he owed me something… love, loyalty, support. And he figured I owed him something. Like an education. But he wouldn't even talk about me financing his dream. That's the point where he figured my responsibility ended and his began. You understand what that means, don't you? I'm responsible for my son's death."

Paul beat me to it. "No, you aren't. There was nothing wrong with the way Matt figured he'd live his life. I admire him for it. Maybe it led him to putting himself at risk, but it didn't kill him. The son of a bitch who drugged him and… and strangled him did that. *He's* the only one responsible for Matt's death."

"I couldn't have put it any better, Juan," I said. "Paul's right, and we all three know it. But that won't stop you from carrying around a load of guilt for the rest of your life. Learn to live with it or it'll eat you up."

An uncomfortable pause built before I said, "Back to Matt's estrangement from his uncle."

"Mutual. Matt began hearing things at school and came home asking questions. For a long time, we tried to shield him, but eventually he knew the truth. I think Zancón wanted to take him under his wing in the Saints, but Matt was repelled by the idea. The boy almost got in some scrapes at school, but in the end, everyone backed down. Probably because they were afraid of his uncle."

Juan paused and moistened his lower lip. "Then one day, Zancón showed up at the house and found Matt in the garage with another boy. He sent the other kid packing and called Matt some names. That put an end to the mutual admiration society."

"Then why did Zancón call me up to the penitentiary?"

Juan shrugged. "In Zancón's eyes, Matt might have been a queer, but he was still family. And that carries obligations." He met my gaze squarely. "Does this change our arrangement?"

"Matt is still dead. And his killer is still out there. Nothing's changed."

He nodded his thanks. "Is… is it likely you'll be able to find my son's killer?"

"The fact he's a serial killer makes it even more likely we'll be able to identify him."

"But you hear about serial killers who evade capture for years."

"One or two, maybe. But the vast majority are discovered within a reasonable amount of time."

As we pulled out of the car lot, Paul clapped me on the shoulder. "Proud of you, Vince."

"Thanks. You didn't do so bad, yourself."

WHEN WE returned downtown, Paul claimed a computer in our spare office and set to work on his *Sports Illustrated* story. He usually carried his laptop with him, but when he came to the office, he knew our system was available to him, so he merely brought his thumb drive.

I settled down with Hazel and Charlie at the table in my private office. The buzzer on the front door would alert Hazel if anyone entered the outer office.

After I filled them in on our visit to Juan Zapata, I asked if there was anything new on their end.

"I think I found Neville," Hazel said.

"Think?"

"Couple of dog-walkers came across a John Doe down near Socorro. Body's about six months old, and the size is right. No fingerprints. Scavengers saw to that. But the sheriff's deputy told me OMI's sent DNA to the state lab to try to ID him. Also trying to get prints off his clothes."

"So he wasn't naked."

"Nope, but no billfold or other ID."

"Any sign of his car?

"Uh-uh. I checked with Motor Vehicles. His Jag bears NM license plate SND-555. And it hasn't shown up anywhere."

"What makes you think the body is Neville?"

"Right time, about the right size. I don't know how he was killed, body's in too bad shape. We'll have to wait for OMI to tell us."

"What about his credit card being used in Gallup? That's considerably west of Socorro."

"Maybe the killer drove there and filled his own car before disposing of the wallet and card. You know, to make us think Neville was headed for California."

"That would mean his killer would have to know he was heading there. You think it's someone who knew him?"

"I don't know. I just have a feeling."

"I trust your feelings, Hazel. We'll proceed on the basis it's Neville until we know something different. What does it mean for our case?"

I went to my desk and used the intercom to call Paul. He needed to sit in on this. As he took his seat, I gave him Hazel's news. He asked the same question I had.

"What does that mean to us?"

"I'm going to make an assumption," Charlie said. "I think Neville held on to a second key to his apartment. Might have been accidental or might have been deliberate, but that's the connection."

"So you're saying Neville's killer is someone he knew. Have to be for a key to mean anything to him," Paul said.

Charlie nodded. "Fits in with Hazel's assumption the killer knew he was headed for California. Has to be someone who knew him."

"We'll ask Roy and Glenann to check if the Gallup service station has videotapes," I said. "I'd like to see the Neville who used the card. Maybe it's someone we'll recognize. In the meantime, we'll keep on digging into the Park House connection."

Hazel picked up the photos of our four victims and arranged them in front of her.

"What is it?" I asked.

"If the next victim turns out to be a Native American, he'll have covered all the races," she said.

"You may be onto something. An Anglo, a Black, a Hispanic, and an Asian. We may have been wrong about the fourth murder. Lieu may not have simply been a target of opportunity. He may have been picked because of his race."

"Meaning?" Paul asked.

"Maybe something cultural. Maybe the killer's looking for some cultural trait and hasn't found it yet."

"Like what?" Paul pressed.

I stood from the conference table. "I have no idea. But it's something to store in our heads to take out and examine now and then."

I barely had time to settle at my desk after the meeting broke up before Hazel dropped a list of names in front of me.

"Mr. Zapata sent this by email. Friends of Matt's, I gather."

"The ones they knew about. Promised it by tonight, but I guess he's anxious. Is Paul still here?" She nodded. "Ask him to come in. He might know some of them."

A moment later Paul answered the summons. He did in fact know four of the names on the list and promised to try to reach them. Zapata had given us phone numbers but no indication as to whether they were cell phones or home phones.

Most of the numbers proved to be cell phones, so we had run through most of the list by that afternoon and finished off the remainder by nine the next morning.

Chapter 8

WE'D RUN down every lead we had without success. Matt's friends, family, schoolmates.... None of them appeared to have a motive for strangling the kid. Jealousy, maybe, but the circumstances of his killing didn't lead to such a conclusion. A check and a recheck of Barkley Pierson showed a clean slate. There was no violence in his background. So far, I hadn't tied him to the Park House, but I needed to flash his photo to the people there.

I sat back to review the circumstances of Matt's death. His killer had sex with him, which would have provoked feelings ranging anywhere from triumphant exhilaration to intense remorse—and anything in between. But drugging Matt led me to the conclusion the killing was preplanned and deliberate. This wasn't merely a sexual tryst gone wrong.

Greene's murder probably fit the same mold. More than likely, the street kid was a sex-for-pay victim too. Yet he was drugged and strangled as well. It made no sense. And despite the fact serial killings *often* made no rational sense, I couldn't help but look for a reason. Besides, the intuitive side of my brain still believed Greene had done something to set the killer off on his murderous path.

Perhaps it was nothing but desperation, but my mind kept flashing on Neville. He'd pulled a disappearing act around the time of the first murder. I'd told Hazel I accepted her conclusion he was lying up in the coroner's office, but it hadn't been confirmed as yet. Further, I couldn't get Jules McClintock out of my head. A fellow named Jules struck down by some sort of illness. Too much of a coincidence to ignore, even though there appeared to be years between Jules McClintock and the Jules of Neville's infatuation. Time to go back to Willow and Wally… with a detour to Quint James, the manager of Park House.

A call to his office got me nothing but a message my call would be returned if I saw fit to leave a name and number. Quint was probably in class, prompting the question of how a college kid got a job managing an upscale apartment house. I called Charlie on the intercom and asked him to check out ownership.

No use calling Willow and Wally until after business hours, as they would both be at work. That left me free until Hazel dropped a background-check case on my desk. The client was the law firm of Stone, Hedges, Martinez, Levishon, etc., which told me my ex-lover Del Dahlman had sent it to us. Del had been active in the gay community before I met him on a case while I was at APD. The Blah's request—that's what I called the Stone, Hedges firm because of the long list of partners—was a light background check on a Baltimore attorney they were considering hiring. They'd already done their professional precheck and wanted another look at his character and habits.

By early afternoon, I had the information I needed and called Del. It had been too long since we talked. He sounded harassed when he came on line.

"What's wrong? You sound more like a frustrated used car salesman than a lawyer."

"I should never have agreed to become managing partner," he said. "Four more months and then I can lay it on someone else and go back to being a lawyer. What have you got for me?"

"Your applicant looks solid. No evidence of excessive drinking or drugs or chasing wayward women… or men. Doesn't seem to beat his wife. Cusses moderately, but never at the judge."

"Great. Send me the report."

"Hazel's printing it out now. Be in this evening's mail."

"How've you been doing, Vince?" He was the only individual besides Paul who used that moniker for me.

"Thriving and striving to keep off the excess weight."

"You and Paul still doing all right?"

"Great. I've got a keeper there."

"I agree. If you ever get tired of him, let me know."

"Fat chance." An idea struck out of the blue. "Tell me, do you know a fellow by the name of Jules McClintock?"

"Knew him at one time. He was a knockout. Really something special."

"Until?" I probed.

"Until he got transverse myelitis."

"What the hell is that?"

"Don't know much about it, but it's an inflammation of the spinal cord. It put him in a wheelchair. Damned near killed him. Then I lost track of him. Last I heard he was tutoring math students."

"Can you make a living at that?"

"His folks left him a bundle." Del let out an audible breath. "Not as big a bundle as someone else I know." That was a swipe at the twelve mil my folks left me in trust by virtue of an early investment in Microsoft. "But it's enough so he doesn't have to work if he doesn't want to. Haven't seen him in ages."

In ages. That's what Willow had said about seeing Neville's Jules last. "What does ages mean?"

"Three or four years, at least. Why?"

"Someone named Jules came up in a murder case I'm working."

"Murder? Doesn't sound like the Jules we know. I don't think he can even get out of a wheelchair."

We spent a few minutes catching each other up before closing the call. The phone receiver was no sooner back in the cradle than Hazel walked in with a phone slip.

"That Park House office manager returned your call while you were yapping at Del. Said he'd be there for about an hour."

Charlie was right on her heels. "The Park House is owned by a real estate investment trust. Here's the number for the managing partner."

I said my thanks and reached for the phone to make an appointment with the building manager this evening when I thought Willow and Wally might be available.

After that was done, I contacted the manager of the REIT and learned Quinton James was the nephew of one of the partners. It paid to have good relatives.

QUINTON JAMES looked no more like an apartment manager and no less like a college boy than the last time I saw him. He shook hands, first with me and then with Paul. We took seats opposite his desk in a nice office. I scanned the beige-and-burgundy walls. Commercial reproductions of paintings. Nothing personal. Quint probably didn't spend much time here.

I tried to view him as I imagined the cutie-pie killer would see him. Early twenties, slender but with definition, cute... but not cutie-pie. No ring, no photo of girlfriend or wife and kids evident. He pinged on my gaydar. The blip grew stronger when he smiled at Paul.

I directed his attention back to me. "Quint, what can you tell us about the former tenants in 4201?"

"There's only been one," he said without referring to any records. "Fellow by the name of Burton Neville. He was one of Park House's first tenants."

"What was his occupation?"

"Engineer of some kind at Sandia Labs."

"When did he leave?"

He fingered the keyboard of his computer a moment before answering. "Tuesday, September 13, of last year."

"About six months ago," Paul said.

"Right. Broke his lease, paid the penalty, and moved out."

"Why?"

Quint repeated what Willow and Wally had told us about a new job in California, but it wasn't wasted effort. It was corroboration. After Quint ran down, I questioned him about some of the other tenants of the building, but he needed to refer to his records to answer those queries, confirming—at least for me—that he took more interest in tenants who might have been gay.

"Have you heard from Neville since he left?"

Quint shook his head. "No. Although I should have. He has some money coming back on his deposit and was going to call with a forwarding address when he was settled."

"Has anyone called for a reference, like another apartment complex in California or a Realtor?"

"Nobody. I'm still holding a check for him."

"What can you tell us about some of the roommates Neville entertained while he was here?"

Quint averted his eyes. "No roommates. He was the only one on the lease."

A silence built until he buckled. "You must mean his guests. He had a few overnights."

"Lady friends?"

Quint's cheeks reddened enough to notice. "Boys... uh, men."

"Some of them stayed for quite some time, I understand."

"You can have guests for up to two weeks."

I opened the folio I'd brought and spread five photos on the desk in front of him, the killer's four recent victims and the copycat, Pat Aragon. "Were any of these his guests?"

I'd provided snaps of the men while they were alive and attractive. Quint took his time studying them. So far as I could tell, he devoted the same amount of interest and attention to each before looking up and shaking his head.

"I don't recall ever seeing any of them."

I tapped Zapata's photo. "This is the man who died in 4201. Sure you've never seen him before? With Neville or in the lobby or on the street?"

He shook his head again, his eyes back on the photos.

"None of them were Neville's guests?" Paul asked again.

"No. At least I didn't see them."

"Ever seen them with Willow or Wally?"

His flush was different this time, signaling anger, but he swallowed it. "Nope. Like I said, I've never seen any of these men. Anywhere, anytime, with anybody."

"Do you know if a young man named Jules spent any time in Neville's apartment?" I asked.

"No. But like I told you, I never saw any of Mr. Neville's guests."

Paul looked quizzical. "Then how do you know there were any?"

His mouth firmed. He was having trouble holding on to his calm. "Just talk. I heard people mention he had guests."

Paul pushed the issue. "People. Willow and Wally, I imagine."

Quint's complexion turned a deeper scarlet. "Among others. Look, I've told you all I know. I've got work to do, okay?"

"One more thing before we go," I said, handing over Barkley Pierson's photo. "How about this man? Have you seen him in the building?"

As Quint studied the image his face crumbled into a frown. "Yeah. I've seen this guy."

My heartbeat sped up. Paul and I exchanged glances.

"But it wasn't here. This guy's an UNM student. Yeah, yeah… I remember now. He's an artist. The U had a showing of some of the art students' work. I saw him there. He's good."

"Do you remember his name?"

"Peterson or Pearson or something like that."

I cleared it up for him. "Barkley Pierson. They call him Bark. But you haven't seen him with Neville or any of the other tenants?"

"Like Willow and Wally, you mean? Uh-uh. Just saw him at the exhibition. Talked to him for a couple of minutes. Almost bought one of his pictures."

"Did he offer to do a portrait of you?" Paul asked.

Quint looked surprised at the question. "No. He was pitching a landscape he'd done of Sandia Peak."

I thanked Quint for his help and collected the photos on his desk before we left and took the elevator to the fourth floor.

When Wally opened the door, the taller Willow hovering over his shoulder, I was struck by how cheerful and contented the two seemed to be. Here were a couple of guys not the least intimidated by the larger straight world hovering outside their door. They invited us in with broad, welcoming smiles. Wally ushered us to chairs while Willow rushed about pouring tea. All of five minutes elapsed before we were seated facing one another. Finally I was able to start asking questions.

"Any word from Burton Neville?"

Willow substituted a frown for a smile. "Nooo! And I'm beginning to worry. Especially since you asked about him."

"It's not like him to ignore old friends," Wally said. "I know he'd be busy getting settled in a new job and a new home, but *six months*? We'll give him the dickens when he finally remembers us. And we'll let you know too."

"Thanks." I took out photos of the five victims and spread them on the coffee table between us. "Do you know any of these men?"

Willow's eyes widened as he scanned the pictures. "No, but I'd sure like to. Can you introduce us?"

Wally favored his partner with a cocked eyebrow before turning back to the snaps. "Who are they?"

"Five murdered young men."

Willow flapped a hand over his eyes. "Oh heavens! Poor babies. Who'd do such a horrible thing to beautiful boys like these?"

I tapped Zapata's photo. "This one died right across the hall."

"He's the one murdered in Burton's apartment?" Wally's voice came out in sort of a gasp. "Lord, I hope I wasn't sitting over here while that poor boy was dying across the hall."

"It most likely happened during the day," I said, without certain knowledge but to ease his mind. "You were probably at work."

His frown turned into a weak smile. "Doesn't change the poor boy's suffering, does it?"

"No, but you won't go around thinking that if you'd heard someone in the hallway you might have done something to help the victim."

"Victim," Willow said. "It sounds so… so *clinical* when you hear it on those television shows"—he gave a visible shiver—"but when it's right across the hall…." He left the thought unfinished and turned away to stare out the window down on East Central traffic. "I wish I had known him. Said a kind word to him."

Willow—and to a lesser extent, Wally—wore their emotions on their sleeves. Yet the moment seemed overdone. These two lived across the hall from the murder scene. Was it possible they had a key to Neville's old apartment? Possible *and* plausible. The couple moved up on my list of suspects. I'd ask Charlie to check and see if either or both had been missing from work on the day Matt Zapata died.

I cleared my throat. "The last time we talked, you mentioned one of Burton Neville's houseguests was a fellow named Jules. When I asked when you saw this Jules last, you said something like 'ages.' Can you be more specific? A week? A month?"

Willow turned from the window. "Oh heavens no. It was years ago."

"Let me understand. Neville only lived at this address for six months or so."

Wally took over the explanation. "Jules came around while we all lived over on Montgomery. Simply eons ago."

"Like in 2000, maybe?"

"Possibly. We moved in the Montgomery complex in 1999, and Burton was already there. So, yes, that's about the right time frame."

"And you don't recall Jules's last name?" I pressed.

"He was just beautiful Jules to Wally and me," Willow said. "And I do mean beautiful. Despite having Wally all to myself, I couldn't help but be a little jealous of Burton and Jules." He laid a hand on Wally's arm. "Sorry, sweetheart."

Wally patted the hand. "Don't be. I would have jumped his bones in a minute and confessed it later."

"You don't happen to have any pictures of Burton and Jules, do you?" Paul asked.

"No, but I wish we did. Come to think of it, we don't even have one of Burton. Strange, isn't it? Known him for years, and no snapshots." Willow waved a hand in the air. "Guess it proves we're not shutterbugs. Don't even own a camera."

"Sure we do," Wally said. "On our phones."

I stepped in before it became one of those parry and riposte sessions they seemed to engage in. "Does the name McClintock mean anything to you?"

Blank stares before both men shook their heads.

I tried again. "Jules McClintock."

Willow moued his lips. "You know, that sounds right. Jules McClintock. I know it was 'Mac' something."

Bingo. It was the Jules I remembered from the U. But what did it mean other than proving once again Albuquerque is an overgrown town where you run into people you know all over the place? Jules McClintock was thirty or so now… providing he survived his illness. Even so, I needed to run him down and mine his memory.

"Do you fellows have a key for 4201?" I asked.

"We did," Wally said. "Not a key, of course, but a card. The locks are electronic."

I recalled Hector Valdez had mentioned a key card when we questioned the maintenance man the other day. Now it made sense.

"The keyholes are a diversionary tactic," Wally went on. "You know, so would-be robbers waste their time trying to pick a lock. Nice touch, don't you think? It fooled you, and you're a professional detective."

I smiled. "That it did. This card, what happened to it?"

"We gave it back to Burton before he left. And he returned ours. We shared cards in case of emergencies."

"You're certain you returned the card?" I pressed.

"Oh yes. Handing over the card was virtually the last thing we did before Burton left. I remember it clearly. We were all bawling like babies. I can show you the card to our apartment he returned if it would help."

"That won't be necessary." I hauled out Pierson's photo. "What about this man? Was he one of Neville's guests?"

Willow grabbed the picture while Wally studied it over his partner's shoulder. Willow frowned. "Interesting. Not in the same class as those other boys, but it's a good face. Nice planes and good eyes. Some people don't like eyeglasses, but I think they lend character to a face. Intelligence."

His scrutiny wasn't going the direction I wanted. I hoped Wally didn't….

"Oh, yes. Makes a person seem more intense. More sophisticated. Definitely—"

I cut Wally off. "Do you recognize the man?"

"No. Never seen him before to the best of my knowledge," Wally said.

"Me neither. He certainly wasn't one of Burton's boys. Please don't tell me he was murdered too."

I retrieved my photos. "No, he's very much alive. Thanks for your help."

Paul and I took our leave and stopped at the office on the first floor. It was locked. I poked the doorbell to his apartment, and a distracted-looking Quint answered the ring.

"Did Burton Neville return his key card before he left?"

Quint nodded. "The last day he was here."

"Both of them?" Paul asked.

The manager blinked. "Both of them? He only had one."

"According to the tenants in 4202, he had a second one he left with them in case of emergencies."

"I don't see how." Quint's features puckered. "Wait a minute. I gave him a second card when he said his was damaged."

"Did you retrieve the damaged one?" I asked.

"Actually, he said it was destroyed. Son of a gun. He wanted an extra one. Why didn't he say so?"

"Maybe because you might think it was for his overnight guests," Paul suggested.

"Did you change the electronic lock codes after Neville left?" I asked.

Quint dropped his eyes. "He was leaving town, so I didn't think it was necessary. Besides, as I told you, we were going to use 4201 as a corporate apartment. But I'll change it right away."

Paul couldn't keep the sarcasm from his voice. "Might be a good idea."

After we exited the building and walked to my Impala, parked in a metered space in front of Park House, Paul spoke to me across the roof of the car.

"We have three new suspects, don't we?"

I scooted into the driver's seat. "Could be. Maybe four."

"Pierson, you mean. Because Quint admitted recognizing him."

"Thin, but enough to require a deeper search."

"Not sure Willow or Wally could overpower a pumped guy like Matt Zapata."

"No, but Matt was drugged, remember. All the victims were. Besides, they might have double-teamed him."

"Then wouldn't there have been three samples of cum on the body? Matt's and his two killers."

"Maybe one left his seed on Matt, and the other left his on his partner."

Paul nodded. "Could be. And I guess the same goes for the manager. Quinton might not take Matt head-on, but if he was drugged...."

"Exactly."

"It's pretty gutsy to kill a guy in your own apartment house."

"It's risky to leave your semen on a body," I pointed out.

"If he knew he didn't have sperm in the semen, that's not so risky."

"But the killer made no effort to clean the bodies. Didn't seem to be concerned over stray hair or skin cells."

"Maybe he didn't know about those kinds of things," Paul suggested.

I laughed. "If he watches TV, he does."

"The CSI Effect."

"Right. It's played hell with prosecutors."

"Juries expect every case to be tied up in a ribbon with forensic evidence, right?"

"Too bad it doesn't work that way in real life."

"Not every time, anyway."

We headed home so Paul could complete his article for *Sports Illustrated* and I could bring my notes up-to-date and listen to the digital recording I'd made of the day's interviews to see if I'd missed something.

WEDNESDAY MORNING, Paul decided to work from home to talk to some of Matt's friends again while I headed to the office. After parking the Impala in my space in the lot behind the building, I climbed the back stairs to my office, where Hazel let me know OMI had confirmed the murder victim in Socorro County was Burton Neville.

"Drugged and strangled," she said, "but no evidence of sexual activity."

"Zopiclone?"

"Right. Looks like the cutie-pie killer. Except there was no sex and the victim wasn't exactly cute. Or naked," she added with a distasteful look on her face.

"No, but he was the connection."

"To what?"

"That I haven't figured out yet," I acknowledged. "Probably linking the killer to something that happened at Park House. Makes it likely the killer was one of Neville's roommates."

"Oh, by the way, APD sent over a list of Neville's credit card activity. He had two other cards in addition to the American Express."

"The two Willow and Wally told us about?"

"Right, a Visa and Mastercard."

I accepted the envelope she handed over and told her to locate Jules McClintock for me. I also asked her to have Charlie trace the movements of Wally and Willow on March 5, the day of Matt Zapata's death. For good measure, I added the task of digging a little deeper into Quint James, the Park House manager. Charlie was already taking a more thorough look at Pierson's background.

I entered my private office to review Neville's credit card charges and was immediately struck by regular expenditures at a place called Jack's. An internet search led me to a bar on East Central. Deciding on a personal call rather than a telephone interview, I headed for the Impala.

The small, nondescript bar, located in an equally featureless stretch of the old Route 66, would have been easy to miss. A blank door with a faded sign painted on the brick wall above it proclaimed it as Jack's. Hard to see as a favorite watering hole for a prosperous engineer, especially when a popular diner sat a few blocks down the street.

The interior left me equally puzzled. While small, it could hardly be called cozy. The obligatory flashing beer signs were the most distinctive items in the bar. The booths and tables were old but serviceable. A fellow with a graying Vandyke looked up from swiping the bar with a nearly white rag.

"Mornin'," he rumbled in a baritone. "What'll it be?"

"Some information, if you would. My name's Vinson. I'm a confidential investigator. Who am I addressing, please?"

His enthusiasm waned. "Harvey. Harvey Fisk."

"How long have you worked here, Mr. Fisk?"

"About as long as the place has been open. What can I do for you?"

"I'm making inquiries about a man named Burton Neville."

His interest visibly revived. "How is old Burt?" He chuckled, seemingly to himself. "Don't never call him Burt to his face. No siree. You call him Burt, and he sets you straight right fast. Wonder why that is? You have any thoughts on it?"

"He's an engineer. Maybe he feels Burton's more professional sounding than Burt."

Harvey nodded as if we were discussing a serious matter. "Makes more sense than my idea on it. I just thought he was stuck-up. How is the old dog? Ain't seen him in a month of Sundays. Is this about the job he was looking at out in California?"

I pulled the digital recorder from my belt and flipped it on after he nodded agreement. Perhaps introducing a mystery would motivate the stocky bartender, although I didn't want to reveal Neville was dead and perhaps trigger a reluctance to point a finger at anyone.

"In a way it has to do with the job. Burton accepted employment but never showed up for it. He seems to be missing."

"That so? He always seemed like a steady sort to me."

"From what I've learned, he was. Which makes his disappearance puzzling. What can you tell me about his companions? Who did he drink with? Regulars, or anyone who happened to be here?"

"Not old Burt. He always come with someone." Harvey didn't actually arch an eyebrow, but he came close to it. "Men. Young fellers."

I spread photographs of the five murdered men on the bar. "Any of these young men?"

Fisk frowned, pursed his lips, and studied the photos a long moment before shaking his head. "Nope. None of them, but they's definitely his type."

"What kind of patron was he? Quiet? Troublemaker?"

"Quiet as a dormouse. Old Burt never raised his voice except to call for another drink. We got a waitress at lunch and evenings, and he talked to her more'n to me. Him and his drinking buddies talked quietlike and never made no fuss."

"Did your other customers ever raise a ruckus over Neville and his companions?"

Neville's attraction to the place became clear with Fisk's reply. "Nah. Around here, it's live and let live. And if any of them said anything to me about it, I stepped on them. Jack's is a peaceable place, and that's the way I wanna keep it."

"Do you know the names of any of the men he brought with him?"

"You oughta talk to Brunie about that."

"Brunie?"

"That's our waitress. Real name's Brunhilda, but everybody calls her Brunie. She might know some names."

"What time does she come on duty?"

"She's in the back getting ready for lunch. We don't have a big menu, but what we serve's good food."

"Would it be all right if I spoke to her?"

Brunhilda Waterson proved to be a hefty, outgoing woman in her forties with a hoarse voice that almost reached Fisk's register. When she called out an order, it likely could have been heard halfway down the block. It almost seemed wasted in the tight confines of Jack's.

She took a stool beside me at the bar and stared at me through green eyes while she recalled what she could of Burton Neville.

"Course it's been a while, but the last laddie he had was called Sonny. Never heard a last name. Sonny was the way he was introduced." She tapped the photo of Pat Aragon. "Looked a lot like him, but this ain't Sonny." She pointed over her shoulder at a corner booth. "They'd sit over there for hours, pulling on beer and talking with their heads close like they was telling secrets. I'll tell you one thing. Sonny had a sense of humor. He could get old Burt to giggling something fierce."

"Can you describe Sonny? Was he Hispanic like the man in the photo?"

"Nope, but he had black hair and soulful brown eyes. Almost too pretty to be a man, but he was a man all right. Pinched me a couple of times."

She reacted to my raised eyebrows. "Oh yeah. I know what him and Burt was up to, but that Sonny, he'd tumble a gal in skirts as quick as he would Burt."

I accepted the word of an experienced barmaid without question. "How old was Sonny?"

She squinted and looked off into the distance. "Hard to say. He was one of those guys who looks like a teenager but you know they's older. Twenty-one, twenty-two, I'd say."

"Did Sonny ever come in with anyone else? Man or woman?"

"Uh-uh. This was him and Burt's place."

"What about anyone before Sonny?"

"Oh yeah. Four or five of them. Some only come in once, others lasted 'most as long as Sonny. I recollect a Darrel and a Joe, but I couldn't tell you nothing about them. Except they was all pretty as a picture. Dunno how Burt done it. He was all right looking, but you couldn't call him spectacular."

"Free spender?"

"Yep, and that musta been it. He treated them right, so they treated him right."

"Did they appear to be call boys?"

"You mean pros? Naw. Well, Sonny mighta been. Don't have no idea why I said that, but there you are."

After asking all the questions I could think of, I ordered a beer and a kielbasa with chips, discovering another reason Neville might have been attracted to Jack's. The food was delicious and the tab modest.

Once back in the office, I gave my recorder to Hazel for transcription before taking a seat at my desk. When a phone call to APD revealed Roy and Glenann were out, I opted to go all the way to the top. I hadn't spoken to my old APD partner in a while, so I asked for Commander Enriquez. After talking my way through his receptionist, I finally got him on the line.

"About time for another lunch," I said.

"My God, I don't even have time to eat. Why in the hell did you let me take this job?"

"Sitting on top of the Criminal Investigative Division seems like the achievement of a dream," I said.

"A nightmare. Damn, BJ, I don't even have time to breathe."

"So I guess you don't have time to look up a record for me."

"Hell, I have minions for that. Besides, you've got online access to damned near everything I do."

"Roy and Glenann are out, and I'd like the benefit of your long memory. I'm looking for a guy I only know as Sonny, early twenties, black hair, brown eyes, handsome."

"You working a case or looking for a replacement for Paul?"

"That'll be the day. It's the Mateo Zapata murder case."

"We've both run into some Sonnys in our long and storied careers, but nobody stands out. What makes you think he has a jacket?"

"I don't have any idea, but if he doesn't, then I'm at a dead end."

"Since I can't help in the memory department, I'll have my receptionist call you with what she finds. In the meantime, use your own database."

"So no time for lunch, huh?" I asked, even though I'd already eaten at Jack's.

"The only lunches I get to go to are fattening feasts with high-hats or cardboard dinners at mind-numbing functions."

"I saw where you had another police shooting the other day. According to the paper, the victim didn't even have a gun."

"Naw, but he had a Subaru. His car was his weapon. It was righteous."

"Feds still threatening to intervene?"

The sigh in my ear gave me my answer before Gene uttered a word. "It's inevitable. Surprised they're not already here. But they will be, you mark my words."

"You gonna be all right?"

"Should be. Most of the shootings have been by street cops… patrol cops. But it'll involve everybody before it's over."

"The chief going to survive?" The police chief was Gene's mentor.

"Naw. He's decided to go voluntarily. Probably announce it soon."

"Get the feds in and get it over."

"My sentiments exactly."

"How are Glenda and the kids?"

"Thank the lord for Glenda. She's all that stands between me and a pack of teenagers. They're all doing fine. I'll tell them you said hello."

Licensed investigators in New Mexico have access to police databases normally closed to outsiders. As soon as I hung up, I turned to my computer, began a search for felons who went by the pseudonym of "Sonny," and zeroed in on a likely prospect by the name of Morton Delaware, a twenty-two-year-old petty thief who occasionally worked on construction jobs. Mug shots are never flattering, but this kid's front and profile couldn't hide his smoky good looks. I noted his contact information and turned to answer my ringing cell phone. It was Gene's receptionist calling me back.

She'd picked out the same jacket I had identified. She also had a couple of other names, but after viewing them on my own database, I settled on Morton Delaware. Now to run him down.

Chapter 9

AFTER HAZEL secured an appointment for me to see Jules McClintock at his Colorado Street NE home that afternoon, I phoned Paul to see if he wanted to accompany me. He did.

An hour later, we pulled up in front of a brown stucco with a ramp leading to the porch in a neat, middle-class neighborhood of flat-topped pueblo style houses in varying shades of brown. My stomach clinched in shock when the door opened in answer to my ring. Instead of the lean, handsome man I'd last seen, a huge figure loomed in the doorway.

"BJ," he boomed. "Haven't seen you in a decade or so. Come on in. Who's your friend?"

As I opened the screen door, he took a couple of uncertain steps backward and settled his bulk into a wheelchair behind him. I accepted his outstretched hand and turned to introduce Paul. While his attention was centered on my companion, I studied the man in the wheelchair. Time and illness had not been kind to the once slender, incredibly handsome Jules McClintock. His still-arresting blue eyes were now almost lost in a fleshy face. Honey brown hair streaked with premature gray. A trim body now bloated to somewhere around 300 pounds. When he smiled, I caught a hint of the Adonis he once had been, but the image was fleeting.

"Come on in the living room," he said, turning his motorized chair and leading the way. "To what do I owe this pleasure?" He parked in a spot obviously cleared for his wheelchair and indicated seats for us.

"Working on a case, and your name came up."

His eyebrows climbed toward his receding hairline. "My name. You must be kidding. What's the case?"

"Young man by the name of Mateo Zapata was murdered and left on the mesa. Seems he was killed in the apartment of a man you knew. Burton Neville."

"You're dredging up old memories, BJ. This fellow was killed over in Sandalwood Apartments?"

"No, Neville's new place on East Central."

"Didn't know he'd moved. Haven't seen Burton since… well, since I got laid low by my illness." Sadness or something clouded his features. "He abandoned me after that. A couple of visits in the hospital and then nothing."

"Sorry, Jules. I know it cost you a lot."

He rallied and mustered a smile. "Including the man I loved. But I've built a life for myself despite everything that slugged me in the face."

"What are you doing these days?" I asked.

"To keep body and soul together, you mean? My folks left me this house and a little money. Gives me some income. And for these past few years, I've been tutoring math. Be surprised how many kids need help with math. Actually, I do pretty well for myself."

"I never did know what hit you back then. You were in class, and then you weren't."

"Transverse myelitis. I can give you chapter and verse on it, but essentially it's an inflammation of the inside of the spinal cord. Kills some. Renders others invalids. As you can see, it's left me somewhere in between."

"From the way you met us at the door, I take it you're not wedded to the chair," I said.

"I use it ninety percent of the time. When I fix myself something to eat, I walk around in the kitchen. When I shower, I stand up long enough to do the job. I'm mobile, but I've got no stamina." He grimaced. "That's why I look like a whale. I can't exercise. Even the therapists gave up on me." He cocked his head. "When you've got no other pleasures in life, what do you do? You eat. This chair, eating everything in sight, and no exercise is gonna kill me one of these days."

"I admire the way you're coping," Paul said.

Pure pleasure radiated from Jules. "Thank you, Paul. Some could probably do it better, but I get by."

Despite myself, I played detective. "Where do you get your students?"

"For a while, I was a substitute teacher at a nearby elementary school. That was before I got so big it was hard to get around. When I quit, the teachers started referring kids. Guess I'm good at it, because other schools joined in."

"What age group?" Paul asked.

"Grade schoolers for the most part. It's best to catch them early. But right now, I've got two high school girls. Last year, I helped a college freshman for about three months. But mostly, it's the little guys."

"So you haven't seen Burton Neville lately?" I asked.

"Not since I left UNM. My God, that's been twelve years. Hard to imagine." He pounded the left wheel of his chair. "Second thought, not hard at all. Seems like I've been trapped in this thing for a lifetime."

"You didn't keep in touch with Neville?"

"I didn't even know he'd moved from Montgomery Boulevard."

"So you wouldn't know any of his more recent roommates."

Jules shook his head. "Not surprised there are some, but I don't know anything about them. I'm out of touch with the old gang." He mustered a smile. "I came out of the closet before this happened, BJ." The smile died. "Just before it happened. Didn't even have time to really enjoy the freedom."

I hauled out the snaps of the four cutie-pie victims and handed them to him. "You know any of these young men?"

Jules took his time studying the photos before handing them back. "No, but I wish I did. I'd give free math lessons to any of them for the pleasure of looking at them." He glanced at Paul. "You too, if you need any help."

"Thanks, but those days are behind me."

"How about this man?" I asked, passing across Barkley Pierson's snapshot.

Jules pursed his lips as he studied the image. "Interesting face. Not nearly as handsome as the others, but it has a certain sex appeal."

"Do you know him?" I asked.

He handed back the picture and shook his head. "Afraid not. Who is he?"

"UNM art student."

"How does he fit into things?"

"Good friend of one of the victims, that's all."

Jules straightened in his chair. "I'm not a very good host. Can I offer you a drink?"

I got to my feet. "Thanks, but we have to be going. Good to see you again."

"Don't be a stranger."

"We'll see ourselves out. Thanks for your time."

Paul said nothing until we were in the Impala. "Man, that's beat! Can't imagine living like that."

"A lot of people have it worse. At least he can get out of the chair occasionally. But you're right." I started the car and pulled away from the curb. "It's hard to believe Jules was once as fit and trim and as beautiful as Matt Zapata."

"I could see it every once in a while. When he smiled, for example. But now?" Paul shivered. "Gross."

After a moment of silence, he said, "I noticed something kinda odd."

"About Pierson?" I asked.

"Yeah, right. You showed him four dead guys, and when you handed over the next photo, he didn't ask if he was the fifth."

"Interesting reaction."

"True. So guess it doesn't mean anything. I noticed you didn't mention Neville was dead."

"We came to get information, not give it. Besides, I was waiting to see if there was any indication he knew."

Returning to the office was a mistake, but Paul's car sat in the parking lot, and as long as I was there, I might as well go upstairs. As soon as I entered, Hazel put me to work pacifying an irritated client. One of the local engineering firms had asked us to do a background check on a man they wanted to hire from an out-of-state firm. Our investigation had turned up a propensity for alcohol. Two- and three-martini lunches, after-hour barhops, and the like. Instead of being grateful we'd discovered a possible problem, the client was upset. He really wanted to hire the man. I reminded the irked voice on the other end of the call he was free to do exactly that, but he was entitled to the facts before doing so. I think he wanted to see how firmly convinced I was the information was correct.

Hazel had located an address and phone number for Morton Delaware, the man I suspected of being Neville's "Sonny," but no one answered the calls or responded to messages I left. I decided to finish the day with a telephone call to Roy and Glenann so we could bring one another up-to-date. They'd made a little progress on the nonrelated murder of Pat Aragon. The young man had had an argument with a friend at a local bar, but the detectives hadn't tied the friend into the killing yet. I took advantage of the call to ask if the forensics people had been able to come up with meaningful fingerprints in Neville's apartment. It had been six months, but sometimes miracles do happen.

"You're not going to believe it," Roy said. "They found one that didn't belong to any of the cleaning crew. It was on the underside of the toilet bowl lid."

"Someone hid his stash," I said.

"Most likely. And that someone had a record. It was a nothing bust, but it was enough to get him printed. Name's Hosea Middleton."

I took down Middleton's contact information and the relevant items from his jacket. Single, twenty-one, nickname "Hose"—probably a corruption of Hosea—public nuisance resulting from a bar fight, no occupation listed.

"And he's a looker too," Glenann said into the speakerphone. "How do you gay guys find all the good-looking ones?"

"It takes some work," I said. "And like with you straights, the really good-looking ones aren't always the ones you want to settle down with."

I heard her snicker. "Yeah, take another look at Paul and tell me that."

"I got lucky."

"Why are you so obsessed with Neville's lover boys?" she asked.

"Zapata was killed in Neville's old place. Who's likely to have a key card to the apartment?"

"His old roommates, I guess," she acknowledged.

"Plus a couple of friends across the hall."

"Surely management changed the code after Neville left."

"Manager claims he didn't because the former tenant left the state."

"Sorta careless. Suspicious?"

"Maybe," I said.

She cleared her throat. "By the way, I'm sending over the DNA hair sample you asked for so you can take it to K-Y Labs."

"Thanks. I'll have Charlie deliver it to them."

I closed the call thinking I had two good-looking men to run to ground, but I'd do that tomorrow. Right now, it was time to go home to my own cutie-pie.

THE EVENING turned out to be as nearly perfect as an evening could be. Paul was pumped because his *Sports Illustrated* article had been accepted, and the editor had suggested another subject Paul might pursue for the magazine. My boy was building a name for himself in the freelance journalists' world.

After some take-out Chinese, we settled in the den to watch *Law and Order*. I like the detail they give the show, but the best part was snuggling up on the couch with Paul for an hour while sipping a little scotch.

My snuggling paid off because later that night I got to watch Pedro play. The little dragon tattoo hanging on to Paul's left nipple got a real workout. Like I said, as nearly perfect as could be.

Chapter 10

I SPENT most of Thursday chasing my own tail, but midafternoon Sonny Delaware finally returned my repeated calls.

The voice sounded rough and irked. "Who are you, and why you filling up my voicemail?"

"If you returned your calls, that wouldn't happen. As my many messages say, my name is B. J. Vinson, and I'm a licensed confidential investigator."

"What does a private eye want with me?"

"I want to talk to you about Burton Neville."

"That's old news. I got nothing to tell you."

"Maybe I have something to tell you," I said. "I want to meet."

"Got no time for it. I'm gonna hang up now, and don't call me no more."

"You hang up, and the police are going to be knocking on your door."

"You ain't no cop. You said you're private."

"But I was one for ten years, and I still have lots of friends on the force. You sound like you have something to hide."

"Don't everybody? I don't like cops, official or not."

"Look, I'll meet you wherever you want. Your place, a coffeehouse, the police station, or my office. Your choice."

The man hesitated a long moment. "You know Jack's?"

"Where you used to go with Neville. Sure do. And I know Harvey and Brunie too."

"Thirty minutes. And you better be good for a drink or two."

I made the seventeen or so blocks up East Central well before the appointed time. It was too late for the lunch trade and too early for the after-work crowd, so Harvey had the place pretty much to himself. He gave the counter a swipe with his ever-present rag and granted me a smile. When I showed him a grainy photocopy of Sonny's mug shot, he nodded.

"Yep. That's Burt's boy. He come in here with the kid up till he left for California."

"How many times?"

"Regular for three-four months. Burt's pattern was to be all hot and bothered for a coupla months, then he sorta ran out of steam with them. This one lasted longer'n most."

"They have any trouble? Spats, arguments, harsh words?"

"Not that I recall. This one knew how to work Burt. Right on the edge of being lovey-dovey, but not enough to get them thrown out. Know what I mean?"

"I do."

"Uh-oh, here he is."

I slipped the mug shot into my pocket before turning for my first look at Sonny Delaware. He was good-looking all right, but if you wanted a wide-eyed innocent, this wasn't your boy. The attitude of nascent hostility he'd displayed on the phone showed up on his face, marring his fine features.

"Hi, Harvey. Long time no see. You Vinson?"

"That's me," I replied, stepping forward and offering a hand. The shake was firm… a little too much so. Like the kid was transmitting his aggression through his greeting. "What'll you have?" I asked.

"Harvey knows. Right, Harvey?"

"Bourbon rocks?"

"Double."

I settled for a soft drink and led the way to the booth Brunie had said was Burton Neville's usual choice.

Sonny scooted his butt across the padded vinyl seat and settled in. "Whaddya wanna know about Burton?"

I sat opposite him. "How did you meet him?"

"Hell, I don't remember. He knew somebody, and I knew somebody, I guess. What does it matter?"

"Okay, let's get to the point. What was your relationship with him?"

"Relationship? We was friends. Nothing more."

We paused while Harvey delivered our drinks.

"It was more than that. Look, I'm not the sex police, so let's be honest here. I just need to understand how things were with Neville."

"Then ask him. To me, we was friends. That's all."

"Look, Sonny, don't try to snow me. I was gay when I served in the Marines, I was gay when I was a cop, and I'm gay now. My gaydar pinged the moment I heard your voice on the telephone."

Not strictly true, but effective. He cleared his throat and spoke in a lower register—probably unconsciously. "I ain't gay."

"I suspect that's true. No emotional involvement. Drinking with him here was probably as close to friendship as you got. But what you did at the Park House was strictly for a paycheck."

"Hey, man, watch what you're saying."

I met his brown-eyed stare. "I know you spent a lot of time in his apartment, including overnights."

The eyes crinkled and a smile touched his lips, easing the hardness and rendering him even more handsome. "Okay, so I hitched a ride for a while. Burton was generous and didn't ask for nothing I wasn't willing to give. He claimed he loved me." The smile widened. "You want details?"

"No, thanks. How long were you with him?"

"Four months. Practically lived with the dude. Couldn't get enough of me. But then he started talking about taking a job in California." Sonny's smile revealed rows of straight white teeth. "He wanted me to go with him. Said he'd take care of me. All I had to do was be a stud for him."

"If the man loved you, why didn't you go with him?"

"Thought about it. But this place he was going was on San Francisco Bay, and he was gonna buy a beach house. I been in California, and it's colder'n a witch's tit on the beach in the morning." Sonny stretched, emphasizing his nice torso. "I dunno. I couldn't see leaving Albuquerque. I grew up here. All my friends—my real friends—are here. And I keep a roof over my head working at construction jobs."

"And you can always find yourself another sugar daddy," I added.

That smile again. "Haven't had no trouble so far." He raised his arms and flexed his muscles. "You interested? That what this is all about?"

"I'm in a relationship. When did you see Neville last?"

"Day he took off for California. He had me come up. You know, for a goodbye fuck."

"After that what happened?"

"When I left, he was getting ready to go down and turn in his key."

"Did you give him yours?"

"Mine? I didn't have no key. It wasn't really a key, anyways. It was a card. An electronic gizmo."

"You never had a key card?"

"No… well, once. He had to take a business trip and was gone for three days. He give me a card so I'd have a place to stay while he was gone. But he took it back when he come home."

"You have friends up to the apartment while he was gone?"

"Thought about it, but I didn't wanna screw up a good thing. So I did my drinking with buddies at a bar and come home alone."

I finished my drink. "You haven't talked to him since he left?"

Sonny frowned. "No, and I thought I would. He was really hung up on me, and I figured he'd be calling and trying to get me to come out for a visit. You know, see if he could change my mind."

"How did he seem the day he left? Was he excited about the new job and the move?"

"Old Burton didn't get excited about much." Sonny flashed a grin. "Except me. But you know, he was down about something. Figured it was because we was splitting, but afterward, I got to thinking. It was more like he was worried."

"You ask about it?"

"Figured it wasn't none of my business. He was clearing outa my life, you know. What's this all about, anyway?"

No reason to withhold the truth. "Burton Neville is dead."

Sonny's eyes went wide. "What? How?"

"Murdered."

"No shit! Where?"

No use telling him everything. "Somewhere on the road between here and California."

"Son of a bitch. Guess I won't be making no visits to California, will I?"

"Not to see Burton Neville, at any rate. Do you know who was with him before you came along?"

He glanced at me, and I saw a touch of sadness in those expressive eyes. Maybe he wasn't so tough after all. "Fellow he called Hose. Think that was his way of saying José or Hosea. Never met the guy, but Burton talked about him some."

"What did Neville say about him?"

"He was a good guy. Kinda soft, but a decent guy."

"How come this Hose wasn't around anymore?"

His lips twitched. "It was me he was looking for. Found me too. Damn, I shoulda gone with him. Maybe he wouldn't of got killed."

"Or maybe both of you would."

He straightened in the booth and thrust out his chest. "Have to be a real man to take on both of us. Hell, to take me on."

"Or a gang."

That sobered him.

I took a shot in the dark. "By the way," I asked, "what did you stash in Neville's toilet reservoir? That's how I found you. You left a fingerprint on the inside of the lid." It had been Hosea Middleton's fingerprint on the bowl lid, but these guys tended to think alike.

"Be damned." Sonny looked amused as he answered the question. "Just a little weed. Got it while he was on his trip and had a little left by the time he come back, so I hid it. Burton didn't cotton to drugs."

After ordering him a second drink and asking some questions about his movements on the day Matt Zapata was killed, I left convinced Sonny Delaware wasn't the cutie-pie killer. Nonetheless, I'd have Charlie look a little deeper into his background.

Since the drive to Sonny's predecessor, Hosea Middleton, wasn't a long one, I opted to see if I could catch the kid at home.

Middleton lived in an apartment located in a neighborhood of duplexes and triplexes in Albuquerque's War Zone, so named by the APD because of the frequency of calls to the area. The individual who answered my knock at the apartment on San Pablo SE caught me off guard. He didn't look old enough to be a man, not even a twenty-one-year-old one.

"Hosea Middleton?" I asked.

"Yessir." The voice sounded older than he looked.

I introduced myself and talked my way into the no-frills, one-bedroom apartment. A ratty overstuffed chair and small settee plus a 19-inch Sony on a rickety TV-dinner tray almost overcrowded the living area. He chose the chair, so I took the couch.

"I understand you knew a man by the name of Burton Neville."

"B-Burton? Yeah, I know him… knew him."

"Which is it?"

"We were friends, but… but not anymore. Well, I guess we're still friends, but—"

"But you're no longer lovers."

Middleton flinched at the word. "I guess that's right. Although…."

"Although what?"

"He called me before he left to take a new job. I went over and saw him for an hour or so."

"When was that?"

"Right before he left."

"You made love?"

His eyes moistened as he nodded.

"Was Sonny there?"

Middleton studied his hands. "N-no. It was just Burton and me."

"Do you think Sonny knew he was going to call you?"

He glanced at me. "No."

"Why are you so sure of that?"

He fixed his gaze on the blank television screen. "Sonny woulda come looking for me. Burton said he was real jealous."

"You didn't know Sonny?"

Middleton shook his head. "But I saw them go into Jack's once. So I know what he looks like."

"Never spoken to him?"

"Never."

"Why not? He's handsome. Sexy."

"Not my type." He blinked before spitting out his next words. "He used Burton. Didn't love him like I did. I-I…." His voice died, and he covered his face with his hands.

"How do you know that?"

He looked up, eyes defiant. "Because Burton told me so the last time I saw him. I-I wish I'd gone with Burton, like he asked."

"He asked you to go to California with him? Why didn't you?"

"I don't know. He took me by surprise, and I didn't know if Sonny was going with him too."

"You're lucky you didn't. You would probably be dead as well."

His mouth dropped; his eyes went out of focus. "Dead? Who's dead?"

"Burton Neville."

Hosea Middleton collapsed then. For a few minutes, I thought I was going to have to take him to the emergency room, but he recovered after a bit. Not enough to answer questions, but enough so I felt comfortable leaving him on his own. As I walked to the car, I mentally crossed Middleton's name off the list of possible cutie-pie killers. But like with Sonny Delaware, I'd have Charlie dig a little deeper into the boy's background.

I returned to the office even though it was after-hours and both Charlie and Hazel would have gone home. I wanted to leave the recorder holding the interviews with Delaware and Middleton I'd surreptitiously taped. Normally I follow the rules and let the interviewee know of the recording, but I'd done it without telling either one of them because of the sensitive nature of the subject matter. Looking back on it, I doubt either of the young men would have objected. In addition to that, I needed to dispose of whatever Hazel had left on my desk to sign and bring my time tickets up-to-date on the Zapata case.

I NO sooner arrived at the office the next morning than Roy and Glenann phoned to say they had arrested a man in the Patricio Aragon killing: the individual who'd fought with the young man in the bar. The problem centered around a woman. Bad blood thickened, resulting in Aragon's death. His killer had read about the cutie-pie murders and attempted to recreate the circumstances to throw the police off the trail. Fortunately, the news articles were short on details, making it obvious the murder was a copycat.

Now the two of them were focusing on the cutie-pie killer again and wanted an update on our investigation. Once I finished bringing them current verbally and promising to deliver transcriptions of my notes, we agreed on how to proceed.

"I'm going to continue to concentrate on Zapata," I said. "I know where he was killed, which puts me a leg up on the other three killings. You concentrate on those, and we'll check for common elements, although to be frank, I don't believe we'll find any. Those three are killings of opportunity, not specific targeted individuals. We know Zapata was targeted because he was lured to the Park House."

"Not necessarily," Roy objected. "The killer could have picked up the kid and taken him there."

"Either way, the Park House is the common element. Frankly, I think one of those burner phone messages was from the killer. Matt walked straight into his killer's waiting arms in the fourth-floor apartment."

I thought for a minute. "Another thing, Hazel believes if there's another victim, he'll be a Native American. Our killer's claimed a victim from four different races. If her prediction is true, we might change his name to the rainbow killer."

"Let's hope we catch him before another killing takes place," Glenann said. "From what you've told us, you're concentrating on gays."

"That's not strictly true. The common starting point in the Park House seems to be Burton Neville—"

"Who might be the cutie-pie killer's first victim," Roy interjected.

"Could be. But I'm not convinced Sonny Delaware, Neville's last lover, is gay. He's more of an opportunist willing to participate for a paycheck. But Neville was gay, and I'm convinced the key to Zapata's killing is tied in to him... or the

Park House. Someone had to have a key card to the apartment. That someone is the killer."

"That should narrow it down to the manager."

"Neville had a duplicate key card. Only one was returned to the manager."

"Or that's what the manager claims," Glenann said. "Besides, he would have changed the electronic code when Neville moved out."

"Shoulda-woulda-coulda. He didn't but he's corrected the oversight."

"Again according to the manager."

"The staff will have a master card," Roy said. "That adds a few people to the mix."

"Six. The manager, maintenance man, and four cleaning staff. But I can't find anyone in that group with a motive, sexual or otherwise. And the missing key card opens all sorts of possibilities."

Roy sighed over the phone. "Okay, you keep on with Zapata, and we'll continue to look at the other three."

"Have you found any other murder sites?"

"Nope."

"Most likely the killer's home or his vehicle," I said.

"Or Park House."

"I doubt that. None of the staff found signs of disturbance in 4201 before or after Zapata died there."

I hung up convinced the two detectives wouldn't make much headway on the other three murders. Forensics had given them nothing useful, and they could talk themselves blue in the face with family and acquaintances. Those three were pickups off the street, targets of opportunity. Unless the killer made a mistake in his next kill, Roy and Glenann would get nowhere. Matt Zapata was different. He *had* been targeted. He'd done something to attract the killer's attention. I resolved to enlist Paul's and Charlie's help in touching base once again with

Matt's telephone contacts made through Ma Flanagan's service to see who the clients shared his name with. If I found one who tied back in to Park House, I'd have my man.

Before leaving for home, I made three quick phone calls. Hilda, Dick, and Morton all denied knowing Burton Neville or anyone at the Park House. For good measure, I threw in the name of Jules McClintock with the same result.

Chapter 11

PAUL AND I try to reserve weekends for ourselves. Doesn't always work, and this Saturday seemed destined to be one of those. My cell phone rang around nine in the morning.

"BJ," Roy's voice said in my ear. "Got another one. Number five. If you'll hurry, you can get here before they remove the body."

"Where?"

"Sandia Pueblo, old road to Bernalillo. Turn right at the old cottonwood grove. You know where I mean?"

"Yeah. Fifteen… twenty minutes."

"There'll be a Sandia cop at the turnoff. I'll tell him to let you through."

Paul and I didn't take time to change from casual clothes. We hopped into his Charger and took off.

The cottonwood grove Roy had mentioned, populated by huge trees older than most living things, was awash in activity. NM State Police, Sandoval County Sheriff's Office, Roy's APD Ford, and Sandia Reservation Police cruisers lined the rough dirt road. The pueblo officer Roy warned me about let us through after we'd identified ourselves. An OMI wagon blocked the way a couple of hundred feet ahead of us. We got out of the Charger and met Glenann at the OMI vehicle.

She held up her hand. "This is as far as we go, but we have permission for you to view the body once OMI brings it."

"Where's Roy?" I asked.

She inclined her head. "Down there arguing. We're in a bit of a jurisdictional pickle. The county would probably give us the case, but the reservation cops are protective of their own."

"That's not all bad. The pueblo will use the state's facilities for forensics. All they have to do is give us access to the information."

"That's a pretty big 'if.' We had to argue our way to the scene. I do have some Polaroids you can look at."

I took the snaps and started thumbing through them. "Who is the victim?"

"Sandia kid named Robert Sandoval. A high schooler. Looks like Hazel was right. The scumbag went for a Native American to round out the count."

"You sure it's our killer?"

"The signature's right. Victim's cuter than hell, naked, no clothing left behind, strangled. But the bastard went younger this time."

"How young?"

"Seventeen." Her face reddened. "He hadn't even lived yet!"

As we fell silent for a moment, I was struck by the atmosphere. The cottonwood grove, filled with more people than it had probably seen at one time in a hundred years, was strangely hushed. A puff of dust, raised by my shoes, rose lazily in the still air. Chirping birds disturbed the eerie peace more than the hushed voices whispering about violent death just beyond our sight. Appropriate. These ancient trees had witnessed more than their share of tragedy and death over the course of centuries.

All of that fell away as the OMI techs rolled the gurney in our direction, bringing a horde of others with them. Roy was still engaged in serious talk with a stocky man in a uniform heavy with gold braid. The local police chief, probably.

Glenann stopped the OMI personnel and had them unzip the body bag so we could get a good look at Robert from the navel up. Beautiful face, slightly underdeveloped physique. Fresh, unblemished skin. I tried to imagine Robert Sandoval, now still and stiff, as the lively, perhaps impish youngster he had been.

"Exactly like the others," Paul noted. "Looks like he used hands to strangle the boy to death."

"Semen?" I asked.

Glenann unzipped the bag a little farther, revealing the stains. "Lots of it."

"From both of them?" Paul asked.

"Have to wait for OMI to tell us that. But there's so much… probably so."

She hastily zipped the bag up to the boy's neck as a car came barreling down the road toward us. The man I'd labeled the police chief stepped out to intercept it. A moment later, he returned.

"It's Robert's family. They'd like to be alone with their son for a moment. Everybody will have to leave."

Roy inclined his head, and we joined him at his departmental Ford well away from the gurney.

"Get everything ironed out?" I asked as we gathered in a small group.

"County's okay with us handling it. Why wouldn't they be, it's Sandia's jurisdiction. The FBI might get involved since the killing took place on Indian lands. At the very least, the pueblo will work with the State Police. So they're stiff-arming us."

"Just so long as we get the benefit of the forensic information. Did you figure out when death occurred?"

"OMI says probably ten to twelve hours ago."

"Anybody see a strange vehicle around about that time?"

Roy shook his head. "The pueblo police chief questioned some of the curious who gathered as soon as word went around. So far nobody's admitted to seeing anything. But the chief needs to ask some of the younger people. They'd be the ones up and moving at night. Damn, I need to talk to some of those kids."

"Show up at Bernalillo High School. The principal can point out kids from the pueblo," I said.

"Good idea, and the All Indian Pueblo Council might be able to help too."

Stymied, Paul and I left with some Polaroids Glenann gave us and stopped at the west-side Flying Star for coffee and brunch. As we ate, Paul looked at the photos. Suddenly, he plunked them down on the table and stabbed one with his finger. "Damn, damn, damn! I'll bet the kid hadn't even been able to use that thing except for pissing."

Crudely put, but his sentiment affected me profoundly. Robert Sandoval had been cheated out of a chance to really live, make his mark, do his thing. Tragic.

As we were about to leave, four youngsters bustled in and claimed the table next to ours. My ears perked up when I heard the name Robert. In moments, it was clear they were discussing the murder of a schoolmate. They fell silent, excitement and fear reflected on their young faces, as I stood and approached.

"Excuse me, fellas," I said, glad Paul stood at my side. He was of an age they could better identify with. "My name is B. J. Vinson, and I'm a confidential investigator. Paul, my companion here, and I just returned from the body dump site at the pueblo. Do you mind if we ask you some questions?"

Curiosity and resentment did battle on the four young faces; curiosity won out.

"Sure. Okay," the larger and perhaps older of the quartet said. "Pull up a chair. Was Robert really raped by some sick bastard?"

Now I knew what gained us entry to the group. Curiosity about sex… sex of any sort, apparently. We accepted his offer and dragged over chairs. Paul sat on one side of the table, and I took the other.

"I doubt it. There was a sexual element to it, but I don't believe he suffered that indignity."

"I heard this guy's killed three or four others like he did Robert," one of the younger kids said, worry clouding his innocent features. I was reminded of Robert's face and slight build.

"That's true. And that's why it's important for you to answer some questions for us."

"Sure, go ahead."

The attitude clouded slightly when I hauled out my recorder and asked each to identify himself. But eventually Johnny Segura and Jim Hightower and Mikey Zamora and Billy Johns identified themselves. Segura and Zamora were Sandians.

To ease the tension, I asked questions to determine who the victim had been. The consensus? Robert was a quiet kid, not quite as ebullient as I imagined, but probably as impish. He was a senior in high school, a decent first baseman, interested in rodeoing but not bold enough to participate beyond watching and cheering. He had an off-and-on girlfriend but nothing serious. When the group loosened up enough to start joking, I tried the hard questions.

"Let's assume Robert's killer was a stranger to him. How would he have enticed Robert into his car?"

"Robert hitchhiked sometimes," Mikey Zamora offered.

"That would have been one way. Would he have been tempted by offers of money?"

Jim Hightower, the eldest of the group, caught on right away. "You mean to do things with the guy? No way."

I turned to one of Robert's fellow villagers. "Do you agree, Johnny?"

Segura looked offended. "You bet! Robert wouldn't go along with something like that."

Billy Johns frowned. "I dunno, he wanted to buy a horse awful bad."

Segura turned on him. "He was working his ass off for that. He wouldn't go sell it."

"He was getting ready to go up to Bobcat Ranch. He had a summer job lined up," Zamora added. "He was gonna earn what he needed for a horse."

"What's Bobcat Ranch?" I asked.

"Ranch the Pueblo owns up in the Sangre de Cristos." After answering my question, Johns moved on. "How'd he get a job up there? I heard they're hard to get."

"His old man's a War Captain," Segura said. "He got it for Robert."

Paul caught my puzzled look and grinned. "These days a War Captain's a civil figure. And kinda a religious figure too."

Neither of the two native boys bothered to expand upon Paul's comments, confirming the Pueblo's notorious reputation for secrecy when it came to things cultural... especially religious details.

Hightower butted in. "You said there was something sexual about it. What did you mean?"

"The details will come out in time, but as I said, I'm pretty sure your friend wasn't raped. Of course, the autopsy will have to tell us for sure."

Segura's eyes flew open. "They're gonna cut on him?"

Uncertain about how the Sandian culture viewed such things, I weaseled. "That's the usual procedure in the case of murder, but I'm sure they'll take the feelings of the family into consideration."

"Where did Robert hang out?" Paul asked.

"Wherever there was a baseball game," Hightower said.

"Or a rodeo," Zamora added.

Johnny Segura waved the comment away. "After school he did yard work and cleaned out barns and stuff to earn some horse money. Spent a lot of his free time at the Boys and Girls Club in Rio Rancho when he could get a ride."

"Sometimes he rode his bicycle there. It's only seven or eight miles."

"Was he on the outs with any of his family or friends?" I asked.

"You mean any of them pissed enough to do that to him?" Billy Johns asked. "No way. Not none of them."

"Who was his closest friend?" Paul asked.

Everyone looked at Segura. "I was," he said, struggling to keep from spilling tears in front of his peers.

"There are two APD detectives, named Roy Guerra and Glenann Hastings, who are going to want to talk to you. You down with that?" I asked.

"Sure."

"Give me your contact information."

After everyone dictated phone numbers and addresses into the recorder, I clicked it off, stood, and dropped four twenty-dollar bills on the table. "I'm going to treat everyone to those fries, burgers, and shakes. Appreciate your help."

"You intend to pursue this latest case?" Paul asked as we left the restaurant and settled into his Charger.

"We'll stick with Matt Zapata's murder, but Roy and Glenann will make good use of what we learned."

OUR SATURDAY was ruined, so we opted to drive straight to Park House and start stirring the pot. Quint James buzzed us in without asking who we were. He was pecking away at his computer when we entered the manager's office, and from the frown, I judged he was laboring over a problem. His expression went south the moment he spotted us.

"You don't look happy to see us," I said.

"Don't have time for you right now. Today's the last day of the month, and I can't get this frigging report to balance."

"Doesn't the software do the balancing for you?" Paul asked.

"That's the problem. I stepped on one of the formulas by mistake and am trying to recreate it."

"Maybe I can help," Paul offered. "I'm pretty good at spreadsheets."

Quint vacated his chair. "Have at it."

I watched the two as they huddled to identify the problem. Then Paul nodded and waved Quint away. He turned to me with a reluctant air.

Time for him to start earning those frowns. "Quint, we've narrowed our list of murder suspects down to someone in this building. At the moment, you're at the top of the list."

His gray eyes bugged. "Me?"

"Think about it. You've got access to every apartment in this building. You're on-site except when you're in classes. And you're gay."

Quint's face turned red. "I'm *what?*"

"Look around you. No pictures of a wife or girlfriend. You answer questions about Neville and Wally and Willow without referring to the record, but you can't do that with your other tenants. And you know how to get from the fourth floor to the ground floor parking garage without any problem."

"I know those guys because of Burton Neville's move-out. You know, more recent. And I have girlfriends. I date girls."

"And I bet they last all of a couple of weeks, a month at the most," I said. "Then you go back to Neville, and more recently to Wally and Willow. Don't try to snow me, guy. I'm gay myself, and I have pretty good gaydar. And I'll top it off with something you might not even be aware of. Every time the two of us show up, you spend most of your time looking at Paul. Not that I blame you. He's good to look at."

"That's... that's—"

"Sorry, guy," Paul said. "He's got you pegged. If I were on the hunt, I'd know right away to zero in on you. By the way, your spreadsheet formula's restored now."

Quint's outrage morphed into curiosity. "Are you two... you know?"

"Absolutely," Paul answered with a smile. "One hundred percent."

Quint sagged back in his chair. "Look, I'm not gay. Well, not all the way. I *do* date women. Enjoy their company. But sometimes… but sometimes…."

Paul finished his sentence for him. "They don't scratch the itch."

"I guess so," Quint muttered. "At least not in the same way. Okay, so I sometimes went up to Burton's apartment. Not too often, but occasionally."

"You ever join Neville and any of his roommates?"

"No! I'm not that…." I waited him out. "Not comfortable with it."

I couldn't resist. "And the guys in 4202?"

"They're too flighty for me," he said.

"Until Neville moved out," Paul said. "Then I'll bet you got a lot friendlier."

Quint went neon again. "Once or twice after Burt left. I mean, they're not really my type, but… but when they both go to work on you, that doesn't matter much."

Now that he was vulnerable, I switched tactics. "Where were you last night?"

He blinked. "Wha-what time last night?"

"Describe your evening for me."

"After my last class about four-thirty, I came straight to the office and caught up on messages and bookkeeping. Found the screwup on the report to the management company, but after futzing with it for an hour, gave up and went to my apartment. Ate something, cleaned up after myself, and watched some TV."

"And after that," I prompted as he paused.

He reddened again. "After the ten o'clock news was over, I-I went up to 4202."

"How long did you stay?" I asked.

"We sat and talked and had some drinks. And… and then they scratched my itch."

"What time did you leave?"

"Sometime after one."

Paul chuckled. "Must have been some itch."

I thought he'd blushed before. He turned an alarming red at Paul's comment.

"What kind of car do you drive?" I asked.

"What?" He turned his attention to me. "My car? A 2000 Mini Cooper four-door hardtop. Why?"

"Does the apartment house have another vehicle you have access to? A van, for instance?"

"The maintenance man drives a van, but it's his own."

"Do you ever borrow it?"

A firm shake of the head. "No. Why?"

"Another young man was killed last night. Same MO. Body dumped on Sandia Reservation."

Now he went pale. "And you think I did it?"

"Did you?"

"No! And not the guy who was killed upstairs either."

"Are you willing to give a semen sample?" I asked.

"A *semen* sample? Can't you get DNA some other way? On the TV shows, they swab a cheek or something."

"The semen the killer leaves on his victims is special. It has no sperm."

"You mean he can't get anyone pregnant?"

"That's right, but no sperm, no DNA."

"How… how would I do it? I mean, lop it out and milk it until it comes? I-I can't do that."

"Bet you could if I left you alone with Paul. But no, you'd go down to the police department and provide the sample to them. Are you willing to do that?"

"I… guess so, if you think it's necessary." He licked his lips. "Would Paul come with me?"

"No, but we can give you a photo of him if you need it."

Paul flushed as deeply as the apartment manager.

I rose to go. "By the way, you can cancel the check you're holding for Neville. He's dead. Murdered."

The shock on Quint's face convinced me he hadn't known of Neville's death… unless he was a drama major at the university.

As he poked the elevator button for the fourth floor, Paul shook his head. "You won't believe the rent they charge to live in this place."

"Did a little peeking while you repaired the formula, did you?"

"Three grand. Three thousand dollars a month. Unbelievable."

"Remind me to have Glenann call Quint for a semen sample."

"Glenann, not Roy? Okay, but I'm not gonna give him a picture of me."

As usual, Wally answered the door with Willow hovering over his shoulder. They broke into smiles at the sight of us.

"I do like it when you bring Paul with you," Willow said, almost but not quite putting his hand on my companion's arm. Paul was probably feeling like bait on a hook about then.

"What can we do for you?" Wally asked.

"Still nosing around and wanted to talk to you."

"To me?"

"Both of you. I understand Quinton James spent last evening with you. Can you verify that?"

"Oh yes," Willow said. "Sweet boy, and quite good-looking too."

"When did he arrive, and what time did he leave?"

"We'd just finished watching the Channel 13 news when he rang the bell, so around ten thirty-five or so."

"How long did he stay?"

"A decent amount of time. We had a nice visit, didn't we, Wally?"

"Very nice."

"Fellas, we've already talked to Quint. So what time did he leave?"

Willow arched an eyebrow. "Quarter of two."

"Kinda late, wasn't it?" Paul asked.

"Well, it was Friday night. So we didn't have to go to work this morning. And Quint didn't have any classes, so we took our time and enjoyed ourselves."

"None of you left the others' presences during that time?"

"We all stayed in this apartment the whole time," Wally said. "Why?"

"There was another killing last night."

"Heavens! How horrible. What happened?"

"Same killer, same method of operation," I said.

"So it was another beautiful young man. You have to catch this beast."

"Doing our best. And may I ask what you gentlemen were doing prior to Quint's arrival?"

Wally sighed. "Same as usual. Came home from work, fixed ourselves something to eat. Watched a rather interesting movie—" His Kewpie-doll smile prevented me from asking what kind of film. "—until the news came on. Then Quint showed up."

After ascertaining what make and model cars the two owned and taking them through some more detailed questioning, we made ready to leave. At the door, I paused.

"You should know your friend, Burton Neville, was found down near Socorro. He'd been murdered—strangled—sometime shortly after he left Albuquerque for his job in California."

"Burton?" Wally exclaimed.

"Murdered?" Willow sang. "How?"

I fed them details and watched them absorb them like body blows. Those men hadn't been aware of Neville's death until that moment. Of that I was convinced.

Chapter 12

MONDAY MORNING, Hazel greeted me with the news Neville's 2010 Jag had shown up in a raid on a chop shop in Denver. That was a surprise. Most of our stolen cars headed south into Mexico.

When Charlie came in, I asked him to see if he could trace how the car got to Colorado. He nodded and gave me the second surprise of the day. He'd dug a little deeper and found a sealed juvie record on Quint James. The Park House manager apparently knew people with a little pull. The jacket had been buried, something hard to do. Charlie, always a thorough cop, had traced down the retired sergeant who'd arrested Quint. The man recalled the incident that earned Quint the record. He remembered it only because of the pressure brought to bear to quash the case. The uncle in the Park House REIT must have some political muscle.

At any rate, the retired sergeant considered the incident enough to have earned the offender jail time, even if it was in juvie hall. Quint had apparently gotten into a fight with another student in high school and, when he found himself on the losing side, whipped out a switchblade and cut his opponent. The injury wasn't serious enough to require hospitalization but did need stitches. Young Mr. James had earned himself a place back on my suspect list. Cutting and strangling were two different things, but both showed a propensity for violence.

The problem was that Charlie had verified most of Quint's movements on the day Matt Zapata died. He was in class at the likeliest time Matt was strangled. He certainly didn't kill Robert Sandoval and dump him on the Sandia Pueblo... unless Wally and Willow helped him do it. Nonetheless, I needed to face him down about the juvie case.

Quint didn't answer the office phone at Park House, so I spent the rest of the day helping Charlie trace the movements of everyone else at Park House even tangentially connected to Matt Zapata. I had already talked to Hector, the apartment house's maintenance man, but I wanted to check something with him again. He was the only one I'd run into so far who had a van, and it was almost certainly a van the killer used to haul around his victims' bodies. Had Hector loaned it to anyone recently? I located him at work by dialing the cell number he'd provided.

"No, sir," he growled into the telephone when I asked him about loaning his van to anyone. "It don't belong to Park House. It's my own vehicle, and they pay me mileage when I have to use it for work. Only one who gets to drive my van 'sides me is my wife, Wilma. Course my son did until he got his own wheels. But nobody else."

"Did Quint James ever ask to borrow it?"

"No, sir. Not never."

"Have you ever known him to rent a van?"

"Uh-uh. He just runs around in his dinky little car."

"Is anyone ever in it with him?"

"Nope. I figure the man don't do nothing but go to school and keep an eye on the Park House."

"Does he ever bring a girlfriend home?"

"Not that I ever seen. Course, I go home at five unless I got a problem with something at the park. So I don't know what goes on at night. He might have parties every night of the week for all I know."

"What do you think of him as a manager?"

He went silent for so long I thought he'd been struck dumb. "Mr. Quint?" His voice caught on the "Mister" part. "He's okay. Little wet behind the ears and kinda light on his feet, but he's okay. Pays the help decent enough. Treats us good. What more can you ask?"

I hung up wondering if the "light on his feet" remark was a reference to Quint's inexperience or his lifestyle. Probably both.

Rather than head directly home from the office, I drove up Central to the Park House. Quint answered his buzzer, and his voice indicated the welcome I was likely to receive. Nonetheless, he admitted me. I met him in the manager's office, where it looked as if he'd been doing homework.

He plopped back down in his chair. "Thanks a lot. I got a call from a detective and had to go down and give a semen sample. Embarrassing as hell. What are you doing here? I thought I answered all your questions."

I took a seat opposite him. "That was before I knew you had a record."

Quinton James wouldn't make a good criminal. His involuntary nervous system would betray him every time. His mouth dropped and he lost color. "I have what?"

"Your uncle did a good job of burying it, but my staff is good at digging up buried treasure. Want to tell me about it?"

"That's supposed to be sealed." His face was red now. Was rose blush his favorite color?

"It is sealed. But the police department is made up of flesh-and-blood men and women with memories. We found the man who arrested you. Mostly, I should add, because of the extraordinary lengths your uncle went to hide it."

"Why is it relevant?"

"Violence is violence. You're gay—"

"Not gay! Exactly."

"Please show me an exact gay, Quint. You had your moments with Burton Neville, and the other night Wally and Willow took care of your needs."

Had the guy's arteries burst? "Okay," I said to calm him down. "You're not gay. Or at least you haven't accepted it yet. But if that's true, you move up on my suspect list."

"W-why?"

"When a man indulges in a sex act he doesn't think is acceptable conduct, he sometimes fights against it. He's mortified by what he's done. Sometimes he's infuriated by it and takes it out on his partner. More than one guy's resorted to violence and tried to blame the other party for leading him on. Strangling a man is violence, Quint. But so is stabbing someone with a knife. A switchblade, no less."

He deflated like a dirigible losing helium. For a moment it looked as if he'd start shedding tears. "I-it wasn't like that."

"Then tell me what it was like."

"He...." Quint swallowed, and then tried again. "He was a senior, and I was a freshman. In high school. I really looked up to the guy. Football hero. Played basketball. And when we got in the fight, he had me belly down on the ground. He was on top of me shoving my face in the dirt. I was suffocating. Couldn't throw him off. I... I guess I was afraid and desperate. I managed to get the knife out of my pocket and stuck him in the leg. Didn't even bother him. Had to do it three or four times before he started yelling and let me go."

"And what started the fight?"

"Disagreement."

"You made a pass at him, didn't you?"

"No! Yes.... I don't know. He thought so anyway."

"Did you cripple him?"

"He recovered. Missed some football games, but he recovered. Claimed I cost him a scholarship to Tulane. They had to transfer me to another school."

"And why were you carrying a switchblade?"

"Everybody had them back then. In my neighborhood anyway. I'd got it a few days before the fight to be like everybody else. Never figured I'd use it."

He almost tuned up again, and as he fought against tears, I could see him for the mama's boy he'd been. Damned if I didn't admire the way he'd turned himself into a seemingly competent individual... until the cracks showed.

"Don't know if it saved your bacon or simply earned you a record. Now let's get down to business."

While grilling him up, down, and sideways, I barked at him, crooned at him. I played good cop and bad cop in tandem, reducing him to tears, but they were stubborn tears. He steadfastly defended himself against my accusations.

On the way home, I was in a thoughtful mood. Even a crybaby could be provoked too far. Maybe tears came after the sex was over, and he went into a rage when someone made fun of him.

I recalled a case I'd had as a Marine MP. This rookie apparently cried himself to sleep in the barracks every night, but when a buddy made a disparaging remark about his girlfriend during a drink-out in a bar, the crybaby tore into him and would likely have killed the guy if we hadn't arrived when we did.

But this was different. The recruit's reaction had been spontaneous. The use of a hypnotic sleeping drug on the cutie-pie victims clearly indicated premeditation. In addition, it hadn't taken much effort to get Quint to acknowledge he turned to Neville for companionship before the man left, and then to Wally and Willow. The guy wasn't as deep in the closet as he thought. It didn't compute.

I'D NO sooner walked through the back door to the house—we customarily entered through the kitchen, which almost got us killed by a bushwhacker hiding in the alley in the case I called the

Voxlightner Scandal—than Paul braced me with a kiss and some news. He'd been rechecking all of Matt's friends and learned something interesting. One of Burton Neville's playmates and Matt Zapata knew each other. At least they'd met. And the circumstances of the meeting were interesting. We took seats in the den where he gave me details.

"This girl—woman—named Beth practically grew up with Matt. They were friends, dated some. You know, casual. She also knew Sonny Delaware and went out with him for a while. Again, nothing serious, according to her. But one night about a year ago, she was with Matt at a dive down on South Broadway. They only went there because the joint didn't question false IDs. Anyway, they were in a booth minding their own business when Sonny came in and spotted them. He stalked over and staked a claim. Things went south from there."

"A fight?" I asked.

He paused to take a sip of his Crown Royal. "Some pushing and shoving. They were headed for the parking lot to get it on when a cop showed up. After that, Matt and Beth left."

"So Sonny lied to me. I showed him Matt's picture, and he said he'd never seen him."

Paul shrugged. "Ships passing in the night. Do you remember everyone you met in a bar?"

"Everyone I had a beef with, at any rate."

Paul's grin was devastating. "I suspect Sonny gets in a few more scrapes than you did."

"Fair assumption."

After a meal of Paul's excellent cheese enchiladas and refried beans, we settled in the den for a peaceful evening of reading and cuddling. That bucolic mood lasted until ten o'clock, when the evening news program put an exclamation point on Monday, April 2, by reporting a man named One Goh, a former student at a Korean Christian school called Oikos University, had opened fire inside the university and killed seven people at random, wounding several others. Such an act of violence shocked the world, and properly so. But our homegrown cutie-pie killer had slain five healthy young men, and the world—at least the larger world outside of New Mexico—didn't even know about it. Paul spoke what was on my mind.

"I hope we find our guy before he kills that many."

"The way he's escalating, we'd better hurry up."

TUESDAY MORNING I set about running Sonny Delaware to ground once again. I didn't anticipate much trouble. He knew who I was and likely didn't consider me a threat. In fact, because of his offer at Jack's, he might consider me an opportunity. I was right. He called me back within an hour of my message on his voicemail.

"Jack's," I said. "Thirty minutes."

"Two drinks minimum."

"Deal."

Sonny was waiting for me when I arrived, drink number one already on the table at his favorite booth. He'd spruced up for the meet. Probably the tightest T-shirt in his wardrobe. Plain white, no decorations. Likely so his nipples would be prominent. He did look good.

I ordered a soda from Harvey and settled on the padded seat opposite Sonny.

"So what's up?" he demanded.

"Wanted to know why you lied to me."

His features settled into something between a scowl and a questioning look, an interesting contortion of the muscles. "Whaddya mean?"

I pulled out Matt's photo and slid it across to him. "You claimed you didn't know this man."

His features morphed into a total frown before clearing. He looked up with a grin as he slid the picture back to me.

"Wanted it to cost you a few more drinks. Knew you'd find out about it if you were any good. From what I hear, you're good… in more ways than one."

"Sonny, let's get something cleared up once and for all. I'm committed to a great guy and have no interest in making a change."

"Not suggesting a change. An addition. You ever had two hunky guys working on you at once?"

"Not gonna work. We're here to discuss the death of a young man and how you fit into the picture."

"Don't. Not in no way."

"But you did know Zapata."

"That's the guy's name? I didn't even know that."

"Beth Turnhill says you did. Got into it with him one night at a bar."

"Don't know everybody I mix it up with at a bar. Do you?"

"Why did you mix it up with this particular guy?"

"He was squiring my girl. And I could tell he was a queer."

"Queer like you, Sonny. He walked both sides of the street."

He shrugged. "Either way, he didn't have no business with Beth. She was taken."

"Not according to Beth."

His cheeks flared, but he swiped at his mouth and shook it off. "That was back when. We went our separate ways since then."

"When Neville came along, I assume. He was worth more bucks than Beth."

He leaned forward, fists clenched on the table, to stare me in the eyes. "I don't take money from women."

I allowed my eyebrow to twitch. "Just from men."

He leaned back in the booth, the tension gone from his muscles. "That's right. I work for my money. With women, it ain't work."

"Was that the first time you saw Matt Zapata?"

"First and only. No… ain't right. I seen him around from time to time. I used to hang out in Zimmerman Library a lot. Good place to meet babes. Good pickup place for guys too, I guess, 'cause I seen him there."

I mentally shook my head, guessing there were two Sonny Delawares. One was reasonably well educated. The other was a street tough with all the fractured lingo that goes with it. I revised my assessment. The reasonable one was Morton Delaware. The thug was Sonny.

"Had you ever spoken to him before? Got with him, maybe?"

"Nah. He might have been as pretty as Beth, but I don't get with guys."

"Unless they pay for it," I added.

He shrugged. "Whatever. Anyway, I never got with him. Not before the dustup and not after."

"What else did you lie to me about?"

"Nothing. Preached the gospel… except for that. I got nothing to do with offing him or those other dudes. Not a frigging thing. We good now?" he asked.

I hauled out the photo of Barkley Pierson. "How about this guy?"

Sonny snatched it up and frowned. "I seen him at the U too. With the other guy, the one I laid on his ass. Seen them in the Zimmerman. Got the feeling they was lovey-dovey, know what I mean?"

Might as well yank this guy's chain. Make him pay for the drinks I was buying. "According to Beth, the queer fought you to a draw."

"Hadn't even gone outside for the real fight before a cop showed up."

I indicated Pierson's photo. "Do you mean they were cozying up in the library?"

"Nah. But I took one look and figured out what they was up to."

"More likely tried to figure out how to join them."

He fooled me. "Wouldn'ta been a bad deal. One of them looked like sex-on-a-stick, and the other one—the one with glasses—you could tell he was built for stamina. You know, slender but with muscles."

"You're showing your true colors, Sonny."

"Whatcha mean?"

"Neither one of them would have paid you, but you'd have jumped in the middle of them in a minute."

He shrugged and grinned. "We done?"

I nodded and called an order for his second drink before I stood.

"No need to rush off," he said. "You're good to look at, even if nothing comes of it."

"Thanks, but I've got to go look good somewhere else. I have a murderer to catch, remember."

"A four-times murderer, as I remember."

"Five. He killed another one. Watch your six, Sonny. He goes for good-looking young guys."

"Guess that's me. But I ain't worried. I can take care of myself."

I nodded at his empty glass. "What if I'd drugged your drink? Could you take care of yourself then?"

That sobered him a little.

SINCE I was not far from the War Zone, I took a run by Hosea Middleton's small apartment, but he wasn't home. As long as I was there, I canvassed some of the neighbors. To the lady on his left, Hosea was a sweet, quiet boy. To the beer-belching guy on the right, "Hose" was "that little queer" who brought all his boyfriends home and probably germed up the place so everybody in the neighborhood would likely come down with AIDS or something. Neither neighbor recognized Matt's picture, but the beer-guzzler said it coulda been one of Hose's pickups. He added it was about time the cops came to check up on the dirty bastard. I didn't bother to point out my license was private. Wouldn't have mattered to him anyway.

Just before I crawled into the Impala, I spotted Hosea Middleton walking down the street carrying a small bag of what appeared to be groceries. He stopped on the sidewalk beside me.

"Hello, Mr. Vinson."

"Hello, Hosea. Or do you prefer Hose?"

He shrugged, rattling the bag. "Doesn't make any difference. I picked up the tag Hose when I was in grade school, so I'm used to it now."

"Hose, I'm going to ask you some very personal questions, but I want you to know I'm asking them as a professional. I'm not asking for any other reason. All right?"

"Yes, sir."

"Do you want to go inside?"

"No, do it here." He put down the bag and pulled out a Coke. "You want one?"

"Thanks, but no. How do you make ends meet? How'd you buy those groceries, for example?"

He looked at me through soft, soulful eyes. "Truth?" I nodded. "I take care of him. The landlord, I mean."

"On a regular basis?"

He popped the tab and took a sip of the pop before swiping his upper lip with the back of a hand. For a moment, we both watched a bee, attracted by the sugary drink, buzz the top of the Coke can before flying away. The scent of the cola reached me. When I was a kid, I was addicted to Cokes, grapes, strawberries—anything carbonated and full of sugar—until my mom put her foot down and banned them from the house. I've regressed a little... but not much.

Hose cleared his throat and answered my question. "Yeah, I take care of him whenever he wants. And... and sometimes he sends someone to me."

"To service?"

He nodded.

"He's your pimp."

After a momentary flinch at the word, he nodded again. "I guess you can say that. Anyway it helps him, and it helps me. So I get by."

I couldn't resist moralizing. "Don't you aspire to something better?"

"Mr. Vinson, all my life I've been a punching bag. And Luis takes care of me. The guy who lives next door would like to gouge my eyes out every time I see him, but he doesn't lay a hand on me. That's because of Luis. He's good to me, and he doesn't send anyone who wants to hurt me—" His mouth turned sour. "—like some of them used to do."

"Like Burton Neville?"

"Oh no! He was good to me."

"What's Luis's name?"

Doubt showed on Hosea's face, but he haltingly provided the name. "Luis Andretta. But please don't tell him I told you."

"Did you ever take him to Neville's apartment in the Park House?"

"N-no! I didn't even know Luis then. I met him the...." He stuttered to a halt, swiped at his eyes, spilling a little of his soda as he did so. "I met him the day after Burton left for California. He-he found me moping around in Indian Alley. I guess I was crying. Anyway, he took me home and, well, you know. He saw me a couple of times after that, and we made an arrangement. Not as good as what I had with Burt, but it's okay."

"Did you give Andretta your key card to Neville's apartment?"

"My key card? I didn't have a key card."

"You never stayed in the apartment while Neville went on a business trip?"

He shook his head so hard he spilled Coke on the ground again. "Never. He only took one trip while I was with him. Two nights in Taos. And he took me with him. We had a great time."

"Then why did the police find your fingerprint on the underside of the bathroom commode lid? You hid your stash there, didn't you? That indicates you partied while he was gone."

He dropped his gaze to the sidewalk. "That wasn't it at all. It was me checking to see if Burton hid anything there."

"Why? You needed a fix?"

"Uh-uh. Right after I met him, he was down on drugs so much it made me wonder why. So I checked the toilet tank once when I took a leak. Wasn't anything there." Hose looked thoughtful for a moment. "Lucky for me I met Luis when I did. I've got my own place to stay and groceries and a TV. What else could I want?"

I refrained from telling him. Instead, I handed over the photo of Matt Zapata. "Take another look. Are you sure you never got with him?"

His eyes were soft and brimming when he handed it back. "I wish I had. He'd of treated me good."

"How do you know?"

"I can just tell. He's not only handsome, he's good."

"That he was."

ALL THE way back to the office, I fought a wave of frustration. This case *had* to be connected to Park House. In some way, somehow. But none of the players fit. Quint James would have been strong enough to lift his victims if they were drugged or dead. But I couldn't see him loading them in a Mini Cooper. Besides, he had no motive. Of course, serial killers don't always have a motive, merely a causation. Something kicks off the urge... the need to kill. Even so, he was in class when Zapata died.

Wally and Willow struck me as squirrely, but it was hard to see either one of them capable of killing. Together? Maybe. But Charlie had confirmed both were at work on Monday the fifth. Burton Neville was already dead when Zapata died. Valdez, the maintenance man, had the day off the Monday Matt was killed but had been with his family. Neither of Neville's "boys," Sonny nor Hosea, appeared likely suspects.

Now there was a new name, but it didn't look promising. I'd have Charlie check on Luis Andretta, but I expected nothing to come of it.

That was everyone I could connect with apartment 4201 at Park House.

Except—

My mind snapped back to Jules McClintock. He wasn't connected to the Park House, just with the former tenant of 4201. And the onetime cutie-pie was now a hulking, semi-invalid man.

Chapter 13

THE NEXT morning, I went for swim therapy at the country club. I'd been avoiding the water, but the old wound in my right thigh was beginning to stiffen, warning me not to take it lightly. Paul had other plans but agreed to join me in the office later so we could review Matt Zapata's killing to search for anything we'd missed.

When I arrived, his Charger was already in the parking lot behind my building. I entered through the back doors and mounted three flights of stairs. As I reached the mezzanine on my floor, I wondered—not for the first time—why taking the stairs rather than accepting the convenience of the elevator didn't serve the same purpose as my swim, and arrived at the same conclusion I always did. The stairs delayed the need for the swim, but both were necessary for my welfare.

When I pushed through the door to Suite C, housing Vinson and Weeks, Confidential Investigations, Charlie and Paul were already in the main conference room, together with Roy and Glenann. Hazel rose from her desk and preceded me into the glass-fronted room.

I claimed my chair at the end of the big table and glanced—as I always did—at the oil painting of three mounted Apache warriors staring into the distance at something one of them was pointing to. It was part of my dad's early Americana art collection. "Morning, all."

A chorus of varied greetings came back at me.

"Anything new on the other killings, Roy?" I asked.

"We've charged a man named Bruno Aisling in the murder of Aragon, the copycat victim. No solid leads on any of the cutie-pie murders. We're counting on you to break the case by solving Zapata's murder. How's that coming?"

"It isn't," I said. "That's why we're here. To make sure we've covered all the bases." I fixed my gaze on my partner's bald pate. "Charlie, have we heard back from K-Y Lab on the DNA sample APD gave us?"

"Yep. Male, of course, aged thirty plus or minus, West European, maybe Celtic. But plenty of French."

I nodded. "Were you able to trace Neville's car backward from the Denver chop shop?"

"Did a little better on that one. The gang the Denver police busted knew the guy who delivered the car. The chop shop had done business with him before. A punk kid in Socorro with a jacket for car theft. The kid claimed he found the car on a Socorro street with the keys in it and a billfold on the seat."

I nodded. "The Denver police didn't know the car in question was connected to a murder. Roy, should we send someone up to question the chop shop operators more thoroughly?"

"I've contacted Denver PD and let them know of Neville's murder. They'll hit the gang harder. If they learn anything more, I'll let you know, and we can decide then."

"What about our Socorro thief? Where is he?"

"Back home," Glenann said. "Socorro PD's picking him up. Roy and I will run down to interview him."

"Are we sure he didn't kill Neville?" Paul asked.

"Don't worry, we'll lean on him, as will Socorro. After all, the case is theirs. But in all honesty, the guy looks good for theft, not murder."

"A Porsche's a pretty pricy ride," Paul said. "Maybe it was worth it to off the guy."

Glenann leaned forward in her seat. "If it was, we'll find out."

"Okay," I said. "Do we know what the thief did after he found the car on a Socorro street... if that turns out to be the case?"

Roy picked up the tale. "Drove the vehicle to Gallup, filled it with gas—that was the charge on Neville's Amex card—and decided he liked the drive to Denver better than the one to Phoenix."

"Long way to drive without another fill-up or two."

"He got some cash off the card at the gas station. Plus I imagine Neville had some in the wallet. At any rate, the thief tossed the card and the wallet afterward. Figured he was lucky the first time and didn't chance it again."

"That part of his story check out?" Charlie asked.

"He's spotted big as life on the Gallup mart's camera," Roy responded. "And like Glenann said, he has no history of violent tendencies. So yeah, I'd say he told the truth."

The weight of my morning swim bore down on me. I fought an urge to grab Paul and go home for a nestle and a nap. Instead, I sat where I was most of the morning while we reviewed everything we'd done and rehashed the leads we'd developed and chased until they'd died. We reviewed the background of everyone at Park House, Matt's friends and family, Barkley Pierson. All the calls made through Ma Flanagan's telephone service. Telephones, computers, credit cards. And then we rechecked them all. Nothing added up. Park House was the key, but so far Park House was also a bust.

"You know what this means?" I asked when everyone had run out of steam.

"Yeah," Charlie answered. "Start the footwork all over."

"Okay, Roy and Glenann, are we agreed you leave Zapata's killing with us while you pursue the others?"

They nodded.

"Charlie, you and Hazel start recontacting people. Paul and I are going to yank the one loose thread we haven't tugged yet."

"What's that?" Paul asked.

"Jules McClintock. He's not directly connected to Park House, but he was to Neville, even though the connection was broken some time ago. We've interviewed him, but I want to talk to him again."

When the group broke up, Hazel reminded me we had other cases and plopped one of them down on my desk. I spent the rest of the day on the telephone tracking down a young woman with Santa Fe connections who'd run away from her Boston home. At 4:00 p.m., I found her and earned a big grin and a peck on the cheek from my office manager. She'd hit up the back-East law firm who'd contracted with us for a lot more than that.

PAUL AND I arrived at Jules McClintock's house at 9:00 the next morning. The big man's eyes flickered in momentary surprise as he answered our ring in shapeless pants and a gaudy Hawaiian shirt that closely resembled a tent. His lips stretched into a smile as his eyes flicked to my companion.

"Paul... and BJ. Welcome. Won't you come in?"

This time he insisted on acting the proper host by bringing us hot tea, the cups riding on a serving tray propped on the armrests of his chair. In the midst of my first sip, I recalled the zopiclone found in the bodies of the five cutie-pie victims. My reaction must have been noticeable because Jules glanced at me.

"Too hot?"

"No, it's fine, thank you."

Paul eyed his cup before setting it untasted on the table beside him. If I was being doped, at least he could call for help. I fought to keep from laughing aloud at the thought.

"And to what do I owe this pleasure?" Jules asked before taking a healthy slug of his tea. That was little comfort. He wouldn't dope his *own* drink.

"We're back to ask more questions about Burton Neville."

"Ah, good old Burton. Gone... but he won't leave us alone, will he?"

"What do you mean, gone?" I asked, my heart rate beginning to accelerate.

"He left for a job in California, I gather…." He ran a hand vigorously across his scalp. "None too soon, if you ask me."

"That's sorta uncool for someone who was once your main squeeze," Paul said.

"*Once* is the key word in your statement, my young friend. Once I became ill, he dropped me like a hot stone. Shook me off like a nettle pricking his fingers." Jules's great sigh seemed to shake the rafters. "I understood, but understanding didn't make it hurt less."

Paul nodded to a framed photo hanging on the wall. "Is that you back in your college days?"

Jules didn't bother to follow his look. He kept his eyes trained on Paul. "Again, the word *once* comes into play. That was once me. Now…."

Paul smiled. "I can still see you in the picture."

Jules beamed. "Kind of you to say such a thing."

"It wasn't just words. I meant it."

Still hung up on Jules's characterization of Neville as "gone," I tried a gambit. "You're certain you haven't seen Neville lately."

His look clouded as it swung back to me. "He came to the hospital twice. Exactly twice, and then I neither heard from nor saw him again."

I tapped a forefinger against my lips. "Strange. He told friends he'd seen you recently."

There was no change in his bland features, but his eyes sharpened. "I saw him once as I was entering Walmart. I said hello, and he deigned to pause long enough to at least acknowledge me. Come to think of it, he's the one who told me he was leaving Albuquerque for the Bay area. New job, as I recall."

"When was that?"

"Six or seven months ago. I'm surprised he even mentioned me to his friends. His manner said I was nothing to him anymore. Not even a pleasant memory." Jules frowned. "And we had plenty of those, I can tell you."

"How long were you with him?" Paul asked.

"Something over three years."

"Was it a regular thing right away?"

"Casual. But I knew it would build into something. While my folks were decently well-off, I knew he'd help me with my education. I never paid a penny. By the time I met you, BJ—and I must say you were quite a dish too, even though you were a cop at the time—he was totally supporting me and happy to do so."

"And that's why you stayed in the closet," I said.

"That's the way Burton wanted it, so that's the way I played it." He frowned. "I think he didn't want others to know I was gay, to reduce the competition."

I smiled. "Didn't work, did it? The way you looked, they came for you left and right."

He glowed. "All too true. I could have had anyone I wanted, but I stayed true to Burton." His smile faltered. "Well, almost faithful. There were a couple of others who wouldn't take no for an answer. As I think I told you, I slipped out of the closet toward the end."

"Are you sure that's not why he dropped you?" Paul asked.

"*That* I could have understood. But it was obvious he couldn't handle my illness."

Paul toyed with his teacup. "How did he find you?"

"I was a junior in high school. Does that surprise you, BJ? I was quite mature for my age, and it didn't take much to convince him I was eighteen. Of course, he wanted to believe, so that made it easier."

"How old were you?"

"Sixteen. And without being egotistical, a knockout."

Paul frowned. "He came right on the school campus and picked you up?"

"He came to a football game with a friend." Jules laughed. "Can you imagine that? A high school football game. He didn't care a whit about football, but he got a bang out of the players. He shook his friend and hung around until I came out of the locker room. Picked me up on the spot."

"And now you're bitter about it," Paul said.

Jules favored him with another smile. "Bittersweet is more like it. Memories are good, but the present stinks."

I entered the conversation. "What can you tell me about his other boyfriends? Particularly those who came after you?"

"No idea. As I said, there was no contact."

"May I use your restroom?" Paul asked.

"Certainly. Straight down the hall on the right."

He turned his chair enough to watch Paul's graceful stride before turning back to me.

"Okay, so you had no contact with Neville, but you had friends," I said. "Surely you heard things about him now and then."

Anger flashed in his still-beautiful eyes. "I lost most of my so-called friends as well. Disease drives away all but the stalwart. And there weren't any stalwarts among my circle."

I flashed back on my breakup with Del Dahlman when he was unable to deal with my recovery from a gunshot wound. I spoke to clear the thought from my mind. "I remember bumping into you at the university, but so far as I know, I never set eyes on Burton Neville."

"He didn't come on campus. The day was mine, but I went home to him." Jules's features hardened. "As I said, I was faithful to him, BJ. Except for a couple of weak moments. I got propositioned all over the place by people you wouldn't even suspect, but I never strayed far from Burton." His features softened. "But I'm wasting my words. You were really a handsome guy, BJ—still are." The final words held a certain bitterness. He brightened. "Ah, but your friend...."

As his voice died away, I nodded. "And here he comes."

Paul entered the room with a questioning look on his face.

"I was explaining the unnecessary," Jules said. "About how attractive you are."

Paul—who was no stranger to compliments—had the grace to blush. "Two ears, two eyes, a nose, and a mouth," he mumbled.

"And put together in such a delicious way," Jules said.

I got up. "Thank you for your time. Paul, would you take our teacups to the kitchen for Jules? Then we need to be on our way."

Jules heaved himself out of his chair and waddled to the door with us, claiming we were welcome anytime. He held Paul's hand a beat too long in a parting handshake.

Once in the car, Paul shuddered. "He gives me the heebie-jeebies."

I pulled away from the curb before eyeing my companion. "Why?"

Paul was silent for two blocks. "I don't really know. His physical condition, I guess. Not really his disability. The way he's let himself go. He was everybody's wet dream in that picture. Heck, if I'd met him back then, I'd probably have thrown you over for him."

I chuckled. "Back then you would have been about fifteen years old."

"I still had eyes."

"True."

"And I was beginning to fill out and discover... things."

"Also true."

Paul dragged out a soggy napkin. "I poured tea from a cup on it. We can check for the drug the killer uses."

"My cup or yours?"

"Mine." He flashed a smile that roiled my loins. "He was giving me longer looks than he was you."

"You obviously ring his chimes."

Paul shivered visibly. "While I was in his bathroom, I snuck a look in the medicine cabinet and wrote down a couple of prescriptions. I got the name of his doctor and the drugstore where he filled them. You know, there weren't as many meds as I thought a guy in his condition would have."

"I suspect there's another bathroom off his bedroom he uses most of the time. The meds were probably in there."

"Yeah. Shoulda taken a look in the other room."

"Too risky. Your instincts were right. But let's get back to your reaction to Jules."

"Gross," he said.

"Is that it? His weight?"

Paul took another minute to think. "That and maybe his attitude."

"Meaning?"

"Meaning he's smoldering inside. He likes who he was and detests who he is. Plus the fact he wouldn't take his eyes off me."

"People watch you all the time. You're very watchable, my friend."

"He doesn't watch me. He devours me."

UPON ARRIVAL at the office, I sat at my desk with my fingers on the computer keyboard without pressing a single button for a long time. What rattled around in my head probably bordered on the unthinkable. Was it even possible? Could Jules McClintock divorce himself from his motorized chair long enough to meet, have sex with, and then strangle and dispose of someone afterward? We often equate body mass with strength, but that is not always the case. Even so, I suspected he had the muscle power to kill a drugged victim. Carrying a dead body any distance was another matter.

But how far did he have to carry them? Matt Zapata was probably the biggest challenge. The killer had engaged the victim through a telephone service to meet in a highly unlikely place. A multistory apartment building. But there were laundry carts available for the hard work.

The murderer had taken a significant risk. Someone might have seen him on his way to or from apartment 4201. And Quint James might have shown the apartment to prospective lessees at any time. Yet no one saw him in the hallway or in the garage. Lucky or careful?

I called up a police database and began my hunt. Charlie had done preliminary work on Jules earlier, but I started over again. No jacket. No complaints at the school where he worked until his illness and obesity forced him to quit.

In New Mexico, confidential investigators don't have the right to check an individual's credit cards or banking details, so I called and asked Glenann to do it. She phoned back later with preliminary information. No unusual charges on credit cards. Ditto his banking reference. I learned Jules enjoyed a monthly income of around $5,000 from his parents' trust. Seemed adequate for normal living, but would it handle his medical bills? No matter, the killings weren't done for monetary gain. Although all the victims' wallets were missing, along with their clothing, no one had tried to use stolen credit cards.

I ran into a roadblock while attempting to look into Jules's medical records. I didn't bother calling Glenann back. The cops would have the same problem. The medical profession is a stickler for privacy laws. A superficial check confirmed Jules suffered from the transverse myelitis he described but little else. Maybe Roy or Glenann might be able to get a warrant for a list of his prescriptions, but thanks to Paul, I knew where he filled them, and I was confident there were more than the ones he had found. Of course, I was looking for a specific drug, the one used to control the five victims: zopiclone, a powerful sleeping aid that might well have rested on Jules's bedside table.

According to MVD, Jules owned a 2010 white Chrysler Voyager. Photos on used car dealers' websites showed a reasonably nondescript vehicle perfect for transporting dead bodies.

THE NEXT day, Paul had a chance meeting with Jules, which shook him a bit. As he explained it to me afterward, he was coming out of Staples in Cottonwood Mall and ran into Jules entering the store. The man paused his chair long enough to hail my companion, talk a minute, and invite him for coffee in the food court. Paul pled a previous appointment and left before Jules could make an alternate suggestion—as Paul was certain he would. My lover has seen a lot in his twenty-seven years, but the encounter obviously rattled him.

"I wonder why he was at Cottonwood?" I mused. "The Staples on Montgomery would be closer to his home ground."

Paul answered the question. "Said he'd just finished a tutoring session nearby."

"Still, it's a hell of a lot easier to get to Staples in a stand-alone store rather than in a big shopping mall."

Paul shrugged. "Guess he's adapted to his condition. Goes wherever he wants."

"Still, I wonder…."

"Crap, Vince, don't creep me out. You think he was looking for me instead of Staples?"

I shook my head and eased off. "Not too likely he could follow you and stay close enough to determine where you were going for such a long distance without you noticing. So… chance encounter, most likely."

"Better be," the light of my life muttered.

Jules McClintock—disabled or not—deserved a look-see, even though his connection with Park House ranged from tenuous to nonexistent. I went to Charlie's office and asked him to arrange for Alan Mendoza and Tim Fuller, our other part-timer, to set up surveillance on Jules.

His eyebrows expressed surprise. "Isn't it premature? Why is he any more apt to be the killer than a dozen other guys?"

"You show me the dozen other guys to surveil, and maybe I'll listen."

"Hell, BJ, there's the Delaware kid and that other one… Middleton. There's the manager at the Park House, and—"

"And we've traced them into the ground."

"Are you sure?"

"Reasonably certain." I shrugged. "You never know until you know, but they don't seem right to me."

"But a three-hundred-pound man confined to a wheelchair does?"

I sighed. "He knew Neville, and Neville's tied to Park House."

"But he knew Neville before Park House."

"Met him at least once in the past six or seven months. And consider that he hates Neville and—"

"And Neville's dead. Murdered."

"Right. And Neville had a spare key card to Park House that's missing. That key card is—pardon my expression—key to the case."

"I'll give you that. But Delaware and Middleton both claim they saw Neville the day he left for California. They could have copped it then."

"And finally," I said, "we can't trace Jules McClintock's movements. Consider the irony of that. The man's in a wheelchair, and we don't have any idea of where he was when those boys were killed."

"Get him down to the police station and grill it out of him."

"Jules is the kind of guy who'll yell lawyer right off the bat. After that, what do you think are the odds of our grilling a pitiful invalid confined to a wheelchair?"

"Yeah, especially when you're accusing him of killing healthy young studs and then heaving their dead bodies all over the place." Charlie shook his head but surrendered gracefully. "All right, but it won't be easy to surveil 3661 Colorado Street," my partner said. "No alleyways in that part of the Northeast Heights. It's a quiet neighborhood. A car's gonna be noticed."

"True. Have them switch off. Change cars too. Authorize a couple of rentals."

"Okay," Charlie said, doubt riding his voice.

SATURDAY, I got one of those early morning calls I was beginning to dread. I dug sleep out of my eyes and answered.

"Sorry, guy. Know it's early, but we've got another one."

I sat up in bed at the sound of Roy's voice. "Another body?"

"Exactly," he said.

"Where this time?"

"Way out at the gate to the west side shooting range. You know it?"

"Yep. That's only a couple of miles from where Lieu was found."

"Turn west there, and it's more like three miles."

"It's the cutie-pie killer?"

"His signature right down to naked, semen-saturated, and strangled."

"Who is it this time?"

"Don't have an ID, but…."

My back prickled. "But what?"

"At first, I thought it was Paul."

I let out a breath I didn't know I was holding. "He's right here."

"Yeah. Closer inspection told me this guy was younger. My first impression was wrong."

"Hispanic?"

"Probably coyote. Mix of Anglo and Hispanic."

"Just like Paul," I said. "We'll get there as fast as we can."

"No need. The county's giving us some static on this one. Might have to fight them over it. I've got plenty of photos I'll share. On second thought, I probably shouldn't have bothered you."

"Glad you did. Something I want to check as fast as I can."

I hung up, ignored my companion's "What's like Paul?" and dialed Charlie. I couldn't tell if I woke him or if he'd been up for hours. He simply sounded like Charlie. "The killer was working last night. Have you heard from Alan or Tim?"

"Tim's out of town, and I didn't reach Alan until a few minutes ago. We didn't get the surveillance set up yet."

"Damn! Maybe we could have saved a kid."

Charlie's voice was unruffled. "There's another one?"

"Dumped out by the city's shooting range on the west side. Crap, maybe we could have saved him."

"Doubt it. By the time you called me last night, he was probably already dead. Besides, there's a lot saying this McClintock character isn't the perp."

I told him about Paul's encounter with Jules yesterday afternoon and how Roy had initially mistaken the latest victim for my companion.

"You figuring him hankering after Paul sent him on the hunt for a look-alike?"

"Possible, or it's as likely the victim was totally random."

BY THE time I reached the office around eight, APD had identified the latest victim as a University of New Mexico student named Peter Baca. The photos Roy emailed showed an extremely handsome young man of about twenty who did put me in mind of Paul. However, when he examined the pictures, my mate failed to pick up on any strong resemblance other than hair, eye, and skin color. And, of course, height and weight. What else did he need?

"That ID was fast. He was in the system?"

"Went to the state's facial-recognition system and ran it against New Mexico drivers' licenses. Got some possible hits and winnowed them down to Baca. Plus we had some help. Baca's mom called the Louisiana SE station yesterday and reported him missing. The sergeant there told her it was too soon to put out a missing person's report, but he was smart enough to put the kid on the be-on-the-look-for list."

Charlie appeared at the door, and I beckoned him to join Paul and me in my office, where I had Roy on the speakerphone. "What's the kid's background?"

"High school football jock. But didn't come to UNM on an athletic scholarship. Paying his own way. Popular at school. Scored with the ladies regularly. No sign of him walking the other side of the street. And he didn't need to sell himself to keep a roof over his head."

"Live on campus?"

"Nope. In the family home in the Southeast Heights area. The forensics guys are at the house now. Don't have a report, but they're already pretty sure it's not the murder site."

"You said the county was giving you some problems. How do you stand with them on this one?"

"The sheriff gave it to us. The county's merely the dumping site. He was giving me grief because we haven't managed to stop the killer." Roy made an exasperated sound into the phone. "Six! This guy's taken six human lives, and we're no closer to catching him than after the first one."

"Seven," I said. "I'm convinced he killed Burton Neville down near Socorro, but his death might have been for a different reason. You any closer to solving any of the other killings?"

"Not much. Talked to those Bernalillo High students you gave us. They confirmed Sandoval as a quiet, shy guy. Nothing squirrely."

"That's the way this killer likes them," Charlie said. "He's not looking for troublemakers. Probably the closest he came to that was his first one."

"Greene, you mean?" Roy asked. "The street kid?"

"Yep. He might have given the killer some trouble."

"The perp's steered clear of vagabonds since then," I said.

"True," Charlie agreed. "Zapata was a call boy but not a ruffian. Even so, it looks like our killer's staying clear of pros now. The rest of them are targets of opportunity."

"And there are plenty of those walking around," Roy said.

"But how does he lure them in?" Charlie asked. "We know one of them was stranded. But what about the others?"

"John Lieu might fit the same description," Roy suggested. "He walked away from his ride at the bar and was hiking. BJ, have you figured how the killer contacted Matt Zapata?"

"I'm convinced the babysitting request through Ma Flanagan's telephone service was from the killer. But it was from one of the two cell phones we can't locate, possibly burner phones. But you're asking if I've found how the killer obtained that number."

"Other than picking out good-looking young guys and going through each of the races, strangling them after administering dope, and having sex, have you picked up any patterns to the killings?" Roy asked.

I consulted my notes. "Not really. Ignoring Neville for the moment, there were almost three months between the first and second killings. Then he waited a little over three months for his third killing. After that, it's only a matter of days or weeks between the last three killings. Something's revving this guy's motor."

"Looks like we're no closer than before," Roy said.

I thought of Jules's lusting looks at Paul. And his meeting in Staples. And of the last victim's resemblance to Paul.

"Maybe we're closer than you think."

I filled him in on Jules McClintock.

Chapter 14

CHARLIE AND I began Monday morning by canvassing Jules McClintock's neighborhood, looking for anyone who had used Matt Zapata's services—personal or otherwise—who might have mentioned the young man to Jules. Paul harped on me to let him join in, but I didn't want him anywhere in the vicinity of the man.

My fellow investigator and I went about the procedure openly, making no effort to shield our activity from Jules. I wanted him to know we were on his case. We called on every house in any direction within three blocks of 3661 Colorado. The results fell into three distinct patterns: "Don't know the guy." "Oh, you mean the fat guy who rides around in his electric gizmo." And closer to his address, "He's really a nice man. Tutors those little kids and makes sure they don't get into the wrong car when they leave. They all love him."

And then I knocked on the door to the right of Jules's house. A woman with the sharpest nose I'd ever seen answered the door and identified herself as Mrs. Mercy Hormel. She opened the screen but didn't invite me inside. At first, she bristled when I quizzed her about her next-door neighbor.

"What's this all about?"

"Just doing a required background check for the system." Maybe she'd connect "system" with Albuquerque public schools. Apparently she did.

"Well, I can tell you without compunction," she said, her nose twitching as if it were looking for an odor it could sense but not quite smell, "he's the grandest man alive. Those little darlings come over dragging their heels and come out all smiles and thanking Mr. Mac—that's what they call him—for making arithmetic understandable."

"All of them come out smiling?"

"Some of the little dears don't make the connections regardless of who's teaching them. But I know for a fact he helps most of them more than their regular teachers."

"No signs of… trouble with any of them?"

"Of course not." Her eyes and her mouth both went wide, and her nose wiggled like it was trying to escape. "Oh, you mean *that* way? Absolutely not. Jules is a righteous man. He has no perversions like that."

I feigned an embarrassed smile. "Sorry, but it's a question we have to ask in such a check. You know, when dealing with little innocents."

She and her nose both smiled. I'm not sure how I came to such a conclusion, but I did. "I understand. There's nothing like that going on. In fact, one of the little tykes had a family tragedy yesterday. The little boy came in sobbing this morning, and Jules sent him home smiling."

"What kind of tragedy?"

"The little boy's brother got killed." She dropped her voice and stepped closer, bringing her nose dangerously near. "Murdered, in fact. Perhaps you read about it in this morning's *Journal*. They found the poor thing out on the mesa somewhere." The voice dropped lower, the nose, closer. "Naked he was." She stepped back across the threshold. "Shameful. No respect."

"I read about that," I said. "That was one of Mr. McClintock's students?"

An impatient look claimed her features. "No, young man. You don't listen well, do you? I said it was the older brother of one of his students. He used to pick up his little brother all the time. Handsome boy. They both were. The little one too."

"Do you know their names?"

"The paper said the family name was Baca. I just knew the little one, poor dear, as Jimmy. Jules called the older one Petey."

"Did Petey ever go inside Mr. McClintock's house?"

"Sometimes, but mostly he only came to the front door." Her eyes flicked and the nose twitched. "Are you still harping on *that*? I told you Jules isn't interested in… well, you know. Given his ailment, I question whether he even thinks about such things. Oh, that came out wrong. With ladies, I mean. Anyway, I have to go. My husband will expect a meal on the table when he gets home, and I haven't even peeled the potatoes yet." With that, she started to close the door, but I forestalled her.

"Just one more question, please." I held out the now well-worn photo of Matt Zapata. "This young man does odd jobs for extra money while he's at the university. Have you ever used his services?"

She snatched the photo and peered at it intently. "My husband takes care of the outside of the house, and I do the inside. Don't have any use for such a tradesman." She thrust the photo back into my hands.

"Did you ever see him at Mr. McClintock's house? Or anywhere else in the neighborhood?"

"Never."

"Did Mr. McClintock go out yesterday and perhaps return late?"

"Young man, I believe you misled me. You're not doing a background check. You're trying to slander a good man. I'll have no part of it!" She hesitated. "He did go out yesterday afternoon—which is not unusual—but I have no idea when he returned."

This time, she managed to get the door firmly closed.

I walked next door and tried to peek inside the garage, but the row of tiny windows showed me little other than that the van was inside. Jules jerked open the door before I rang the bell.

"What the hell are you doing?" he asked, hanging on to the doorframe. His chair was right behind him.

"My job." I held out Matt's photo. "Take another look. You've never seen this man?"

"I told you no, and I mean no." His eyes fixed on the photo. "And I would have remembered him. Almost as dishy as your friend. Is Paul with you?"

"No, he's doing his own thing over at Zimmerman Library. Just me and my business partner today."

"Learning anything?"

"Some," I said, giving him a tight smile. "More than I expected at any rate."

I left him looming in the doorway as I turned and walked to my car, noting Alan Mendoza's gray Chevy parked halfway down the street.

Your move, Jules.

But Jules McClintock didn't take the bait. Alan later reported he went out shortly after I left his door but only to go to Walmart. Came home and remained there until Tim Fuller—who had returned from his out-of-town fishing trip on Sunday—relieved Alan Monday evening.

CHARLIE HAD no better luck than I did. We failed to discover Jules's connection to Matt but had found a direct link to the killer's sixth victim, Peter Baca. I'm accused of sounding like a broken record when I say Albuquerque's a big overgrown town where almost everyone knows almost everyone, even if it's true. This particular connection could be coincidental. But like most investigators, I don't like coincidences. They stink, and so did this one. But would Jules take such a risk striking so close to home? Why not? He—at least the cutie-pie killer—had taken enormous risks leaving semen, body hair, and skin cells on his victims. He'd risked having everyone in a four-story apartment house seeing him remove a dead Matt Zapata and load him in a vehicle. And the dump sites were public places. This killer wasn't risk averse. And if Jules were the killer, it wouldn't have been difficult to lure Pete Baca into his house or his van. After all, he was the little brother's beloved tutor.

Dammit, we needed to get into Jules's house and vehicle, but there wasn't enough for a search warrant. And if I did get access, what would it prove? We already knew Petey Baca had been in Jules's house. According to the feisty neighbor with a nose, the older brother had gone inside on occasion when picking up Jimmy. So evidence of his presence in the home could be explained away… unless it was found in the bedroom. Same for the white van. My skin crawled in exasperation.

I took a mental step backward. We had reasonable evidence Matt Zapata was killed at Park House. Jules McClintock had a connection to the place, no matter how tenuous. And he damned sure had a connection to the last victim. A direct connection. No one else on the horizon linked with two out of six victims. That was enough for me. Jules McClintock had earned my attention.

I went down the hall to Charlie's office and reviewed my thinking. He took a moment to swivel back and forth in his chair and consider the situation before agreeing with my conclusion.

"That means Alan and Tim better keep a sharp eye out," he said.

"Maybe they better call in a couple of their cop buddies to beef up the surveillance."

Charlie cocked an eyebrow at me. "You wanna get inside the house? The van?"

I hesitated before shaking my head. "Getting inside won't tell us much without a forensics-level search."

"Unless he keeps mementos. We know serial killers often do. What does he do with his victims' clothing? And maybe he takes photos."

"Not worth the risk of screwing up a case for the prosecutor if it ever comes to that. No, nothing illegal, but I want to know everywhere he goes."

"He's no dummy. He'll catch on soon enough if he hasn't already."

I rubbed my chin and discovered a bit of stubble I'd missed with my shave this morning. "That's not all bad. If he's our killer, he won't have much opportunity to kill again."

Charlie sighed and leaned forward to pick up a crystal letter opener. Like me and a lot of other cops and ex-cops, he tapped it against his desk blotter while he thought. "We can't stay on him forever. And he's apt to overreact when we have to stop watching. Might be nasty."

I noticed he hadn't added the caution *if he's our guy*. Maybe Charlie was a little more sympathetic to my thinking. "Or maybe we'll get enough to trip him up before we have to withdraw."

"I hate to say this, BJ, but our chances of tripping him up are not good." Charlie fixed a steely blue eye on me. "Unless we catch him killing someone else."

"Be a little more upbeat. He might get so frustrated he tries it right in front of us… and we can stop him. Let Tim and Alan know we think this is our guy."

"Will do."

I returned to my office and contacted Roy Guerra to bring him up-to-date. He didn't totally agree with my assessment of the situation but nonetheless pledged to ask for some departmental resources to back our effort, including manpower to supplement a round-the-clock watch on Jules. He also agreed to reinterview all of the individuals who'd used Ma Flanagan's telephone service to engage Matt. Dammit, we needed to know how the killer had identified and zeroed in on the young man.

After I closed the call, I phoned Juan Zapata and gave him a verbal update on his son's murder. I shared that we had a suspect, although I refrained from identifying him, ever mindful of Matt's Uncle Zancón waiting in the state pen.

"BJ," HAZEL'S voice floated through the intercom. "Call for you on line one. Won't say who it is but sounds like something you oughta take."

When she buzzed the call through, I understood what she meant. The voice quailed in tone, making it difficult to know if it was male or female.

"Yes, who is this?"

The speaker gained strength and the answering voice sounded more masculine. "Sir, I didn't know who to call, but you left your card so—"

"All right, I left my card with you, but who are you?"

"Hosea, sir. Hosea Middleton. You came—"

"Yes, I remember you. Is something wrong?"

"I can't afford to pay you."

"First tell me what the problem is, and then we'll discuss that. What's the matter?"

"I-I lied to you, Mr. Vinson. I did know Matt Zapata. We spent a night together. It was wonder.... Uh, anyway, I lied to you."

"Why?"

"At first, I just didn't want to get involved. But when I told my landlord about your visit, he told me not to talk to you anymore."

"I believe you said your landlord was Luis Andretta. Why didn't he want you to level with me?"

"I-I don't know. But he insisted I couldn't tell you."

"Insisted how?"

"He slapped me when he said it."

"Does he slap you often?"

"Sometimes. When I don't do what he wants fast enough."

I recalled the soft, handsome young man whose birth certificate said he was twenty-one but who looked and acted more like a shy teenager. "You told me he treats you okay. Now you say he beats you."

"Yes, sir. I lied to you about that too. But—"

"I understand. Go on."

"Luis slaps me mostly. But when he really gets mad, he punches me. Still, he's not as bad as some. My neighbor would like to kill me."

"You're kidding yourself, Hosea. Time to leave the guy."

"I-I can't, Mr. Vinson. I wouldn't have any place to live. I've lived on the streets before, and that's lots worse."

"I can put you in touch with some people who'll help you, providing you're willing to work to earn your keep."

"Yes, sir. I'll work. But that hasn't been too good for me in the past."

"What do you mean?"

"The people I worked with picked on me. Made me do things."

I got pissed at the kid at the same time as my heart went out to him. I remembered my tender years. The way I solved my problem with the prevailing society was to go out for football—and take my beatings—and join the Marines—and fight to hold my ground—and join the police department afterward—and take the guff. In short, I'd proved myself to me and to the gay-bashers I ran into. Hard to see Hosea doing anything like that, but he either had to stand up for himself or be a punching bag for the rest of his life.

"Son, you're preaching to the choir, but I survived it, and so can you. Do you have something to write on?"

"Yes, sir."

I thumbed through my Rolodex and found the number for Bishop Gregory of the Temple of Our Lord on High, who'd helped my friend Jazz Penrod after we rescued him from a sex-trafficking ring. I cited the number and told him to ask for the bishop. "Tell him I told you to call. Then do exactly as he says. In the meantime, pack up everything you need to carry with you. He'll send someone to pick you up."

"I-I don't know...."

"Your choice, guy. Man up or remain Andretta's victim until you die or you're too old to make him money."

"Maybe I can find someone like Burton."

"Neville's dead. He can't help you. Maybe there's another one out there, but you can't afford to hang around Andretta. Whatever you decide, I need to know more about your connection with Matt."

"It was only one night."

"Where did you hook up?"

"I was thumbing through some records at the secondhand shop on Central down near the university. He started talking to me about what kind of music I liked. And then he invited me for a cup of coffee, and then...."

"Then you went to his place."

"That's right. And he was...." I thought I heard him swallow. "He was a great guy."

"I'm coming to understand that. But tell me, how does Andretta know of your night with Matt?"

"Whenever he looks for me and can't find me, he always asks me where I was."

"Afraid you're holding out on him."

"Yes, sir. That's it. When I wouldn't tell him where I was the night before, Luis started beating on me until I told him. Then he was mad because I didn't charge Matt anything. It was just a thing between me and him. But when Luis found out, he went over to Matt's place to collect from him."

"What happened?"

"Matt told him to go to hell, and they mixed it up. Then Luis came back here and beat on me some more."

"Why did he tell you not to mention you knew Matt? Why should he care?"

"I-I guess he read in the newspaper about Matt getting killed, and he didn't want to be connected with him."

"Hosea, I've made up your mind for you. Call the bishop and let him send someone for you, because tomorrow morning I'm getting in Luis Andretta's face about Matt Zapata."

"Please don't...." I hung on while he got ahold of himself. "Okay, Mr. Vinson. I can see you have to do that. Be careful. Luis is a bad man." I heard a muffled sob. "He wasn't at first. He was good to me. But then...."

"But then he showed his true colors."

"I guess."

"After he had you hooked, the real Andretta showed up. Hosea, hang up and call the bishop right now. Do you have enough change to make another call?"

"I'm calling you on my cell phone. Luis gave it to me so I could keep in touch."

"Yeah. So he could line you up for his clients, most likely."

BOTH PAUL and Charlie wanted to go with me to confront Hosea's pimp the next morning, but I wanted to face Andretta man-to-man. I needed to take his guff because I wanted his cooperation, and I was afraid he'd clam up if we ganged up on him.

The pimp lived in a small home not far from the apartment units he owned in the War Zone. I'd phoned the bishop last night and learned Hosea was safely tucked away in one of the church's safe houses, but I didn't know if Andretta knew I'd cost him a source of income.

I still didn't know when he opened the door with a studied look of indifference on his features.

"Are you Luis Andretta?"

"Who's asking?"

"Call me BJ, Mr. Andretta."

"I don't want none."

"None what?" I asked.

"None of what you're selling."

"What if I'm not selling? What if I'm buying?"

"Buying what?"

"Agreeable company, perhaps?"

"You looking for a boy?" He gave me the once-over. "Yeah, you're the type. Ain't sure you're gay, but you crave something you ain't getting."

"That pretty well describes it."

"Why you coming to me with that kinda problem?"

"Because I was told you could help me scratch my itch."

"Hell, I ain't—"

"Not you. One of your boys."

"Who says I got boys?"

"Come on, we're grown men here. You know the word is out you're the man to see. Do you mind if I come inside? I don't feel comfortable discussing this sort of thing standing out in the open."

He backed away. "Have at it."

I didn't need to ask if he was married. The inside of the house was all man. No feminine touches at all. In addition, it was closely akin to a pigsty. Something crunched beneath my shoe when I stepped over the threshold. My passing disturbed dust on a coffee table. I stood in the middle of the room and faced Andretta.

"You looking for rough or pansy?" he asked.

"I wouldn't say pansy, but I'm not into the rough trade. A nice, handsome, accommodating boy. Nothing illegal. Eighteen or older."

He smiled, revealing crooked teeth. "But not much older."

"You have the idea."

"I got a kid that fits the bill right down to a T. Name's Hose. Don't get the wrong idea. Hose don't describe his equipment, but he ain't bad in that department neither."

So he wasn't aware Hosea had flown the coop.

I held out a photograph. "I'd like someone as close to this young man as I can get. If you can supply this one, that would be worth double the fee."

I watched him as he examined the image of Matt Zapata I'd handed him. His features hardened.

"What is this? What you trying to pull? You a cop?"

"Private. You have some information I want. Give it to me, and I'll be gone and out of your life."

"I don't know this kid from Adam."

"Yes, you do. You confronted him at his place on Princeton trying to collect some money from him."

"He tell you that?"

"You know he didn't. He's dead. Murdered. And I'm trying to find his killer."

Andretta flushed. His body language changed. My antennae went up.

"I didn't kill the creep. I went to collect what he owed me."

"And collected a beating, instead, I understand."

"Fucker didn't beat me. We tussled, but I walked outa there on my own two feet."

I put in the needle. "Without your money."

His eyes narrowed. "And you think I killed him over a measly fifty bucks?"

"Did you?"

He charged, aiming to get me in a bear hug. I'd boxed in the Marines and was a fair hand at it, but I wasn't a street fighter. I did what I usually do when someone comes barreling at me. I dropped to all fours. Unable to stop his momentum, he tripped over me and went crashing into his glass-covered coffee table…

face-first. He rolled off onto the floor, leaking blood from a number of cuts. His nose looked funny.

"Bastard!" he muttered. "You broke my nose."

"*You* broke your nose. Are we going to talk now or fight?"

"I'm bleeding, and my nose is broke. I need a doctor."

"Do you want me to take you to one after we talk?"

"Shit no! I'll take myself."

"After we talk."

He didn't reply, so I walked into the kitchen and brought him a filthy dish towel to staunch the blood before going back and washing my hands thoroughly. As I dried them on my trousers, I stood beside the groaning man, who'd hauled himself up on his couch.

"Andretta, did you know Matt Zapata?"

"Who?" he wheezed.

"The man in the photo I gave you." So reminded, I picked it up from the floor and put it in my pocket.

"Only seen him once. Man, I'm bleeding here." His voice sounded like he was holding his nose… which I guess he was.

"Hold the towel to your nose tighter." Could he smell the sour dishcloth? Probably not with all the blood. "Did you know a man by the name of Burton Neville?"

"Nev' 'eard of 'im."

"Do you know anyone at a place called Park House?"

"Doh…."

His speech was deteriorating. Nonetheless, I asked all my questions before walking out the door and leaving him bleeding on his sofa. I'd made one last offer to take him to the hospital, but he'd declined and was now on his own.

Although I wasn't finished with Luis Andretta, there was no reason not to tip off Glenann and Roy about his pimping operation.

Chapter 15

THE BACA family's house looked to be in mourning. The dirt-brown stucco reminded me of a tomb. The Moroccan arch leading onto the front porch and the equally crescent-shaped walnut carved door both brought gravestones to mind. The woman who answered the door Wednesday morning did nothing to relieve the impression. Small and walnut hued, she looked damaged but enduring.

I let Paul take the lead. He had such an open and sincere attitude that most people reacted favorably to him.

"Mrs. Baca?"

She nodded mutely.

"My name is Paul Barton, and this is my friend B. J. Vinson. May we offer our condolences about Petey? I wonder if we could talk to you about him?"

"Are you the police?"

I spoke up to spare Paul from explaining he was a journalist, which might not have gone over too well with a grieving mother. "I'm a confidential investigator, ma'am."

"Why are you asking about Petey? Are you looking for his killer?"

"We're investigating a series of killings of young men, and your son's death seems to fit the circumstances."

"I read something about that. You think that horrible serial killer murdered my Petey?"

"It's possible. And I want to put a stop to it."

"Come in, and let's see if I can help you." The "and him" she added in a whisper probably referenced her dead son.

From what Roy and Glenann had told me, the Bacas were solid middle class, but their modest home in a not-so-affluent Southeast Heights neighborhood reflected both frugality and pride of ownership. Afghans in bright colors covered inexpensive furniture in a sitting room obviously used only for visitors. A vase of pink roses on the mantelpiece surprised me until I figured out they were probably plastic. The delicate attar permeating the room was likely an air freshener. The family lived in other parts of the building. In fact, I heard a child, probably Petey's little brother, somewhere in the back of the house.

Once we were seated and served with particularly good cups of hot tea, Mrs. Baca leaned back in her chair and waited expectantly.

I took a sip and placed the cup on the small coffee table in front of me. "Is your husband home?"

She shook her head. "He's at work. He works for the public school system. And lately, he's been putting in long hours. You know, to take care of expenses we didn't know were coming."

I understood her to mean Petey's funeral expenses. I cleared my throat. "Could you introduce us to Petey? Let us see him for the young man he was?"

With a great deal of dignity, Mrs. Baca led us through Petey's brief life. Bright, quick to anger but rapid to forgive, he appeared to be a decent youth willing to work hard and keep his nose clean. He'd been both patient with and exasperated by his little brother, Jimmy. Although the murdered youth had been in his freshman year at UNM, he lived at home in order to save money. And as Jules's nosy neighbor had told me, Petey often picked up little Jimmy at his math tutor's house when the older boy had no classes that interfered.

As Petey's life unfolded between tears and sniffles and frequent photographs of the two boys, I grew even more incensed at the heartbreak and misery this killer had spread over Albuquerque. Even seasoned lawmen often became so wrapped up in seeking justice—or retribution—for the killer's victims, they sometimes missed the tragic effects on the victims' families. Murder not only brought death, it also rent families apart, ruined ambitions, and caused health problems and anguish. My resolve to bring this to an end stiffened and brought back the memory of my exchange with Charlie the other day. I'd said, "Nothing illegal." Now I was willing to reconsider. I wanted this bastard found and put away.

Once Mrs. Baca had purged her soul talking about her son's life, I started with the questions. The first one was about Matt Zapata. She scanned the picture and said she'd never seen him.

"Of course, Petey might have known him at the university. He was a freshman, you know."

"Yes, ma'am, that's a possibility. Did he have any friends at an apartment house in the 4200 block of East Central known as the Park House?"

Her brows knitted, deepening the crease between them. "Not that I know of. But...."

"Yes," I finished for her, "he might have known someone from the U."

"You said you called his friends. How about friends from the university? You know any of them?" Paul asked.

"He talked about one or two of them, but he never brought them home. Maybe my husband knows some names. Is it important?"

I placed my card on the coffee table. "It could be. Perhaps you'll ask your husband and let my office know if he comes up with any names. What about girlfriends? Was he going with anyone?"

"He did in high school. Got quite serious, but her family moved to Las Cruces. They tried to keep in touch, but you know how it is at such an age."

"Did Mr. McClintock ever tutor Petey?"

"Heavens no. Petey was always a good student." She looked abashed at her outburst. "Of course, Jimmy is too, except in math. But Mr. McClintock has helped him a great deal."

Jimmy ambled into the room with a football under his arm and stopped dead still. He stood for a moment without speaking before blurting out, "Who're you?"

"Don't be rude, Jimmy. These men are investigators asking about your brother. They want to help catch the monster who killed him."

Paul reacted faster than I did. "I see you're a football player. What say we go outside and throw some passes while your mom and Mr. Vinson finish up."

"Yeah. Sure."

"Be careful of traffic," Mrs. Baca called as they headed out the door.

That told me Jimmy and his friends played ball on the residential street in front of the house. When the door closed behind them, I turned back to the grieving mother.

"Did Petey ever spend any time with Mr. McClintock? You know, go over early or stay late when he was picking up his brother?"

"Not that I recall. Sometimes I had to poke at him to get him to get over there in time to pick up his brother." She frowned again. "Most of the time he went directly from his classes or the library at school to pick up Jimmy. It's quite a drive from here, and Petey saved on gas that way. He didn't want to be a burden. He worked evenings at a café not far from here to help pay his expenses at college."

"Was he able to contribute much?"

"More than I thought. He waited tables, you see, and was usually tipped decently. Petey had a good way with people. They liked him, so they left him good tips."

"Ma'am, I'm going to ask you a question that might offend you, but it has to be asked, and I'm doing it in the most respectful way possible. You've told me about Petey's girlfriends. Did he have boyfriends?"

"Of course he had boys as friends. He—"

"No, ma'am. Did he have *boyfriends*?"

Her mouth dropped open. "*Dios* no! He went to church with us regularly. Went to confession. He… wasn't like that."

Her unconscious prejudice saddened me a little. The coming enlightenment hadn't reached everywhere. Maybe someday.

"Thank you, Mrs. Baca. It was something I had to ask. But think about it for a moment. It's not something he would have admitted or made obvious. Are you certain?"

She gnawed her lower lip for half a minute, telling me her mind was flashing back over her late son's life from birth to death. She'd give me an honest answer.

"There was a boy who lived next door a few years back. They were close, like brothers, really. But I'm certain there was nothing like that going on. No, definitely not."

"Again, thank you, ma'am. What can you tell me about the day he disappeared? A Thursday, I believe."

Maria Baca swallowed audibly. Her eyes moistened. "Yes. Thursday. I was at work all day. I housekeep for some families up in the Heights. I came home and found his car in the driveway with the hood up. He'd been working on it, you see."

"What did Jimmy say about it?"

"Jimmy was still at school. When he got home, he said his brother had been having car trouble. So we assumed he was off getting a part he needed."

"Petey wasn't in class that day?"

"He only had morning classes on Thursday."

"And when he didn't return home?"

"I didn't start to worry until after dark. Then I called all his friends, but no one had seen him all day. So I asked the neighbors. Mrs. Samuelson next door saw him start up the street toward the Gas Mart. Waved to him in fact."

"When was this?"

"Around two, the best she could remember."

"Aside from calling his friends, what did you do?"

"I called the police station over on Louisiana Street, but they told me there was nothing they could do. He hadn't been gone long enough. Promised to keep an eye out for him, but that's all."

"That's true, ma'am. Then what?"

"I called our church. Petey'd been to confession the Sunday before that, so I thought maybe the father could tell me if he was disturbed about something. Of course, he couldn't tell me anything, but I wanted to know if Petey was worried about something. He... he said no, Petey seemed okay. His usual self." A tear spilled from her right eye. "My husband and I spent a sleepless night. Even called his father up in Denver to see if he'd heard anything."

"Your husband isn't Petey's father?"

She shook her head. "We were divorced. But my husband's been Petey's father for the last six years. He loved Petey as much as he loved Jimmy."

"Had your ex-husband heard from Petey?"

"He hadn't." Her voice almost failed. "And then... and then the next morning, they called and told us... they'd found him."

I allowed her to recover before spending another fifteen minutes asking questions that gave me nothing new. I terminated the interview, and when we stepped to the porch, she smiled— the first one I'd seen from her—at the sight of Paul throwing passes to an obviously delighted and coltish Jimmy Baca.

Her voice sounded strong when she called out to her son. "Time to go to the school bus, Jimmy." In a near whisper, she added, "Time to move on."

As we drove to the office, Paul told me of his talk with Jimmy Baca.

"He swears by Jules McClintock," my hunky mate said. "Thinks the guy walks on water. Jimmy's math skills apparently have soared under his tutelage."

"Nothing funny?"

"Naw, I'm convinced of it. Jimmy talked about Jules too readily. No hesitation, no thunderclouds overhead when we spoke of the man. Jules wasn't molesting the little guy."

"Prepubescents are not his thing," I said. "What about the older brother?"

"Jimmy said Petey sometimes came inside while Jimmy put books in his backpack, but he never stayed. And if Petey was seeing Jules on the side, his brother sure didn't know about it. In fact, I'm convinced it didn't happen."

"So am I. Petey was lured to his death another way."

"He wasn't a hitchhiker. He had an old Saturn he drove to classes and to pick up his brother."

"There was a Saturn in the driveway when we drove up."

"Petey's. Jimmy said Petey'd been having problems with it. His mom drives a Chevy. Petey's dad's a construction worker in Denver. He and Mrs. Baca are divorced. Jimmy and Petey had different fathers."

"Any problems between stepfather and son?"

"No indication. And Petey changed his name to Baca, so that kinda bears it out."

"You got more from the kid than I did from the mother. Dammit! We have a direct link to McClintock but can't connect the dots."

"Do we canvass the neighbors around this neighborhood?" Paul asked.

"The police did that. I want to talk to Roy and Glenann before we plow that ground again."

More frustrating news greeted us when we pushed through the door to Vinson and Weeks.

Hazel looked up from her computer screen. "Gloria called from K-Y Lab. Your tea wasn't laced with zopiclone. It was tea and a little lemon. She's sending the written report to us."

"Damn," Paul said as we entered my private office, "I walked around with a wet pants pocket for nothing."

"Not for nothing. You learned you weren't about to be ravaged by a mad killer."

Paul's voice held a sarcastic lilt. "That's a relief."

Charlie followed us into the office. "McClintock's on the move. Earlier and more than usual, according to Tim. He took over surveillance this morning from Alan. McClintock didn't go anywhere last night but pulled out of the garage right after Tim went on duty."

"Where'd he go?"

"Still out. Stopped at a Smith's, came out with a bag of groceries. Went to a lamp shop on Fourth. Filled up the van with gas. And according to Tim two minutes ago, seems to be headed your way."

"To the office."

"To your house."

"Damn, I'm going to have to take my home listing out of the white pages."

"You've been saying that for years," Paul said.

"Time to do it," I came back at him.

Charlie's cell phone rang. He answered and listened for a minute before hanging up. "That was Tim. McClintock parked in front of your house."

"He go to the door?"

"You don't have a wheelchair-friendly porch. He pulled into the driveway, got out, and put a jug of something on the edge of the porch. Then he stood in full view and made a phone call."

"Probably to the house," I said.

Paul took out his phone. "I'll check." A minute later, he tapped in a code and listened again. "Yup." He closed the call.

"Left a voice message saying we like his tea so well, he brought us some. Claimed he was trying to be neighborly."

"Trying to get neighborly with Paul," I said and yelled for Hazel to delist my home phone and address from the local directory.

"I'll see what I can do," she called back.

Paul, Charlie, and I moved to the small conference table in the corner of my office, where we sat while I used my cell to run down Roy and Glenann.

"Just got back from talking to your boy Luis Andretta," Roy said after making it clear he had his partner with him on a speakerphone. So reminded, I punched the speaker button on mine. "Special Victims had him on their radar for a while," Roy said.

"Under surveillance?"

"No. But they know he has a ring of boys he farms out. They aren't hot and bothered about him because he doesn't prostitute underage kids, but they'll make a case on him one of these days."

"How'd he come to SVU's attention?"

"Beat up one of his boys a year ago. Kid wouldn't file a complaint, so nothing came of it. But it put him on their radar."

"Can they tie any of our victims to his stable?"

"Uh-uh. They know about the Middleton kid, and while he might look fifteen, he's damned near twenty-two."

"Was he the one Andretta beat up to get their attention?"

"It was another guy. Andretta has a record of petty theft, assault, and the like, but nobody's ever testified against him. So he's still on the street doing his thing."

"You might be able to turn Hosea Middleton. The kid was pretty shaken when he called me for help."

"Good move getting him with the bishop, but odds are he's too scared to stand up to his pimp."

"What can you tell me about the investigation of Petey Baca's murder?"

"Not much. I know you want to connect him with Jules McClintock, but all we can do is confirm he picked up his brother from McClintock's place several times."

"I know. We visited Mrs. Baca this morning. Hazel will send you a transcript of my conversation with her, but we didn't canvass the neighborhood. Figured you did that."

"We did," Glenann said. "Roy and I didn't want to leave it to patrol officers, so we did it ourselves. We probably know how the kid was lured by his killer. At least when it was done."

"How?"

"One of the women near the Gas Mart was in her yard. She saw him get off a city bus and start walking home. Apparently, she knows the family, and he stopped to talk to her. Said he'd gone to the auto store for a part to fix his car. Then he headed on home. But she saw a white van stop about a block away, and Petey got inside. Then it drove on toward the Baca home."

My pulse rate soared. "A white van! That's it. We've—"

"Don't get your shorts bunched up," Glenann said. "It was a white van with blue panels on the side. Jules McClintock's van is white, no blue panels."

"Magnetic signs?"

"The witness said it wasn't a sign, just blue paint covering the rear side windows. She thought it was a friend of Petey's because he smiled and waved before stepping to the side of the van and talking to the driver. Then she thought it was somebody asking for directions, because Petey motioned on down the road before he walked around the van and got inside."

"She see the driver?"

"Not even his elbow sticking out the window."

"I don't suppose she got a license tag number."

"No, but she said it wasn't a New Mexico tag. Too far away to be sure, but she thought it might be Arizona. And before you ask, we checked all the motels and hotels on the east side of the city. Found a couple of vans, but not the right one."

"We now have the how but not the why and the who."

"The autopsy showed one other thing," Roy said. "A small hypodermic puncture on Petey's upper left leg."

"And that's new," Glenann added. "The kid was incapacitated, probably before he got to the end of the block. So it wasn't a friend. He was lured in by someone asking directions and offering a ride home."

"That lets out your favorite suspect, Jules McClintock," Roy went on. "His van's registered in New Mexico, and the Baca kid would have known him."

"I'm not so sure. Maybe the neighbor was right the first time. It was someone he considered a friend... or at least an acquaintance. Do we know if Jules knew where the Bacas lived?"

"No idea," Glenann said. "According to Mrs. Baca, Jimmy always went to his tutor, not the other way around."

"I guess Jules reserves home visits to his more affluent clients," Paul said.

"If he hadn't been to the Baca home before, Jules might have spotted Petey on the street and offered him a ride home. Petey's arm wave might have been motioning to where he lived."

"But that doesn't explain a multicolored van and out-of-state license plates," Roy cautioned.

"License plates can be stolen. Any complaints from tourists over losing their plates on the way through Albuquerque?"

"We can check," Roy said. "But you're reaching, aren't you? Someone would notice if he was driving around without plates."

I snorted. "The thief likely provided them with another set."

"Yeah, and the owner wouldn't notice until he renewed his registration."

"Roy, I can't tell if you're arguing with me or against me. But I'm not ready to let go of Jules McClintock and his white van, blue windows and Arizona plate or not."

AFTER TALKING it over, Charlie and I agreed to keep Tim and Alan on watch, although Roy pulled his APD help other than ordering an occasional drive-by. Decision made, Paul and I drove home to check on the tea left on our porch by the prime suspect in six murders… possibly seven.

Our one-woman neighborhood watch, Gertrude Wardlow, came flying out of her white brick house across the street as soon as I pulled into our driveway behind Paul's Charger. Jules must have gotten a thrill out of spying Paul's car and figuring he might have some time with his enamored without me around. That explained the phone call to the house.

"BJ," Mrs. W's thin voice reached us as we got out of the Impala. "This huge man stopped at your place and left something on your porch."

"Yes, ma'am. He phoned the house and said he was leaving some tea."

"Looks like sun tea to me," she said, revealing she'd already checked the place out. No surprise. Within the past five years, she'd witnessed two fire bombings to my porch and been involved in a street gunfight with two thugs.

"Most likely. He does make good tea."

"Since you already know about it, I'll be about my business. Huge man." I detected a ladylike shiver. "Gross. Poor man," she added.

Paul scooped up the gallon jug as we walked to the back, our traditional way of entering the house. I immediately grabbed a tumbler from the cabinet, popped some cubes from the ice maker on the refrigerator, and poured a glass of tea.

Paul's eyes went wide. "Vince! You're not going to drink that, are you? It might be drugged... or even poisoned."

I took a deep draft. "You don't think Jules is dumb enough to spike the tea, leave it on the porch for anyone to see, and then call the house and admit he'd left it, do you?"

"Maybe not, but I'm not having any so I can call the ambulance to save your butt in case you're wrong about McClintock's intelligence level."

I smacked my lips. "Your loss. This is good. Do we have any lemon in the fridge?"

I had a second glass with the excellent fajitas Paul was so good at making. I sort of liked the way he eyed me for the rest of the evening. And Pedro enjoyed the romp when we turned in for the night.

As I lay recovering afterward, I recalled an incident from my APD days when Gene and I caught a case of a blue-collar guy named Abel Waxfelter beating his lover to death. The lover—a young construction worker named Todd—had been with him for over a year. There wasn't much question Abel had killed the younger man, but it took a while to figure out why. When we arrived at their apartment in response to a 911 call, Waxfelter was in tears and totally devastated. In the days when it was dangerous to admit to a homosexual relationship, the man loudly proclaimed his love to anyone who would listen.

Gene and I spent two days trying to find out if Todd had run around on Waxfelter, but got nowhere. It was only when we started grilling the older partner that we tumbled to the truth. Abel Waxfelter had finally met a woman who sparked his interest, but he was physically unable to make love to her. Enraged, he returned home, blamed his lover of the last twelve months for corrupting him, and beat Todd to death with his own hammer. There is no accounting for the human mind's reaction. Paul and I had recently spent an hour engaging in some of the same actions as Waxfelter and Todd, but there was nothing but love and respect and trust between the two of us.

Just before I surrendered to the sandman, the final irony struck me. Paul's semen was on me; mine, on him. We were both naked. The difference was… we were still alive. And it had been an act of love. Pure unadulterated love.

Chapter 16

THE NEXT morning, Paul expressed the frustration I was suppressing. He got up from his computer in our home office as I was checking appointments Hazel had loaded onto my PC calendar.

"Jeez!" he said. "We're getting nowhere. How many more guys are going to die because we can't figure out the situation? I'm afraid to pick up the paper or watch the news. Every time Roy or Glenann call, I add another ulcer."

"Figuratively speaking, I hope."

"So far. But I can feel the acid eating away. Can't we do something? Can't *I* do something more?"

"You can check the online dating spots and see if you find anything suspicious."

"Hell, I've already done that. They're all suspicious. Guys wanting to part other guys from their money."

"Or looking for a little companionship."

"That too. But okay, I'll do it again," he said.

I cocked an eye at him. "Just don't find somebody *you're* interested in."

He gave me his most devastating grin. "Not unless I find your profile in there."

Twenty minutes later, I walked through the downtown office door to find an agitated Luis Andretta stewing in our small reception area.

Hazel inclined her head. "This gentleman's here for you. He doesn't have an appointment."

"That's okay. Come on in, Andretta."

He tromped on my heels until I sat behind my desk and then dropped uninvited into the chair opposite.

"Hey, man, wha'd you do to me? Hose is gone, and the cops been hassling me. And you done it. Don't claim you didn't."

"What makes you think that?"

"'Cause it all started when you come to see me."

"How's the nose?" I asked to prod him a little.

"Ain't broke, but it's sorer'n hell. I got payback coming for that."

"Why? You attacked me."

"You come in my private pad and tried to whingding me."

"Whingding?"

"You know, pull a con. Making like you was looking for a boy. You was looking for trouble."

"Looking for a killer is more like it."

His eyes flickered. "Already told you, I ain't no killer. You got that straight?"

"Just because you say it, doesn't make it true. Tell me what you were doing on Monday, March 5."

"How'n hell I know that? You remember what you done back then?"

I took a moment to recall the date of Petey Baca's death. "All right, then, how about Thursday, April 5th? That's only a week ago."

"Same thing, man. What was you doing then?" He wrinkled his brows and rubbed an eyebrow. "Got up around noon. Work late, you know. Made some calls. Went and met some dudes at a bar."

"See, it's coming back to you. Who, what bar, and when?"

He racked his brain and came up with some more information, and finally made a call on his cell to ask a friend what time they were at the bar last week. He departed after half an hour, leaving a reasonably complete re-creation of his April 5. He'd gotten so wrapped up in providing details he forgot to rail at me about Hosea's disappearance and the cops hounding his trail. I gave everything to Hazel to check as much as she could before I'd go look up his drinking buddies.

After the pimp was gone, I picked up the summary of Tim and Alan's report Hazel had left on the desk. Jules had four tutoring clients yesterday. The kids arrived separately, went inside, and stayed for something under an hour before emerging bathed in smiles. Nothing suspicious. The neighbor with a nose rang his bell early afternoon and delivered what looked like a home-baked upside-down strawberry cake. She departed looking smug. No nighttime excursions. Yardman came around 1:00 p.m., departed an hour later. Lights out at 11:00 p.m.

I asked Hazel who was on stakeout this morning and dialed Tim's cell. "Reading your report," I said. "Tell me about this yardman."

"He's not no cutie-pie, I can tell you. Hispanic, in his forties."

"Good physical shape?"

"Fair. Carries a little roll around the middle, but yeah, I'd say he's strong enough. What are you thinking?"

"How often does he come around?" I asked.

"Once a week."

"You have his name? Know how to get in touch with him?"

"Yeah. What—"

"Maybe he acts as Jules's muscle."

"Oh, I see. Might be the case, but you couldn't pay me to get in the car with Hank."

"That's the yardman's name?"

I heard Tim flipping through his notebook before answering. "Enrique Dominguez. Goes by Hank."

"What kind of vehicle does he drive?"

"Black Ford pickup so old I can't even tell you what year it is. He does some of the other yards in the area. I see his rattletrap truck two, three times a week."

"You see it now?"

"Uh-uh."

"Get Alan to go look him up. See if Hank can account for his time for the most recent killings."

"Okay."

I closed the call, fighting a temptation to dangle Paul in front of Jules to see if I could start something, but what if I lost control of the situation? Petey Baca may have died because Paul's visits stimulated the killer. Besides, I sure as hell didn't want Jules coming for Paul. My love was a grown man and capable of taking care of himself, but the same could probably be said of most of the six young men this monster had killed.

That thought brought me up short. I was certainly vested in believing Jules McClintock was the cutie-pie killer, but why? His connection with Park House was tenuous at best. There was no evidence he'd ever set foot in the place. His connection was with a prior tenant of the apartment where Matt Zapata died. No, I'd wager Neville was dead before Matt was strangled to death. Was I suffering from tunnel vision?

Hazel interrupted my contemplations by ushering in a topic I didn't like to discuss. The company's tax returns were waiting to be signed. The accountant had also prepared my personal taxes. The trustee took care of my trust, so I didn't suffer the agony of seeing the bite IRS and the state took from that one. It was bad enough signing the returns and checks for the company and me.

"Don't know why you always wait until the last minute to do this," Hazel complained as she waited for me to sign the returns.

I tapped the checks. "Because of these. Besides it's only the twelfth. And we have an extra day because April 15 falls on Sunday this year."

She sniffed. "I'm perfectly capable of holding on to checks until the due date. One of these days, you're going to be out on a case and miss a deadline, then where'll you be?"

"Hazel, you and Charlie are both officers of the company. You can sign the returns and the checks." Her persimmon look caused me to add, "Okay, we'll do it earlier next year."

She probably didn't believe that. Not sure I did.

"CONGRATULATIONS, YOU'RE a witness in a criminal case," Glenann said to me over the phone the next morning.

"How so?"

"We arrested Andretta this afternoon. He was beating up one of his boys when someone called 911. We'd tagged Andretta's name, so we got called in."

"Damn, Andretta was waiting for me when I got to the office yesterday. I musta stirred him up some. Who'd he beat up?"

"A kid named Bushnell. So long as we were going to haul in Andretta for the assault charge, Roy leveled promoting prostitution for good measure. He's gone up for pimping once, so maybe he'll get the full eighteen months and five grand fine this time."

"So how am I a witness?"

"Remember your confrontation with him in his apartment you recorded? And your conversation with Hosea Middleton... also recorded."

"Okay. So I'm a witness."

"Heads-up. You remember the sex-trafficking ring you took down a couple of years ago? Well, it's back. Or one that looks like it."

"The Bulgarians?" I asked.

"So they say, although neither one of us has ever seen a Bulgar in these here parts."

"So Andretta's connected?"

"It would appear so."

"I'd better warn the bishop to hide Middleton. You ought to do the same for this Bushnell kid."

"In process."

I hung up the phone in a thoughtful mood. Testifying was no big deal to me. I'd done it a hundred times as a cop and as a confidential investigator, but it wouldn't be easy for a kid like Hosea. A defense attorney would shred the young man and reduce him to tears in minutes. Not all bad, of course. Might generate some sympathy for him and hostility for Andretta with the jury. Of course, Hosea had to make it to trial first. In the case Glenann was building for the prosecutors, Hosea would be a major player. I wasn't certain the kid was ready for a starring role.

THAT FRIDAY was a calm day—no surprises, but no progress either. Roy and Glenann assured me Bishop Gregory was doing a good job of shielding Hosea, so perhaps he would eventually make it to the witness stand in good health. The surveillance reports on Jules McClintock were dull reading.

Alan had run down Hank Dominguez and put him through the wringer. The yardman was meticulous, writing down all of his jobs, together with detailed notes on starting and quitting times. The man had no jacket. In fact, he had no record at all, not even a driver's license. Alan figured he was undocumented. My operative would pursue the matter further, but at this point we concluded Dominguez was another dead end.

Saturday, Paul and I braved a chill wind to get in a game of golf at the country club. He pinned me for twenty bucks on the course and the entire gin table for around a hundred later in the cardroom. I hoped his journalism career was going as well as his hustling business.

Sunday, the television reminded everyone listening Tax Day was upon us. I asked Paul if he'd done his.

"Filed in March," he said. "Made more money than I realized in 2011, so had to cough up some."

"Geez, I didn't hear your cries of pain."

"I suffer in silence, thank you. Shield the world from my woes."

"You okay? For money, I mean?"

I saw his hackles rise, but he controlled it. He was touchy about paying his own way in the relationship, despite my multimillion-dollar trust fund.

"Peachy. Still have some in the bank after the government's bite." He hesitated. "But thanks for asking."

Pedro must have been pleased as well, because he romped for a good part of the afternoon, bringing both his master and me to a state of exquisite exhaustion.

MONDAY MORNING I took time for a therapeutic swim before driving to the office. As I got out of the Impala in my spot in the Sixth Street parking lot, a stocky man possibly a bit older than I was stepped up to me. My antenna went up, and I resolved for the umpteenth time to stop leaving my Ruger in the car's trunk.

"Mr. Vinson?"

I studied his features before answering. Broad face. Dark. Vaguely foreign appearance, although I detected no accent in the two words he'd spoken. "Yes."

"You are causing a friend of mine some problems. I think maybe you ought to back off."

"And who might your friend be?"

"Luis Andretta."

"Oh, the pimp."

"That is the one. You cause him problems. You cause me problems. You do not want to do that."

No accent, but no contractions either. Was I face to face with one of those mythical Bulgarian sex traffickers?

"And who might you be?" I asked, not really expecting an answer.

"Mr. Smith. And you do not want to make Mr. Smith unhappy."

"Sometimes I think that's the business I'm in, making people unhappy. But tell me, Mr. Smith, do you want me to stop interfering with Andretta when it comes to managing his stable of call boys or in his killing those who won't join his team?"

For a millisecond, I saw something like surprise in the man's dark eyes. "You do not interfere at all."

"And if I choose to ignore your threat?"

He looked at me without speaking for all of thirty seconds before walking away, turning north on Sixth and going west on Tijeras. I made no attempt to follow him, but I told Charlie about the impromptu meeting as soon as I reached the office. He insisted I call Roy at APD and report the incident.

After that, we slogged through the next several hours, checking and rechecking facts, rumors, databases, gossip—the works. No fortuitous break showed up like in every gumshoe movie I'd ever seen. No nothing.

As I was about to leave for lunch, Hazel answered a call and put a hand on my arm to stop me. "It's Roy. He says it's important."

I returned to my office and took the call.

"It's Andretta," the detective said. "He bonded out late this morning. About half an hour ago, we found him in an alley in the War Zone… garroted."

My legs gave way, dropping me in my chair. "I'll be right over. Have a forensic artist ready."

"No need. We already identified the fellow who accosted you this morning. Name's Petrov Arsov. Originally from South Dakota. Has a long record as an enforcer for the mob. Also learned he left on a flight for Mexico early this afternoon. From there, he'll go somewhere he's safe from extradition. Guess you won't need to be a witness for us after all. I'll let the bishop know Hosea won't be needed either."

After Roy hung up, I sat grappling with one burning thought. Had I cost a man his life by a careless, probably baseless, comment made to a gangster?

Chapter 17

MIDAFTERNOON ON Monday, Roy phoned again to ask if he and Glenann could come over. Once I agreed, he hung up, leaving me to puzzle over the call. When the two detectives arrived ten minutes later, Hazel ushered them into the conference room where she, Charlie, and I joined them.

Roy's face was grim as he moved his eyes over each of us. "We may have another one."

"Another killing?" Hazel asked. "A cutie-pie killing?"

"Possibly."

"Possibly?" Charlie asked.

Glenann took up the tale. "We don't have a body. We have a missing person's report."

"Then why…?"

Roy slid a photograph across the table. "This kid's family says he left home to meet friends three days ago and hasn't been seen or heard from since."

"Even if your fears come true and he turns up dead, why do you think it's the cutie-pie killer?" I asked.

"Take a good look at the photo."

Hazel and Charlie hovered over my shoulder as I picked up the picture to gaze at one of the most stunning young men I'd ever seen… with a couple of notable exceptions. Dark, wavy hair. Hazel eyes, square chin. Handsome wasn't strong enough to describe him.

"Take a guess at his age," Roy said.

"Nineteen," I answered.

"Turned seventeen two months ago."

"Mature for his age."

"He's exactly the kind of target the cutie-pie killer would go for," Glenann said.

"What's his name?" Hazel asked.

"Strumph. S-t-r-u-m-p-h. Wesley Strumph."

Charlie frowned. "Any kin to Amos Strumph of Strumph Lumber?"

"Grandson."

"Any record?" Charlie asked.

"Two parking tickets. Which he paid. Unofficial and off the record, he had a problem with drugs. Got hooked on heroin a couple of years ago. Amos put him in rehab, and it supposedly took."

"So his grandfather fixed the record, I assume," Hazel said. "The kid lives at home?"

Glenann nodded. "With his grandparents. He lost his parents three years ago."

"In a plane crash, as I recall," I said.

"Right. On paper, the kid's a paragon. Goes to Albuquerque Academy with all the right kids. No signs of excessive drinking or recent use of drugs. He doesn't even smoke if you believe what they say. Going for a football scholarship. This kid has his own wheels. A Porsche, yet. He wouldn't get in a car with just anybody."

"Gay?" I asked.

"Not so you'd notice. Going steady with a girl. Girlfriends since he started noticing the difference between males and females."

I dropped the photo on the table and sighed. "He fits the mold, but the pattern's all wrong. Missing for three days but no body. No dump."

"True," Roy said. "But since you have Jules McClintock tied down tight, we'd like to see what your reports say on his activities."

Hazel left the room and brought back a binder. "Two days ago? That would have been a Saturday." She thumbed to the right report. "Here it is."

According to Tim and Alan, Jules had remained at home all morning. At 2:00 p.m., he'd left the house in the van, driven to the Rio Grande Vista Center—a small north valley strip mall—parked, and motored in his chair to a restaurant called Pansy's. He sat alone at a corner table in plain view. Alan, who was on duty at the time, took pains to say both Jules and his van were clearly visible to him at all times. Jules ate a solitary lunch, answered a phone call, paid, and went back to his van. He used a motorized lift to place the chair in the back of the van, walked to the driver's side door, got in, and drove straight home. He went nowhere else for the remainder of the day or night.

"How about the day after? And the days since then?" Charlie asked.

Hazel scanned the reports for a long second and then shook her head. "Nothing. Had little kids coming for math lessons, went to Walmart once. Other than that, he's been inside his house at 3661 Colorado."

Roy snorted in frustration. "That answers that. Jules is not our killer."

"Don't get your nose too far over your feet," I cautioned. "In the first place, we don't know if this is a cutie-pie killing. Hell, we don't even know it's a killing. Let's at least see if there's any connection between Jules and the Strumph family. Charlie, will you look into that, please?"

My partner nodded.

"Keep the photo," Roy said. "Wanted you to know about this because our guys have been pulled off the McClintock surveillance. Tim and Alan won't have any more APD help."

"Whose decision was that?" I asked.

"Our sergeant's." Roy hesitated. "You want me to take it to Lt. Carson?"

I shook my head. "No, we'll handle the surveillance."

As soon as the two cops left, Charlie and I got Alan Mendoza on the speakerphone. He'd been on stakeout last night, so we woke him.

"Sorry, guy," Charlie said. "But we got a development." He recited the events to Alan in the efficient way cops have of appraising a situation.

"Crap," Alan said. "Couldn't have been McClintock. Saturday, you say?" We heard noises as he thumbed through his notes. "That's the day—"

"We know," I said. "He had lunch at Pansy's. Anything strike you as odd about the day?"

"Just that he drove a long way to have a solitary lunch at a so-so place. Food's okay and cheap. Maybe that's what brought him out there. Course, he spent more'n enough in gas to make up the difference. Unless the café owner was a buddy of mine, *I* wouldn't have made the special effort."

"You have a van, don't you?" I asked.

"Gave it to my son, but it's here. He rode to UNM on his cycle this morning."

"Alan, do you know the Pacific Paradise Restaurant on the northeast corner of San Pedro and Candelaria?"

"Sure, it's not far from Jules's place."

"Can you meet Charlie and me in their parking lot in your van?"

"Sure. Need a little time to clean up. Say an hour?"

"Good enough."

We no sooner terminated the call than Paul dialed my cell wanting to know if there was anything new. I filled him in on developments.

"I wanna be there," he said.

"Okay, meet us at San Petro and—"

"I'm at home. That's closer to the Rio Grande Vista. I'll meet you there."

Charlie and I spent a little time reviewing Alan's and Tim's surveillance reports a few days before and a few days after the Saturday Wesley Strumph disappeared. Then we headed for the Northeast Heights. Alan got out of his van as soon as we pulled into the parking lot. The vehicle looked a great deal like Jules's van, except it was a gawd-awful purple.

"I see Alan Junior got hold of a paintbrush after you gave him the van," Charlie said.

Alan looked embarrassed. "Would you believe he paid eight hundred bucks for that paint job?"

"Well, it does have some nice chartreuse flames scrolling over the hood and along the sides."

"I taught the boy better than that, I swear."

"It'll do for what we need," I said.

"What are you thinking, BJ?" Alan asked.

"I don't know if the Strumph boy's disappearance means there's been another cutie-pie killing, but I do know one thing."

"What's that?" Charlie asked.

"If Wesley Strumph's a cutie-pie victim and Jules is the cutie-pie killer, I know why the signature's all wrong."

"Because we've got him tied down," Alan said. "He couldn't do this killing the same way he did the others."

"Right. APD pulled their people off today, Alan. You and Tim have the stakeout all to yourselves."

"But he *couldn't* have taken the boy," Alan insisted. "What time did the kid disappear?"

"The police can't narrow it down very much. Wes Strumph played tennis Saturday morning. Ate an early lunch with his girl and some buddies. They broke up about noon, and nobody saw the boy after that."

"There you go, then. At noon, Jules McClintock was home. Stayed there until he headed for the shopping mall with me tailing him every inch of the way. That was about 2:00 p.m.

He didn't stop anywhere from the time he left his house until he parked at the mall and went to Pansy's for a late lunch."

"Alan, I want you to drive the exact route Jules took to the Rio Grande Vista mall. Charlie, you ride with him. We'll keep an open telephone line between us until we get there. Okay?"

"Where do we start from, Alan?" Charlie asked.

"Right here. He came straight down Candelaria, picked up I-25, and headed north."

"Let's do it," I said.

I trailed the purple van out of the restaurant's parking lot and west on Candelaria. My cell phone was synched with the Impala, so I made a legal, hands-free call to Charlie as we drove. Charlie punched in his speakerphone. When we exited the freeway in the far northwest part of the city, there was one place when the passenger side of the van was invisible to me for a long moment.

"Alan, are you certain Jules didn't stop on that last exit ramp?" I asked. "There was a point at which I couldn't see the right side of the van."

"Nope. I woulda run up his tailpipe if he did."

This looked increasingly like a fool's errand.

When we pulled into the parking lot at the Rio Grande Vista—sorely misnamed as neither the river nor much of a view was evident—I told Charlie to have Alan park exactly where Jules's van had been parked that day.

Paul's Charger picked us up in the parking lot and trailed us to where Alan located his son's van. As soon as Charlie and Alan got out of the vehicle, I called for them to get into the Impala.

"Direct me to where you were parked," I said and took off, drawing Paul along behind me.

Once I parked where Alan said I should, we collected in a group beside the Impala. Even with a few cars in the big lot, we had a clear view of the long building housing Pansy's at the south end, abutted by a hardware store, a sewing shop, an empty suite, and a couple more business establishments in this typical, modern-day urban strip mall. Cheap and unpretentious. Alan was right, the van and the restaurant were both clearly evident. The only strange thing was the van was parked at the extreme north end of the property and relatively deep in the lot.

"How crowded was this parking lot Saturday?" I asked.

"About like today," Alan replied. "Maybe a little more traffic."

"Then why didn't Jules park closer to the restaurant?"

"Anytime I've followed him, he's chosen a spot as far away from other parked cars as possible. I figure it's because he wants to make sure he's got room to load and unload his motorized wheelchair."

"There's a handicapped spot almost in front of Pansy's," Paul said. "The van accessible lane would make sure he had room for his chair."

Alan shrugged. "Can't tell you why, but he doesn't usually use handicap spots. Prefers to park away from traffic. Only time he doesn't is when he's in a hurry or there's no other convenient spot."

"Okay, so that's explained. But what brought him all the way out here to Pansy's? You said it was a so-so restaurant."

"Pansy," Charlie said. "Wasn't she Li'l Abner's girlfriend?"

"That was Daisy Mae," Alan said.

"Pansy was his mom," I added.

"Who's Li'l Abner?" Paul asked.

"Comic strip. Before your time, kid," Charlie said.

Paul shook his head as if clearing it of minor details. "I got here before you guys and had a look around the area. And I can tell you one reason why Jules might drive all the way out here for lunch."

"And what's that?"

"To pick up somebody."

Alan raised a hand in protest. "I already told you he didn't pick up anybody. Drove up, got out of his van, ate, and got back in his van."

"I think your report said he answered a cell phone call in the middle of it all," Paul said.

"Right. But still—"

"I'll bet you ten bucks I can get in your van without being seen from here."

"You're on," I said.

"I'll take ten," Charlie said.

Alan hopped on the pay wagon. "And I'll take another."

"Wow, not a bad payday. Is the van unlocked?" Paul asked.

Alan nodded.

"Okay, wait right here. I'll honk when I'm in the van." He got in his black Charger and pulled out of the parking lot.

I shifted my attention to what lay north of the Rio Grande Vista, another small shopping plaza that looked to be on lower ground. Out near the street where I saw Paul turn into the adjoining mall's parking lot, a small grove of pines towered above everything else. Paul's car disappeared from sight. Had he pulled into the trees?

"Okay, guys," I muttered. "Keep a close eye out. I have a feeling Paul's gonna snooker us."

No one spoke. All eyes were on the atrocious purple vehicle. Five minutes later, the van's horn beeped.

"Son of a bitch," Alan said. "How'd he do that?"

"Let's go find out. He's not into magic tricks, so it's probably pretty simple."

We trooped over to find a smiling Paul standing outside the sliding door to the van, which had been on our blind side.

He held out a hand. "Pay up."

As each of us forked over ten dollars, he continued. "Easy money. There's a retaining wall between the two strip malls. I parked in those trees over there as close as I could get, vaulted the wall, and walked… well, kinda crept to this side of the van. Opened the door, got in, and honked for my money. So long as I kept the van between you and me, no way were you gonna spot me."

The others followed me to the wall. The drop was only about four feet, an easy climb for anyone halfway physically fit. Paul's Charger was almost hidden in the small grove of evergreens.

"Any other vehicles in the trees?" I asked.

"Nope. They're a pretty thin screen, but there are signs it's well traveled. My guess is it's a late-night parking spot for horny teenagers."

I turned and looked at the van, then shifted my gaze to Pansy's. Anyone sitting in the café could easily have seen someone vault the wall and approach the van.

"Okay," I said. "We know how it could have been done. But why would a privileged kid like Wes Strumph surreptitiously crawl into Jules's van?"

"Only one reason I can think of," Charlie said. "He wasn't as off the heroin as everybody thought."

"Maybe," I acknowledged. "But how did Jules make contact with him?"

"Word gets around among the drug crowd," Paul said. "Back in my school days, I was always being offered drugs— and more to the point—drug contacts."

"Is there any sign that Jules deals?" I asked.

"No," Charlie said. "But one of his pain prescriptions is for morphine."

"And heroin's made from morphine," Alan said.

"Yeah, but morphine's a schedule two drug while heroin's a schedule one. No known medical uses… except in rare cases." Charlie rubbed his balding pate. "Still, if a guy can't score heroin, I guess morphine would do in a pinch."

Once again, I took in the scene. Doable. "Let's assume for the moment we're right. Wes climbed the wall and got into the van. Did he take something left for him, get out, and then go his own way?"

"I'm betting he never got out of the van," Alan said.

Paul nodded. "I agree."

I held up my hands in an unconscious police gesture to stop. "Okay, I understand why Jules couldn't simply park and wait for his mark to get into his van, make the transaction, and go his own way. Because Alan was sitting on his tail. But I don't understand why Wes Strumph would agree to handle it that way. Why would the kid agree to such a thing?"

"Come on, BJ," Charlie said. "When a druggie needs a fix, he'll jump through hoops."

"Was the Strumph kid still hooked?" Alan asked.

"If so, he hid it well," Charlie said. "But what other explanation could there be?"

"Maybe we're flat wrong," I said. "But at least let's find out if Wes was using again. He might have hidden it from his grandfather, but *someone* in his social circle knew."

We sent Alan home to complete his recovery from his previous night's stakeout. Because Paul connected with young people better than the rest of us, I asked him to run down the Strumph boy's friends to determine if the teenager was using again… or still.

Once they were on their way, Charlie and I went to canvass the small shopping center to the north of where Alan's van had been parked. We struck out until we stopped in a small eatery called Phil's. The young woman waiting tables and apparently doing everything else but the cooking had worked the previous Saturday and noticed a sports car of some type parked down in the trees near the road. The cook, who looked barely old enough to grow the thin mustache on his upper lip, was more car aware.

"It was a white 2011 Porsche Spyder," he declared. "Bitchin' ride."

"Did you get a tag number?" Charlie asked.

He shrugged. "Why? It wasn't botherin' nobody."

I followed up Charlie's question. "See the driver?"

"Young fella," said the cook, who qualified for the description himself.

"Recognize him?"

"Nah. Just some rich kid."

"What did he do?"

"Climbed the wall to next door."

"And…?" I prompted.

"Dunno where he went. I was busy."

"Did you see him return?"

"Uh-uh. Car sat there all night. Leastways, it was sittin' right there when I come to work the next day."

"How long did it stay?"

"Coupla days. Then one morning it wasn't there no more. Figured the driver come and got it."

More likely, some thieves took it, but I didn't reveal my suspicions. We got the couple's names and contact information and left, convinced Wesley Strumph had entered Jules's van last Saturday afternoon. Had he come out? Doubtful. Then where was he? There had been no body dump reported.

As we crawled into the Impala, Charlie spoke my thoughts aloud. "Looks like the Strumph kid got into Jules's van the way Paul demonstrated."

"I agree. But we can't prove it. See if you can raise Roy or Glenann and determine what kind of car the Strumph boy drove."

A few minutes later, he closed his call with a sour look on his face. "White 2011 Porsche Spyder."

We hadn't yet reached the office when my cell went off. I poked a button on the steering wheel. Tim's voice came through the car's speaker. "McClintock's on the move, and I lost him."

"He evaded you?" I asked.

Frustration made his voice heavy. "Naw. He was driving normal. Crossed San Mateo on Candelaria just before a funeral procession caught me flat-footed. The patrolman escorting it roared up and held up his hand before I could get across. Damned thing's still going by. McClintock's out of sight."

We all three said different dirty words. "Can't be helped, Tim. What's your best move?"

"Go back and sit on the house, probably. I don't have a clue where he was heading."

"Do that. Charlie and I are mobile. We'll head over on Paseo West to see if we can spot the van. If he's dumping the Strumph boy's body, the West Mesa's his favorite spot."

I closed the call and headed west. Charlie mumbled a couple of things before asking, "Okay, I see how Jules might have gotten the kid into his van without us spotting it. But I'm with you... why would the kid stay?"

"Has to be drugs," I said. "Wasn't sex. A kid who looked like Wes Strumph wouldn't get it on with someone like McClintock. He coulda had his pick of partners... male or female."

"So why didn't he pay for the package and scoot out the van door?"

"Just one of several unanswered questions. How did Jules contact Wes? Why didn't the kid buy his merchandise and leave?" I was quiet for a moment. "Heroin. What's the common way of taking the stuff?"

"Most efficient way is mainlining. But they snort and smoke the stuff too."

"And morphine?" I knew the answer but wanted it confirmed.

"Generally orally, but you can shoot it too. I've even heard of them smoking the stuff."

"Wes was an athlete, and his grandfather was on the alert after rehab. So Wes couldn't afford needle tracks."

Charlie shifted in his seat. "Between the toes, maybe. In the groin. But he probably took it orally."

"And you can mix a hypnotic in the stuff any way he chose to take it."

"Simple if you use the liquid or the capsules. Harder if it's tablets. So the kid had a sample of the product while in the van—"

"And never got out of the vehicle," I finished for him. "At least on his own two feet."

We headed for the West Mesa, the place where the killer had done most of his body dumps, and started our search. We found a couple of vans, but none were white or matched the photo of the van Tim and Alan had provided us.

After a while, Charlie asked if we were looking for a white van with New Mexico tags or a white van with blue panels and an Arizona license.

"White van. Jules's white van."

"You can change license plates, but not panels," Charlie cautioned.

"You'll have to convince me of that. I'm still banking on magnetic panels. You know, like magnetic signs they use on some vans."

Not long after that exchange, Tim called to say the van was back at the house on Colorado. I experienced an almost overwhelming desire to go grill Jules about where he'd been but quelled the urge until after we huddled with Roy and Glenann. We arrived back at the office in time for Hazel to transcribe a report of our conclusions and fax it to APD.

Chapter 18

ALAN MENDOZA joined our small procession as we passed him a block south of Jules McClintock's house, making our arrival even more notable. Paul and I were in my Impala, Charlie followed in his own vehicle. Roy and Glenann drove a departmental Ford, but in case anyone missed the significance, they put a magnetic blue light on the roof to drive the point home. The four cars in our little group completely blocked the front of 3661 Colorado, including the driveway. Something— perhaps the slamming of vehicle doors—alerted Jules, because he loomed in the open doorway before we reached the porch.

"Hello, Jules," I said in as pleasant a voice as I could muster.

He pointed over my shoulder at Paul. "You can come in. The rest of you, go away."

"Sorry, but it doesn't work that way."

He plopped into the motorized chair sitting directly behind him. "Then it doesn't work at all."

"Jules, this is Detective Guerra and Detective Hastings of APD. They want to ask you some questions."

"What about?"

"About your whereabouts last Saturday and where you went yesterday afternoon."

He shoved a thick thumb toward Alan. "Hell, ask him or his partner. They follow me everywhere I go."

"Not yesterday. You eluded them by taking advantage of a funeral procession."

"Did I? Didn't notice. I don't pay them any mind. I figure they're a bad smell following me everywhere. As far as last Saturday, I don't even remember. Every day's like the one before when you're tied to a chair just to get from the front room to the bathroom." He smiled, jiggling his fleshy jowls. "'Cept for the days the little guys come for their lessons."

"Do you pick out your victims from the little ones and wait until they're old enough to kill?" Roy asked.

"Don't know what you're talking about. Not any of my boys and girls died that I know of."

"What about Petey Baca?" Glenann asked.

Jules's face fell into a frown. "That was a tragedy. Good kid, Petey." He looked up from his chair and examined each one of us. "But he was never a student of mine."

"We'd like to come inside to discuss the situation."

Jules backed his chair away from the door a foot or so. "Do you have a warrant?"

"No, sir," Roy answered. "But we need to ask you some questions. We can do it here or down at the station, your choice."

"Or in BJ's office, if that's more convenient for you," Paul said.

Jules brightened. "Will you be there?"

"I can be."

"As tempting as that is, I don't believe so. Besides, you've had me under your thumb, so I couldn't have done anything bad. Well, except for the funeral procession, and I went to the grocery store and a hardware store and to have a bite to eat. You need names and places, I'll email them to you. To Paul if you'll give me his email address."

"Send them to my office," I said and cited an AOL address.

Jules went into a pout. "When I get around to it."

"As far as being tied down so tight you couldn't have done anything bad, I'm not so sure. We figured out how you had a hand in that boy's disappearance on Saturday."

"What boy's disappearance?"

"You read the papers, but you didn't need to read about the snatch. Paul figured out how you did it."

Jules shifted his gaze to Paul, but it didn't soften the way it usually did. "Paul?"

"Yes, he gained access to a van identical to yours without being seen while we all watched for him. Never saw him hop the wall and slide open the side door."

Jules's eyes narrowed. He pointed at Roy. "If you wanna talk to me, contact my attorney. Name's Larry Bingman. He'll make the arrangements." Jules cited a phone number from memory before closing the door in our faces.

"Damn," Glenann muttered as we walked away. "We shoulda grabbed him when he was standing in the doorway."

"He wasn't over the threshold, and there was a closed screen door between us," Roy said. "Wouldn't hold up in court."

"And I don't want to do anything the court will throw out," I said. "I want this guy dead to rights."

"And how many more bodies before we get him dead to rights? Keeping an eye on him 24/7 doesn't seem to slow him down much. For a cripple, he's doing a good job of outrunning us all."

"Not sure exactly how handicapped he is," I said. "He can walk. When Paul and I were allowed inside the other day, he walked a bit."

Alan spoke up. "We've seen him walk out the front door and do something on the front porch."

"Like what?" Roy asked.

"Swept it once. Picked up his mail."

"Anything else?" I asked.

"Tim watched from a neighbor's backyard and saw him walk from the house to the little building at the rear of the premises."

"What's the building used for?" Charlie asked.

Alan shrugged. "Looks like storage. His folks lived here before they died, so he probably has some of their stuff out there."

"Roy," I asked, "can you get a warrant to search his house?"

The detective shook his head. "Not enough probable cause. We've got nothing to tie him to Wesley Strumph, so we can't claim exigent circumstances."

"McClintock offered to let Paul in," Glenann said. "Maybe he can spot something to justify a warrant."

"Yeah, I could—"

"No way," Roy and I said at once.

"Why not?" Glenann asked. "McClintock obviously has a hankering for Paul, and Paul looks like he can take care of himself."

Charlie added his objection to Roy's and mine. "If we're right about McClintock, he's taken down a hardened street kid, and Matt Zapata, who was pretty bulked up. You'd think they could take care of themselves too. But they didn't. Besides that, BJ told the killer it was Paul who figured out how he did it."

"Those guys didn't know what to expect, but I do," Paul said.

"No way," I repeated. "Remember the last murder victim had a needle mark. Any number of ways Jules could render you helpless within seconds. It's too dangerous."

"He's not going to let me in his house and then take me down with you guys all watching the front door. He's not crazy."

"I agree with BJ," Roy said. "We'll have to find another way. Let's go somewhere and talk it over."

Curtains twitched on a window of the house next door. The lady with the nose was likely watching. "I kind of like standing out here on the sidewalk in front of Jules's place and talking things over."

Paul laughed. "You like the publicity, don't you?"

"I do, but I'll bet Jules doesn't." I nodded to the window with the twitchy curtain. "Every neighborhood has its Gertrude Wardlow, and she's it for this street. Name's Hormel, Mrs. Mercy Hormel. When we talked, she wouldn't hear anything bad about her poor neighbor, but maybe a yard full of men and women, two riding in a cop car, will shake her faith."

Roy's phone rang, and he turned stone-faced as he listened. He hung up and regarded us with haunted eyes. "They found him. The Strumph kid. It was the cutie-pie killer, okay. Naked, strangled. Oh, jeez!"

"Where?" I asked.

"South UNM Golf Course. Someone tossed him over the fence into the rough. Wasn't discovered until a few minutes ago when a golfer chased a hooked drive."

"We'll follow you," I said as we broke for our cars.

I WILL always wonder if my reaction to the cutie-pie dumps would have been as intense if the victims had been plain looking or unattractive, but I believe I'm human enough and humane enough for that to be true. Nonetheless, my first reaction to seeing Wesley Strumph's naked body was *we've lost another good-looking guy*. But there was something different about this one. The boy was drawn up into a fetal position. Glenann was the one who commented on it.

"Seems odd, doesn't it? Not like the rest of them. You know, all sprawled out as if posed to show their private parts."

Charlie's cop sense kicked in faster than mine. "This young man's been stored in somebody's freezer or some such. Does McClintock have a chest type or an upright freezer? Anybody know?"

No one replied.

"We need to get into his house," I mumbled.

"Agreed," Roy said. "But I don't have probable cause. Just because we know how McClintock could have lured this young man without being caught by surveillance doesn't mean we can prove he did."

"But I'm willing to bet there's evidence in his garage to prove it. There's some evidence this young man was once in Jules's van and garage within the last few days. There *has* to be."

"What are we thinking?" Paul asked. "That Jules brought him home drugged and unconscious, had his way with him, and then stowed the body in a freezer?"

I nodded. "An autopsy will probably show Wesley died the Saturday he was taken. He wasn't dumped until yesterday, which was Monday. But Jules didn't know how long it would take before he would no longer be under surveillance. He probably took the body out of the freezer every time he left his house. When Alan got caught by the funeral procession, he drove to the UNM south course and tossed the cadaver over the fence."

"I can't believe how audacious he is... how careless, really," Glenann said. "He rides around with a dead body in his van. He leaves his semen on the bodies. He does his dumps, and apparently his pickups, in broad daylight."

"And yet he's managed to kill seven men without getting caught," Charlie said. "Eight if you count Burton Neville."

"He doesn't care," I said. "He doesn't care if he's caught or not. That's what this is all about. Jules McClintock hates himself. Hates himself because he's no longer the trim, handsome young man he once was. Because he's mostly confined to a wheelchair. And he hates his victims because they reject him for the way he looks now. Nobody turned him away when he was tooling around UNM collecting admirers and lovers. But they won't have anything to do with him now. So he hates them as much as he hates himself. That's why he leaves the semen on them. His and theirs. His to show he got it on with them. Theirs to show he got them to participate."

Glenann shook her head as the OMI medics brought Wesley Strumph's body to their vehicle. "That's what doesn't make sense to me. If they're repulsed, how can they get it up for him... to be crude about it."

"In the first place," I said, "they're drugged, so they don't fight him. In the second place the hypnotic probably induces some response. And finally, sometimes males respond to physical stimulation whether they want to or not."

"Makes sense to me," Paul said.

Roy sighed. "So now we have the motive."

"Sexual frustration, self-loathing, and revenge." Charlie shook his head. "Pretty potent."

"Roy," I asked, "have they found Strumph's Porsche?"

He shook his head. "No sign of it. If it was abandoned somewhere, it's probably in Mexico by now."

"It was abandoned in the trees at the parking lot next to where Jules parked the van. I'm certain of that. Can we absolutely place it there?"

"No," Glenann said. "We grilled every employee in both adjoining strip malls. All we can get for certain is a sporty, white car."

"The cook at Phil's nailed it as a white 2011 Spyder," Charlie said. "Anything from tire tracks?"

Roy grimaced. "That's a prime after-hours sparking spot for teenagers."

"Did Wesley leave anything of himself on the retaining wall he scaled?"

"If he did, the crime scene boys can't find it."

"So we know how and why it was done but have nothing to prove it. Damn!"

"BJ?" Glenann asked. "If Jules McClintock is into self-loathing, he probably wants to be caught. Why doesn't he make it easy for us? Like invite us to search his house, for example?"

"I said he doesn't care if he's caught, not he wants to be caught. And there's a difference. I suspect by now it's become a cat and mouse game for him. He knows he'll eventually go down for his crimes but will prolong the game for as long as possible."

"So he'll continue to kill," she said, a bitter note to her voice.

"Absolutely, unless we can screw him down so tight he can no longer do so."

"Hate to bring this up," Charlie said, "but there's another kind of danger in that. If he gets too frustrated, he might take it out on one of his students."

I considered his statement. "Right at the moment, they're all prepubescent. I doubt they stimulate him. But if he takes on an older student, that might present a danger."

"Can we take the chance?" Glenann asked.

"If we interfere with his livelihood by warning off the parents, we'll open the department to a lawsuit," Roy cautioned.

Glenann cupped her hands and waggled them as if they were a scale. "Lawsuit… kids' lives."

"I get it," he said, "but will our lieutenant?"

"If we go that route, it won't be Don Carson making the decision," I said.

Charlie waved a finger, catching our attention. "There may be another way. Cheaper too. Get Lieutenant Carson to park a police car right in front of the McClintock house, day and night. It won't take long before some parents get nervous."

"He'll still sue," Glenann objected.

Charlie's smile always transformed his face from cadaverous to puckish. "Not if we make sure someone reports a mini crime wave in the neighborhood. One calling for a police presence."

"You want me to break some windows?" Paul volunteered.

"No need," Charlie said. "When we canvassed the area the other day, I ran across a former cop in the neighborhood by the name of Ames. Knew him when he was in service. If I explain the situation, he'll spread a few rumors around."

"Make sure he plants one with Mercy Hormel, Jules's neighbor to the north. That'll do the rest of his job for him."

AMOS STRUMPH descended on APD like a plague, and he didn't start down at Lt. Don Carson's level. He demanded to know why his grandson was murdered and why wasn't the bastard who'd done it already behind bars.

I deemed it time to report to my client on how his son's case was coming. I shared with him we had a suspect but declined to identify the perpetrator. He must have understood my fear of Zancón's reaction because he didn't press me on the issue. He'd read the newspapers and knew there had been other killings. He said nothing, but his body language urged me to hurry up and put an end to this monster.

I left Zapata's Pre-Owned Cars in a blue funk to return to the task of trying to tie Jules McClintock into the Park House in some fashion. Burton Neville gave us a tenuous connection, but he was dead and could do nothing further for us. If Jules killed his former lover—as I was sure was the case—he must have taken the key card to apartment 4201 that Quint James failed to recover when Neville moved out. That had to be what happened, but how to prove it?

With APD once again helping with the surveillance, we put Jules on an even tighter leash. We adopted the policy of tailing him wherever he went with two cars: one to claim a spot on either side of the van whenever Jules parked his vehicle.

Three days later came the first sign we were getting under Jules's skin. Hazel buzzed me in my office Friday morning.

"Larry Bingman's here to see you."

Larry Bingman was an attorney I'd known since my cop days. Successful, semiaggressive by nature, and ethical. I liked him in a social situation. But this likely wasn't social.

"Ask him in."

Larry came through the door with a half smile on his face, like he wasn't certain how to handle me… good ole boy or strictly professional. We spent a couple of minutes catching up before he got down to business.

"BJ, I've been engaged by Jules McClintock to put a stop to your harassment of him."

"Legal surveillance, not harassment."

"Just what is your interest in Mr. McClintock?"

"Didn't your client fill you in? I'm looking into what the newspaper is calling the cutie-pie murders."

"And this involves him how?"

"Larry, I'm not about to spill everything I know so you can warn Jules. Go fish somewhere else."

"I'm merely trying to determine if your activities are legal. And at the moment, it seems like harassment to me. You've interviewed all his neighbors."

"Legal under the statutes. Friends, family, and associates, as you well know."

"You're following him. In fact, you're double-teaming him."

"Conducting a stakeout and tailing an individual to track his movements are legal pursuits. Again, I'm not telling you anything you don't know."

"Someone checked on his credit cards and his bank accounts."

"Now you really are fishing. I doubt he'd know if someone did that, but if it's true, go talk to APD. They must have gotten a court order, I didn't." I picked up a ballpoint and made a note on a notepad. "But thanks for the idea."

"You've got a police cruiser parked in front of his house, for Christ's sake. If that isn't harassment, I don't know what is."

"Are you asking if I dressed one of my men up as a policeman and decorated his car to look like a police car?"

"Of course not."

I repeated my advice. "Then go see APD."

"I have."

"What did they say?"

Larry waved a hand in the air. "Claimed there was a crime spree in the neighborhood."

"There you go, then. Jules should be pleased he and his neighbors are receiving the protection they're due."

"You trespassed on his property."

"I accompanied two APD detectives to his home to interview him. He declined, and we left, as requested."

"You stood around in his yard for another hour."

"Stood on the public sidewalk to consider our options." I pointed a finger at him. "Incidentally, the detectives received a call about then informing them of another killing."

"Are you accusing Jules McClintock of being this so-called cutie-pie killer?"

"Nope, but the police probably told you he's a person of interest."

"Preposterous!" Larry said. "The man's an invalid."

"Are you sure about that? I was in his house a couple of times—at his invitation, by the way—and witnessed him walking into his kitchen under his own steam."

"Mr. McClintock's obviously impaired. This isn't right, BJ."

"Before you go all indignant on me, Larry, ask yourself one question. You've seen Jules. Would you want to get into a wrestling match with him? The man is stronger than he lets on."

All the lawyers I know are pretty good at covering their reactions, but Larry Bingman's startled expression gave him away.

"Anyway," I continued, "I'm doing nothing illegal or unethical. Nor do I intend to."

"Who's your client?"

"Sorry, that's confidential. But you can go back over the list of young kids brutally murdered by the cutie-pie killer and look over their relatives. You can probably come up with a name."

"I already have. The Brown Saints."

"They no longer exist. I took them down."

"Zancón Zapata still exists. And I heard you paid him a visit up in the penitentiary. You carrying his water nowadays?"

I stood. "I represent the family of a decent kid who was abused and then murdered. If you need anything else, call Del Dahlman. He represents me."

Larry rose from his chair and revealed a side of him I'd never seen before. "Oh, yes. Del Dahlman. I understand you were shacking up with him while you were a police officer." Without giving me a chance to respond, he walked out the door. I might have lost a friendly acquaintance, but at least I was getting under Jules McClintock's skin.

That was reinforced when Alan called to say Jules had wheeled down the street in his motorized wheelchair and cracked Alan's windshield with a brick.

"Call the cops on him. Lodge a complaint," I said. "Cause him maximum distress."

"No need," Alan said. "The cop on duty in front of the house saw it all and came running. They hauled him in for assault."

It would have been ideal if Jules had to stay overnight in jail—better yet over the weekend—but Larry Bingman got a bail hearing the same afternoon. Roy and Glenann joined Paul and me at the hearing, but the judge wouldn't consider any information other than what pertained to the pending assault charge. Bingman was able to load his client into a van and drive him home before the sun even thought about going down that evening.

Saturday morning, while Paul worked on the latest article he was pushing for GQ, I drove to Jules's house, parked, chatted a few minutes with the police officer stationed in front of the house, and went down the block to sit a few minutes with Tim Fuller, who was on surveillance duty.

The following day, I did the same thing. This time Paul accompanied me. My young partner did me one better. He stood on the sidewalk and stooped over to talk to the cop while I sat with Alan, who was back on duty with a brand-new windshield on his 2009 gray Ford F-150 pickup.

Alan grinned at me when I crawled into the seat beside him. "Paul's giving McClintock a good view of his backside."

"And it's driving him crazy, I hope. If Jules even spots him."

"Oh, don't worry about that. I'm convinced the guy has a surveillance system set up so he can see what's going on outside. He's hyperattentive these days."

"Good. Go for it, Paul!"

Damn, I hoped those words didn't come back to haunt me.

MONDAY MORNING, I accepted a collect call from the New Mexico State Penitentiary. Zancón's irritated, unhealthy growl rumbled in my ear. "What's going on down there, gumshoe? You padding the bill or something? Been a month and a half, and nothing's happening."

"Except four more young men have died."

"Thought you'd a put a stop to it by now." He coughed, a wet sound that rattled the telephone. "You ain't figured it out yet?"

"Haven't proved it yet."

I heard a sharp intake of breath. "You know who done it? Who offed Mateo?"

"Yes, but I haven't pinned it down yet. Not enough for an arrest."

"Fuck an arrest. Tell me who done it, and you won't have to worry about no arrest."

"I don't work that way, Zancón, and you know it. So get it straight in your head. When this guy goes down, he's going down legally."

"You ain't gonna tell me?"

"When I have my case tied down all nice and legal-like, I'll tell you."

"Don't make it too long," he said before slamming down the receiver.

Chapter 19

THE TELEPHONE woke me Monday night… or more accurately, Tuesday morning about 3:15. I likely snarled a little when answering, but Roy's voice brought me awake.

"It's Jules, BJ."

"What about him?"

"He gave our guys the slip."

I sat up and snapped on the table lamp. Paul groaned and turned away from the light. "We've got to find him. Right away!"

"Oh, we already found him. Or maybe he found us."

"What do you mean?"

"It's complicated. Why don't you come to the Vista View Urgent Care Center. It's on—"

"I know where it is. Take me twenty minutes."

"We'll be right here."

"What?" Paul demanded as I closed the call and bailed out of bed.

"Gotta go to Vista View Urgent Care. Apparently, Jules is there."

Paul, who usually woke easier than I, was a little crabby at the interruption. "Who in the hell would name an urgent care place the View View?"

"Probably someone who doesn't understand Spanish," I said, drawing on a pair of trousers.

Fifteen minutes later, Paul parked the Charger in the Vista View parking lot. He'd driven because his car was parked behind mine in the driveway. It also let him work off some of his irritation at having his sleep disturbed. Alan, looking sheepish, met us at the front door to the center.

"Sorry, BJ," he said. "It shouldn't have happened."

"What shouldn't have happened? Never mind, fill me in later," I said as Roy, Glenann in tow, strode across the room toward us.

In a few short words, the detective made it clear our two guard dogs, Alan and the patrolman stationed in front of Jules's house, had been caught sleeping. Jules left the house without either of them being aware of the fact. He'd shown up at the clinic—one of the few remaining open all night—complaining of severe spinal pain. Apparently he'd done this before, so the staff handled his complaint and he left, only to return in minutes to report his van stolen.

A haggard-looking Jules McClintock and I stared at each other from across the broad waiting room as Alan made sense of his end of things.

"The officer and I on night duty made a deal. One would keep watch while the other caught some sleep. Not to make excuses, but he was supposed to be on watch and apparently nodded off. Nodded off, hell. He must have been in a stupor. McClintock apparently drove out of the garage right past him and took off. We didn't even know he was gone until dispatch raised the patrolman and let us know the guy we were supposed to be watching was at the clinic raising hell about his van being swiped."

Roy wiped the disgust off his face long enough to speak. "The van wasn't hard to find. Somebody torched it. Made a big bonfire along an arroyo near a well-populated area."

"Where? How far from here?" I asked.

"Five, six miles. We'll take a run out to look at it after we talk to McClintock."

"Before," I said. "I want to see it before I talk to Jules."

Minutes later, we parked at one of those odd little holes in civilization one finds in cities like Albuquerque where arroyos, big and small, break up the terrain as they snake their way from the foothills to the Rio Grande in the valley below. The fire crew was packing up to depart, leaving one departmental SUV holding a couple of firemen behind to talk to us. They walked out to meet us.

"Torched," one with a lieutenant's bars said.

"You know how it was set?" Roy asked.

"Gasoline was probably the accelerant. Can't say yet if a match was pitched in the window or it was something else. The vehicle's still too hot to do much of an inspection. Not much of it left, as you can see."

"How long ago?" I asked.

"The alarm came in an hour ago."

"Any footprints or sign of a wheelchair?"

"Wheelchair? No, but there's paraphernalia in the back that could be a chair lift."

"What are you thinking, BJ?" Roy asked.

"Jules did this."

"How? I checked his arrival time at the clinic. He was already there when the alarm came in. And I can assure you somebody called the fire department as soon as the van went up. Too many houses close by not to."

"Then you better get someone to canvass the neighborhood early this morning. Somebody might have seen him."

"That doesn't make sense. The urgent care center is miles from here."

"Six. Six miles. I clocked it by Paul's odometer."

Roy scratched his head. "What kind of range does one of those wheelchairs have?"

"I don't know, but it's easy enough to check. I'll bet it's more than six miles."

"So you believe we'll find an ignition device activated after the owner left the area," the AFD lieutenant said. "Might be hard to find. Everything's burned up or melted."

"Man, he was taking a chance," Roy cut in. "Anybody spotting a wheelchair that time of night is bound to remember it."

"So you have lots of questions to ask between here and the clinic this morning. Besides, Jules has a propensity for taking risks. And motoring down the street in the dead of night is probably less of a risk than finding evidence in his van one of these days."

GLENANN, WHO'D remained behind with Jules and a patrolman, met us at the door of the clinic. "They've taken McClintock back to one of the rooms. His spinal pain is severe, so they're giving him a shot to block the pain. They'll let him rest for a while before we can talk to him."

Paul struck his palm with a fist. "So he gets to sleep while we stand around and suck our thumbs. He's probably faking the whole thing."

"The pain's likely real," I said. "If we're right, he went for a six-mile trip in his wheelchair down a bumpy street. It's the price he had to pay for getting rid of evidence."

An hour later, an attendant led Jules back into the lobby. As the big man settled up at the desk, I regarded the attendant, a good-looking young Black man, and wondered if Jules had picked out his next target.

A few minutes later, a haggard-appearing Jules wheeled over to where we stood in a small group. "So who's going to get me home?"

"Your chair won't fit in any of our cars. Maybe Detective Guerra will order up a police van for you," I said.

"That's okay. I've got a service I can call. They have the equipment to accommodate my chair."

"Not until we get your report on the van you claim was stolen," Roy said.

Jules nodded to the patrolman. "Already gave it to him. Nothing much to report. I came in when my back muscles started spasming. That happens sometimes. They gave me some e-stim. When I feel better, I go out to get in the van. It isn't there. I come back inside the clinic and call the cops to report it. That's all there is to it."

"Why didn't you use your cell?" I asked.

"I did. But I came inside to see if security had seen anything. Or if they had cameras."

A Sparks Security man standing at the edge of the group nodded confirmation.

"What set off your back?"

Jules shrugged his thick shoulders. "Who knows? Sometimes when I'm stressed, my spinal condition acts up and sets off the muscles."

"Why are you stressed?" Roy asked.

"You guys got me under the microscope. That'd stress anybody out. Hell, I had to get a shot in addition to the e-stim because of all this tonight."

"You eluded the team we had on you. How often have you done that?"

"Eluded? I crawled in my van and drove out of the garage like always. I should honk my horn and wake up your guard dogs?" He gave a coarse laugh. "As to the other? Never done it before. Every other time they were right on my tail. Too bad I was in such pain, otherwise I might have enjoyed the freedom more."

"How?" Glenann asked. "By killing another young man?"

Jules grimaced and leaned forward in his chair to rub his back. "Uh! There you go piling on the stress. You mighta undone everything the electrical stimulation and the shot did for me."

"Too bad."

"You're awfully cynical for such a pretty young lady," Jules said.

"Dealing with killers will do that to you," she responded.

Paul and I left the others to deal with getting Jules home. Alan trailed us outside.

"Sorry, BJ. I shoulda—"

"Not your fault. Sounds to me like you had a reasonable arrangement with the patrolman."

"This was his first time on the stakeout. The other one was reliable."

"I'd like you to get to Colorado Street ahead of Jules. Park directly across the street and see if you can get a peek inside if he enters through the garage."

"What are you looking for?" Alan asked.

"We thought maybe the last body had been stored in a freezer. A lot of the older houses like his in the neighborhood have the freezer in the garage. I'd like to know if it's an upright or a chest type."

"Will do."

Paul and I returned home in time to catch a few more winks of sleep before it was time to get up again. When I arrived at the office later that morning, I found a message from Alan.

"The freezer's a chest big enough for a body."

I HELD a mental box in my head. On one side was a scroll listing all the things a confidential investigator can legally do, and the other side had a scroll detailing all the things a CI cannot legally do. Believe me, the can-do list was a lot shorter than the can't-do scroll. Since I'd pretty well put all my eggs in the Jules McClintock basket, I'd about exhausted the actions legally permitted. If Jules refused to talk to me, there wasn't much I could do except rely on the police department and the fire department to ask questions about the van "theft" for me.

But how did I know he wouldn't talk to me? He'd rebuffed us once, but maybe he got up on the wrong side of the bed that day. Worth another try. And to maximize my odds, I invited Paul to go along. Once we were ready, I phoned Jules and told him we were on the way over because we were out of tea. My jest didn't bring the chuckle I'd expected, but he didn't tell us not to come. When we arrived, I spotted Tim's car parked half a block down the street and gave him a wave. A police cruiser sat squarely in front of Jules's house. How much longer would Roy and Glenann be able to persuade Lieutenant Don Carson the expenditure of manpower was worth it?

I learn—slowly sometimes—but I do learn. I let Paul stand in front of the door and ring the bell. As soon as Jules yanked the door open, I realized he was hurting. He made no attempt to rise, simply leaned forward in his chair and unlatched the screen door. Perhaps his trip to the urgent care center last night was legitimate. It probably was, but once he realized he'd slipped the leash, he couldn't resist taking advantage of it.

As we took our seats in the living room, he backed his chair into place and grabbed a pillbox from the lamp table, gulping a tablet without the benefit of anything to wash it down. Pain pill, likely. Morphine? No offer of tea or anything else in the way of refreshments. Okay, this wasn't a social visit.

"Jules, what time did you get to the urgent care center last night?"

"Check with your cop friends. I got there around two. Couldn't put up with the pain any longer. You guys are beginning to interfere with my life in a big way. Some of my students have dropped off. Mamas tend to be bothered by a police car parked all day right outside my door. I'm having flare-ups in the spine like in the old days. My attorney says I oughta sue."

"If he can find anything illegal, tell him to have at it. Besides, I'll bet I can make a pretty good case it's your own activities that are causing the problem."

"Activities. Like what?"

"Like drugging young men and having sex with them before strangling them to death. You could probably handle all that, but disposing of the bodies requires physical exertion."

"I don't have the spine for that," he said.

"What part?" Paul asked.

"Any of it." Jules's features softened. "Although I'll bet I could muster the energy to give you a good time."

"Good time's one thing. *End* time's something else."

Jules's features closed up.

"Did you see anyone hanging around in the parking lot when you entered the clinic last night?" I asked.

"Nobody. Only three-four cars there."

"Anyone see you arrive?"

"Who knows?"

"Tell me something," I said. "How far can your chair go on a single charge?"

He patted an armrest. "Fifteen miles tops on a full charge."

"Was it fully charged when you left for the clinic?"

"Probably not all the way. I plug it in when I go to bed at night. So it was only on the charger for about three hours."

"Okay," I said, "I understand how you got to the clinic from your van, but how did you trigger the fire? That was dangerous, you know. The gasoline soaked the interior for what? Half an hour before you set it off. You're lucky the fumes didn't explode. But I forgot, you don't really give a damn about anybody's safety, do you?"

"I think it's time for you to go. I got an insurance man coming over to settle my claim for the van. And then somebody's coming to show me a replacement vehicle. Paul, you can stay, if you want."

I didn't give Paul a chance to respond. "Jules, you realize the fire department's going to tell us some sort of device set off the fire in your van, don't you? And when they do, we'll know for sure it wasn't a thief going for a joyride with a bang at the end. No one would have a reason for a timing device except you. To give you time to get to the clinic and establish your alibi."

"You're contemptible, BJ. And you used to be a nice guy. You were a better man when you were a cop. Can't say that about many people. You wanna know why a thief might use a remote to torch my van? 'Cause somebody's gonna call the fire department right quick when it goes up. He didn't wanna be found in the area."

"At least, that's what your attorney's going to claim," I said.

"Like I said, you need to leave now."

Paul spoke up. "Are you up to handling those details with the insurance guy and the car salesmen?"

"I could always use some help. Maybe—"

"Sorry," I said. "I've got Paul tied up the next couple of days. Besides, I'm certain your lawyer will give you all the help you need."

Paul held his tongue until we were in the Impala and pulling away from the curb. "What was that all about? You were needling the guy."

"Absolutely. He's beginning to buckle under the pressure, and I want to help it along."

"But the guy's without wheels. How's he going to get groceries? You know, the essentials. You can't just order a specially equipped van and expect it to be delivered the next day."

"True. But in the meantime, he can motor in his wheelchair to the neighborhood mart or call on the Albuquerque Sun Van. I believe they have a chair lift." I glanced at my handsome young companion. "Sometimes I think your heart rules your head. The guy gives you the creeps, but here you are worrying about how he's going to survive."

Paul flashed a grin that made me tingle. "Merely me being me."

"And don't ever change."

I DON'T mind being awakened for an occasional middle of the night emergency, but two nights in a row are too many nights and too many emergencies. It was Charlie on the phone at 2:30 a.m. this time.

"Sorry to wake you, BJ, but someone broke into our office."

"What?" Visions of stolen computers and recording equipment floated through my sleep-drugged head. "Did they strip us?"

"Stealing information, not loot. Course, he might have stolen the loot after he copped the information."

"He who?"

"Punk by the name of, wait for it… Lothario Stevens."

"Did I hear you right? Lothario?"

Paul groaned, clapped the pillow over his head, and turned over.

"So help me," Charlie said.

"Catch him?"

"He set off the silent alarm when he broke into the building. The security service called the cops. Wasn't hard to find him. Dumb shit not only didn't realize the building was alarmed, but he turned on every light in our office suite. He'd been through your office. Pulled out files left and right. He was working on Hazel's when the cops walked in on him."

"Was he just wrecking the place or was he after something specific?"

"Specific. And he found it too."

"What was it?"

"File on the Mateo Zapata case."

"Son of a bitch! I refused to give Zancón the name of our suspect, so he sent someone to find it. You say he located the file?"

"Had it in his grubby little hand."

"Had he gone through it?"

"Don't think he'd had time. Hell, I'm not even sure he can read. On the other hand, I guess he had to in order to find the right file."

"Where are you?"

"On the landing outside our office. Security called in a locksmith. They're changing our lock now. Then they'll tackle the door downstairs."

"Cops still there?"

"They took Stevens to the station. As soon as I know our place is secure, I'm going over to learn what they pry out of Lo-thar-i-o."

"I'll meet you there."

"No need. I'll find out if he communicated anything to anyone. You go back to sleep."

"After you finish at APD, go home and take the rest of the day off."

Paul emerged from under the pillow as I hung up. "Who's dead now?"

"Nobody. Caught someone breaking into our office downtown." I relayed what I'd heard from Charlie. Paul reached the same conclusion I had.

"Zancón, probably. Sounds like he's still got some sting left in him." He frowned. "You don't suppose it's his brother, do you?"

"More Zancón's style."

"What are you going to do about it?"

"Cut him off. Don't accept any more collect calls from him. Warn his brother. That's about all I can do."

UPON ARRIVING at the office at my usual time, I found Charlie there. The guy was amazing. He'd been up all night, and he looked fresher than I did, except for the gray stubble on his cheeks.

"Thought I told you to take the day off."

"Just got back from APD."

"And?"

"I don't think Lo-thar-i-o"—he stressed the name—"got to read the file before he was caught. He started out in your office, which was logical, and by the time he started tossing Hazel's desk, security and the cops showed up pretty quick."

"So you don't think he found Jules's name?"

"Naw. He had a little camera he was taking photos with." Charlie laughed. "Like in those '40s spy movies. He wasn't far into the file when he got interrupted. I checked, and he didn't make any calls from our phone or his cell. So I'm pretty sure he didn't find the name or pass it on to anyone."

"You willing to bet Jules McClintock's life on that?"

He hid a smile before answering. "Any day of the week."

I held his gaze for a moment. "We need to brief Roy and Glenann."

"Already done. I made sure the patrolmen who collared Lothario knew they'd be interested and why."

THERE COMES a time in many cases when the outcome seems in doubt. Everything shudders to a halt. I had satisfied myself none of the people presently connected with the Park House were involved in the murders, beyond the manager's carelessness in not retrieving Neville's second key card. The card gave the killer access to the suite where Matt Zapata was lured to his death. But Neville was of no help. He'd been killed before Matt met his end.

There was little doubt—at least in my mind—that Jules McClintock was our killer, but I was getting nowhere proving it. And not much else happened over the remainder of the week. According to Alan's and Tim's surveillance reports, unusual comings and goings took place at 3661 Colorado Street NE, but it was insurance people, grocery deliveries, and AFD following up on the arson case.

Charlie and I briefed our surveillance team on the break-in and warned them to keep an eye out for anything strange. If Charlie was wrong about Zancón getting a name from last night's break-in, Tim and Alan were Jules's protectors as well as his shadows.

Tim's Friday observation report indicated Jules had asked him for a ride to the pharmacy, and Tim accommodated him in the hope the lack of a wheelchair would mean Jules would require help in getting back inside the house. No such luck. Our suspect labored his way up his driveway, onto the porch, and through the front door without any aid from my surveillance man. When Tim asked to use his bathroom, Jules told him to use the bottle any stakeout man worth his salt kept in the car for such a purpose.

The final event of the week was the delivery of Jules's new van, a 2012 Caravan outfitted with a chair lift. White like the former van. The arrival of the vehicle confirmed what AFD had already told us. Thus far, they hadn't figured out how the fire had been ignited. They did find a burned book of matches on the ground outside the burned carcass, which seemed to indicate a thief ignited the fire as he left the vehicle in the arroyo. I didn't buy it for a minute.

Chapter 20

I WAS on my way downtown to the office from a therapy swim at the country club on Monday morning when Roy phoned to say the State Police had raided a chop shop over near Tajique in Torrance County and discovered Wesley Strumph's Porsche among the hundred or so cars in the five-acre lot.

"They're still trying to identify all the owners," he said. "Some of the vehicles are junk cars that might be legitimate purchases. About half of them are late model and probably stolen. They got to us fast because we had a BOLO out on the Strumph vehicle."

I knew BOLO to be cop-speak for "be on the lookout for." "Are they giving you access to the landowners?" I asked.

"They've been arrested and are in the metropolitan center. I'm on my way over there now. You want to meet me?"

"No need. You know where I think the car was taken from. If you'll confirm it for me, that's about all we can expect."

"Right. You'll know as soon as I know."

"Have the crime scene boys gone over the car?"

"A team's headed for Tajique now. They want a shot at it before it's moved."

"Doubt they'll find anything we're interested in. I'll wager Jules McClintock's never been inside it."

"No, but maybe we'll find something to connect him with Strumph."

"We can always hope." Likely my tone let him know what I thought of that possibility.

Later that afternoon, I was invited to APD to sit in on an interview with the individual who'd delivered the stolen Porsche to the Torrance County chop shop. It turned out to be the helpful cook named Dominic Evans we interviewed two weeks ago at Phil's Café in the shopping center just north of the Rio Vista mall. He still didn't look old enough to support the thin mustache smudging his upper lip, but it turned out he was thirty-three-years old. Thin almost to the point of emaciation, he probably wasn't much better as a car thief than as a cook. Whereas the last time I spoke to the man he was polite and helpful, today he turned surly.

"I already told you I don't know the kid who climbed the wall to next door. Seen him hop the wall and disappear. First and last time I ever laid eyes on him."

Roy apparently decided to go tough. "Try another story, Dom. We know you saw him return all right. He caught you stealing his ride and you killed him."

The thief blinked slowly, as if digesting the news. "Killed him? I ain't killed nobody in my life. The kid I seen was husky. Wasn't about to take him on."

"Then why did we find his body?"

"Body? Where?"

"Where you dumped him on the way to delivering the Porsche. At the UNM Golf Course South."

"I don't even know where that is, man. You got it wr—"

"Okay, so you didn't know it was a golf course. You found a remote spot and threw the kid over the fence naked as the day he was born. You might as well admit it. We've got your prints all over his car."

"Hey, man, I ain't like that. Why'd I strip the guy? Why'd I kill him?"

"Simple. He caught you stealing his car," Roy said. "So you killed him. You'd read about the other killings of young men and tried to make it look like the serial killer killed the guy. And like I said, your prints are all over the stolen car."

"Course they are. I heisted the car. Already told you that. But I never killed nobody."

"Tell us where the guy went after he vaulted the wall at the shopping center, and I might believe you," Roy said.

"What I gotta do to make you hear me? All I seen outa the café's front windows was this kid parking the car in the trees and hopping the wall. Then he was outa my sight. I'm telling you the truth, man."

I left the interview room believing every word of Dominic Evans's statement. But he'd done one thing for me. He'd confirmed Wesley Strumph was in Rio Vista mall at the same time Jules McClintock was. That put me a giant step closer.

ACCORDING TO Alan and Tim, Jules had settled down after his new van was delivered. He stayed close to home, except for getting groceries. The stream of little kids seeking help in math had slowed to a trickle, so the cop car parked outside had done its intended job. Unfortunately, Lt. Carson saw fit to pull the cop car, relieving some of the pressure on our suspect.

Paul, who's much more knowledgeable about social media—and infinitely more active—than I am, started noticing something on Tuesday, first on his Facebook page and then on Instagram.

"It's not being trolled, exactly," he said when he told me about it. "Nobody's trying to start a fight or controversy, at least not yet. The remarks are off base. You know, sorta personal."

"Show me," I said, moving to his side of our shared home office.

He pulled up his Facebook page, scrolled down, and stopped. "Son of a gun, here's a new one."

I saw what he meant. Below a posting—or whatever they call it on FB—of Paul holding up a check for payment for an article, several of his followers had made congratulatory remarks.

Halfway through them—and there were a lot—someone called Cool Kat had noted while the check was okay, the guy holding it was super, making him wonder what was behind the fly of those trousers. At the end of the responses, Cool Kat had entered, "How about providing us your telephone number?"

"Why don't you scroll through your followers until you find someone suspicious?"

"I post to the public, so you don't have to be a follower to respond. If I limit it to followers, I don't get the public exposure I need for my writing."

"You spend a lot of time on the media, do you get other comments like this?"

My handsome young friend scowled. "Once in a while, but this is the first one who's come back more than once. This is about the sixth time Cool Kat's said something personal."

"You think it's McClintock?"

He shrugged. "Best guess."

"Could be. He's hung up on you, you know."

"Yeah. What did I do to deserve that?"

"Looking like you do would be enough. But you've showed him a sympathetic side a couple of times. That probably made him fall in love. Can you trace Cool Kat to Jules?"

"Don't think so. I found Kat's FB page, but it's got nothing on it. No profile, no photos, no nothing."

"Won't Facebook give him up?"

"I doubt it, they're notorious for privacy."

"How about banning him from your site?"

"He'll just open a FB page under another name. File a complaint's about all I can do. And that's worth exactly zero."

"Then answer the creep and tell him to knock it off."

WEDNESDAY MORNING, Charlie and I reinterviewed all of Jules's neighbors, including the lady with the nose. Mercy

Hormel was less adamant in her support of Jules this time around. Apparently the constant presence of a police car parked next door got her—forgive me—nose out of joint, even though the patrolman was now history.

"Not so much traffic over there now," she said. "Quieter. Although it was terrible what they did to Jules. You know, stole his van and left him with nothing but a wheelchair."

"That wheelchair gets better mileage than my Impala," I responded.

"Just what is it you people think he did?"

I smiled. She'd finally asked the right question. "Killed seven healthy, handsome young men."

The nose took a downer.

"And tossed them out of the van."

It whipped up as she glared at me.

"Naked and posed with genitals prominently displayed."

Someone gasped. Not sure if it was Mercy or her nose.

She tried a couple of times before she got any words out. "You can't honestly believe...."

"But I do. Jules McClintock is not as weak as he leads everyone to believe. He's capable of feats of strength for short periods of time. He eluded both the police and my surveillance the other night. He could have done anything."

"Mercy!" she said before closing the door. *Does she often call on herself like that?*

I'd no sooner walked into the office than Paul rang my cell. "He called me," my mate blurted.

"Who? Jules? How did he get your number?"

"He called on the house phone."

"Damnation! I should have unlisted my number years ago. At least it's done now."

"After the horse is out of the barn."

"What did he say?"

"Said he could use some help making adjustments to his new van. I told him the dealer would take care of him."

"What else did he say?"

"Nothing. I hung up on him."

A shiver ran down my back. "I should never have taken you with me to interview him."

"Why not? I'm a grown man. I can take care of myself."

"I wonder how many times Matt Zapata and Dustin Greene and Peter Baca said those very words in their short lives?"

"Yeah, yeah. I get the message. I'll be careful."

"If you lay eyes on the guy, dial 911 first and then me."

"Don't worry, I've got the panic drill down pat." I heard a sharp intake of breath before he spoke again. "Son of a bitch, a white van just passed the house."

"Where are you?" The office where he usually worked had no windows facing the street.

"Front room. Getting ready to go to the *Journal* to talk to an editor about a story."

"Don't hang up. I'm putting you on hold."

I frantically punched a couple of buttons and got Alan on the line. He was on duty in front of the McClintock place. As soon as he answered, I connected the calls and told Paul to repeat what he'd told me.

"Wasn't McClintock," Alan said. "He's at home."

"You sure?" I asked.

"He came out and got his mail a few minutes ago. Walked, by the way. Had a little trouble getting up the ramp to his porch. Course, it coulda been for show. But there's no doubt he's home." Alan laughed. "You really stirred him up by interviewing his neighbors today. He gave me the finger when he picked up his mail. He usually waves hello or ignores me completely."

"Jules is up to something. He called Paul a few minutes ago. Keep an eagle eye out."

"Tim just relieved me. Want us to double-team him tonight?"

I hesitated before telling him to go home and get some rest.

ONE THING Paul and I learned early in our relationship was not to hold on too tightly. If I went for lunch or dinner with Del Dahlman, my first love, Paul was okay with it. He trusted me. Likewise, he'd kept in touch with some fellow journalism students at the University of New Mexico, and a small group of them had a monthly night out, usually at a bistro where they could both eat and partake of a libation or two or three. That was okay. I trusted him. And Thursday night was the night.

I got home a bit later than usual to find a batch of still-warm green chili stew Paul had whipped up so I wouldn't starve to death in his absence. He was so spruced up and handsome and sexy as all get-out, I experienced a moment's pang of resentment. But dammit, I trusted him, so that was all there was to it. Besides, when he returned from one of these forays, Pedro was usually agitating to come out and play—no matter how late the hour.

Paul sat with me at the kitchen table to discuss the events of the day while I savored some of his great stew. He was relieved Alan had been absolutely certain Jules was at home when Paul spotted the white van passing the house. He got a chuckle out of Jules expressing his pique with his middle finger.

All too soon, the Charger roared out of the driveway, and I was left alone for the evening. I changed into something more comfortable and repaired to the home office to bring some of my notes up-to-date before settling down in the den with a bourbon and water and a good mystery by Joseph Badal, one of New Mexico's better writers.

The house always speaks to me in its own language when I am alone at night. Something creaks here or thumps there. The refrigerator kicks on or off. I can almost hear my father talking in what was his study, now our home office. Mom's laughter hides in corners and escapes in soft chuckles on occasion. I do not believe I would ever be totally "at home" anywhere else in the world.

Along about midnight, my cell phone pinged. A cryptic three-word message from Paul set my hair on end. "Come. Roary's Bar."

Throwing on a windbreaker against the still-cool early May night, I took the time to pull my Ruger .57 Magnum from the trunk of the car before getting in and backing out of the driveway. I reached Roary's on North Fourth in something under ten minutes. Paul's black Dodge sat in the lot with a white van parked beside it. What the hell!

With the Ruger tucked into the waistband at my back beneath the windbreaker, I sprinted for the door of the bar. As I pulled it open, a tall man brushed past me and headed into the parking lot. Ignoring him, I rushed inside, almost running into Paul and two other young men.

"Did you see him?" Paul asked.

"Him who? Somebody left as I was entering. What's up?"

"Gotta catch him," Paul said, squeezing past me. I followed and caught up with him scanning the parking area. "Crap! He's gone."

As the other two men with Paul joined us, I asked what happened.

"Did you see a white van when you pulled in?"

"Parked right beside your car."

"Dammit, he got away."

"Settle down and tell me what happened?"

"A white van followed me into the parking lot when I got to the bar." Paul indicated the two men who'd arrived outside on our heels. "I met Gary in the lot, and Stan was already here, so we got to talking and I forgot about it."

"You know the driver of the van?" He shook his head. "Get a plate number?"

Another shake. "Did you?"

"I parked too far away and rushed to get inside. Hold on a minute." I got on my cell and raised Roy Guerra at home. He agreed to have patrol cars watch for a white van in our vicinity.

"And?" I prompted Paul when I finished the call.

"And my buds and I had dinner and started drinking and talking. After a while, I noticed this guy all by himself at a table in the corner. Big guy. Tall. He seemed to be watching our table. Creepy."

"Did he approach you? Say anything?"

"Not at first," the man I assumed was Stan said. "I was sitting facing him, and after Paul called him to our attention, I sorta kept an eye on him. He was definitely watching us."

"Then a few minutes ago, he came over and offered to buy a round of drinks," presumably-Gary said.

Paul picked up the tale. "I told him thanks, but we were good. So he asked to join us."

"We said no," the other two chimed in.

"What happened?"

"He went back to his table and started watching us again." Paul ran a hand through his hair. "After a while he came over again and asked me to come outside with him. Said he heard I was a journalist and had something outside I might be interested in writing about."

"He addressed you specifically?" I asked.

"Yeah. Pointed at me."

"Then?"

"Then Stan and Gary kept him busy asking questions while I snuck out my phone and texted you. After that, I tried to keep him talking until you got here. You know, asked what it was he wanted to show me. Think he wised up someone was coming for him because he turned on his heel and walked out."

"Did he give a name?"

"Nope."

I paused again to raise Tim on the phone and confirmed Jules hadn't left his house all evening. Then I turned back toward the entrance to the bar. "Let's see if anyone in the place knows who he is."

No one did. We questioned the bartenders, the waitresses, and all the patrons, but no one could help us. The table in the corner had already been bussed, so any fingerprints were lost to us. The busboy had wiped the table down because of beer spilled on it.

When we finally left Roary's, Paul pulled out ahead of me, and I lagged two blocks behind to see if the mysterious van would attempt to follow him. It didn't. Nor was it anywhere in the vicinity of the house. Roy phoned to say no luck on spotting the white van.

I considered the evening a disaster, not only because we failed to nab the curious character from the bar, but also because Paul was so upset, Pedro failed to come out and play.

Chapter 21

I CONSIDERED last night's incident in the cold light of morning and found it not only frustrating but also conflicting. The white van was important to the cutie-pie murder cases only because I'd made it so by fixating on Jules McClintock as the likely killer. No one else had mentioned a van except for the lady who'd seen Petey Baca get into one on the day of his murder. It was also clear Jules was developing a *thing* for Paul. In fact, he made no secret of his interest. He'd denied us all entrance to his house—including two police officers—but openly invited Paul inside. He'd come by the house and left tea. He'd called Paul on our home phone. To be fair, he'd dialed our phone and it was Paul who answered. But I had no doubt he wanted Paul to come help him... not me.

This new van and its driver made no sense. The man obviously knew who Paul was. Probably followed him to Roary's. Knew he was a journalist. How?

Good lord! Was I goading a physically impaired man into insanity because I believed him guilty of something he didn't do? As was my practice, I added up the pros and cons, and the verdict still came down to Jules McClintock. *He* was the connection to Park House where Matt Zapata died. *He* was present when Wesley Strumph disappeared. He was the former lover of the murdered Burton Neville. This was not the time to take the pressure off Jules.

I WAS on the office phone bringing Roy Guerra up-to-date on our progress on the case—or lack thereof—when Tim called on my cell. I told Roy to hold while I answered my operative's call.

"BJ, get over here right away."

"What's going on?"

"A kid just went in McClintock's house."

"By a kid you mean…?"

"A big kid. Twenty or so. In the right age range for the murdering bastard."

I switched back to Roy and told him what was going on.

"Not against the law for someone to visit." His voice didn't match his words. He sounded worried.

"Maybe not, but I'm heading over there."

"Meet you there."

When Charlie and I arrived at Jules's Colorado Street address, Roy, Glenann, and a patrol cop were already standing on the sidewalk, talking to Tim.

"He's been in there about half an hour," Tim told us as we joined them.

"Hope he's still alive," Glenann said.

An itch played down the back of my neck. "Something's not right here."

"Do you think we have exigent circumstances?" Glenann asked her partner.

"Don't think so."

"So what do we do?" she came back at him.

"Maybe go ring the doorbell and ask to speak to McClintock's guest." Once again, Roy's words didn't match his tone.

"Something's not right," I repeated. "Roy, why don't you send the patrol car away. We're attracting attention."

"Hell, BJ, you had us park a patrol car here for a couple of weeks to *attract* attention."

"That was our doing. This is his move. I've got a bad feeling about this. Jules McClintock may be bold—reckless even—but he's not suicidal."

Glenann didn't want to let it go. "If we believe the man's in danger, don't we have a duty to act?"

"Uh-oh," Tim said. "Somebody's coming out."

We turned to watch a tall, pleasant-looking young man exit the house and step off the porch. We intercepted him as he headed for an aged Volkswagen bug parked across the street.

"Hold up a minute," Roy said, flashing his shield. "We want to talk to you."

The youth, who looked a little older on closer inspection, halted in the middle of the street.

"Yeah?"

"What's your name?" Roy asked.

"Hal Clarkson. Why?"

"Why were you in Jules McClintock's house?"

"Hey, man, it's a free country. I can visit anybody I want."

"That didn't answer my question."

"That's personal, man. Not none of your business."

"Are you a friend of his?"

The kid shrugged. "Kinda. Yeah, I guess you could say that."

I glanced at the house. Jules stood in the doorway, watching the confrontation with interest. My unease increased.

"How long have you known him?" Roy persisted.

"What's going on? I gotta go."

"Not till I say you can."

"Am I under arrest or something?"

"No, we want to talk to you about—"

"Well, I don't wanna talk to you. I'm leaving."

Glenann stepped in front of the youth. "We can have this conversation down at the police station if you'd rather."

Before the kid could get the words out of his mouth, the pin dropped. He was going to ask for a lawyer.

"I wanna call my lawyer."

"Who happens to be Laurence Bingman, I'll bet," I said.

The kid glanced up from a piece of paper he'd fished out of his pocket. "How'd you know?"

"Guys, we're being set up. Jules lured us here on purpose."
I threw a thumb at Clarkson. "He probably found this guy on a
call-boy website and—"

"Who you calling a call boy?" Clarkson interrupted.

"Would punkass whore sound better to you?" Glenann
snapped. "Shut up and let the grown-ups talk."

"Jules wants us to make a scene so Bingman can claim
police harassment. Bingman's Jules's lawyer."

"All right, get outa here," Roy told Clarkson. "And
consider yourself lucky."

"Yeah, right. Lucky," the kid said as he stalked away.

"He doesn't know how lucky," Charlie said. "Let's clear
out before Bingman shows up. Jules has probably already
called him."

As we drove back to the office, Charlie got Hazel on the
line and asked her to check a Hal or Harold Clarkson. By the time
we arrived she'd found his record. Two busts for prostitution.
Slap on the wrist for both. She'd also located his website, where
a considerably slicked up young man in a revealing muscle
shirt stared into a camera and offered his personal services
to all comers. That's likely where Jules found the kid—kid,
he was twenty-three according to his jacket. I wondered how
much it cost Jules to have the guy ignore his gross obesity. But I
suspected sex wasn't Jules's primary goal. It was to provoke us
into doing something rash.

Before the afternoon was out, Larry Bingman called to
lodge his harassment complaint, but it didn't have the effect
Jules intended because we'd backed off from the situation.

PUNCH, COUNTERPUNCH. Was that what this was coming
down to? Jules was likely enjoying this a lot more than I was,
regardless of the eventual outcome. Was this an additional
motive for the killings? Was this a grotesque game of cat and

mouse? Whatever, it was time for another punch. I got on the intercom to Hazel.

"Bring me the morgue photos of all the cutie-pie victims and ask Charlie to join us in my office, please."

A minute later Charlie strolled in and took a seat at my small conference table in the corner. We sat mute until Hazel bustled in with photos in hand.

"What's up?" Charlie asked.

"Time to apply more pressure to Jules McClintock."

"How?"

I reached over and tapped the morgue pictures lying in front of Hazel. "With these."

Charlie's eyebrows climbed. "By…?"

"Reinterviewing his neighbors and asking if they've ever seen these men at Jules's house."

"We've already done that."

"Not with these pictures."

Hazel sputtered before getting the words out. "That's… that's grotesque."

"And likely to get us sued," Charlie added after leafing through the photos.

"Not only that, but I want Alan and Tim to intercept every pupil arriving for math lessons and ask the same question of the adults delivering them."

"That *will* get us sued," Charlie said. "You might as well outright accuse the man of murder. And he's already had a lawyer contact us twice."

"We're not doing anything prohibited by law."

"Maybe not. But his lawyer's gonna yell harassment and interfering with the man's livelihood and who knows what else."

"He'll use the city's public nuisance ordinance," Hazel said. "Or the two state ordinances."

"City shouldn't be a problem. We're not hiding or intruding on private property without permission." I wrinkled my nose. "State might be more of a problem. Those cover public property, which probably includes the street. But they do have a 'without lawful purpose' clause. Preventing a murder should cover that."

"He could get a restraining order," Charlie said.

"So we'll move down the street. But we'll have shown his neighbors the pictures by then."

Hazel gave me the fisheye. "You're determined to do this, aren't you?"

"I want to, but you're partners in this firm, so you have a stake in it as well. I won't do it without your consent."

Charlie slapped the table. "Do it."

Hazel was slower to agree.

That evening when I told Paul what I intended, he high-fived me and insisted on participating in the new canvass, even though I didn't want him within five miles of Jules McClintock.

BRIGHT AND early Monday morning, Charlie, Paul, and I—armed with photocopies of the morgue pictures—descended upon Jules's neighborhood to knock on doors. Alan parked in front of the house and intercepted the parents of arriving students. When I ultimately reached the Hormel door, Mercy took one look and turned pale. Her nose did everything but speak. She closed the door on me halfway through my spiel, opened it again quickly to shove the offending photos into my hands, and slammed it again. The message had been delivered.

I was stepping off the Hormels' porch when Larry Bingman arrived... with *his* nose out of joint. "What the hell are you doing, B. J. Vinson? You're tromping all over my client's rights."

"How, pray tell?" I said, keeping my face straight. "I'm conducting a legal and ethical investigation of Jules McClintock as a person of interest in the murder of seven young men. Eight, if you count his former lover."

Larry blanched. "Wh-what?"

"Didn't your client tell you what this was all about? You've contacted me twice before on his behalf. Didn't you even know what was going on? Here, take a look." I shoved the photos into his hand.

He blinked several times as he scanned them. "This is virtually accusing my client of murdering these men. You can't do that without some sort of proof."

"Not so. I'm asking the neighbors if they've ever seen these men with Jules McClintock or at his home."

Larry shifted from foot to foot, his face turning red enough for me to worry about his blood pressure. "Photos of *dead* men? This has gotten out of hand. I'm seeing a judge this afternoon for a restraining order."

"Fine with me."

He eyed me for a moment. "You'll move your stakeout a block down the street."

"Possibly. Or perhaps we're about finished here."

"Are you?" he pressed.

A car pulled into Jules's driveway and disgorged a tyke for his math lesson. Fortunately, Alan had sense enough not to confront the mother delivering him.

"To answer your question, I'll have to check with APD detectives Roy Guerra and Glenann Hastings. We're working on this together."

Larry's complexion had returned to normal, so I ceased to worry about his health. "Are you seriously telling me Jules didn't tell you he was being investigated as what the press is calling the cutie-pie murderer?"

"Not exactly."

"Meaning?"

"He said you were trying to tie him to the murder of a young man at the Park House, a place he's never set foot in. One young man, not seven." He ran a hand through his hair, mussing it and ruining his image of a buttoned-down lawyer. "But what we're discussing is your harassment of my client."

"I don't see it that way. I'm doing my job and trying to keep any other young men from being killed."

"You'll have the restraining order by this afternoon."

"Just leave it with Hazel at the office, and I'll consider it served."

When we arrived back at the office, Hazel gave us a sour look when I told her what to expect. She didn't exactly say "I told you so," but her frown was about as expressive as Mercy Hormel's nose.

"Any luck in finding the driver of the white van who approached Paul at Roary's Thursday night?"

"Not with the information you gave me. You're a trained investigator, BJ. You should have been able to give me more. Like a license plate, for example."

"Sorry, but I wasn't close to the van, and I was intent on answering Paul's distress call. But it was a Caravan."

She sighed and rubbed her upper lip. "I've tried matching all the registered owners I can find with police records but can't find anyone who comes close to the description of the driver you and Paul gave me."

"I remember something I forgot to tell you," Paul said. "The guy had a tattoo on the back of his hand."

"What kind of tattoo?" I asked.

"Which hand?" Charlie said.

Paul held his hands out, palms down, and shifted them back and forth with his eyes closed. "Right one. An anchor. Black and red."

"And I noticed a scar on his right cheek when he rushed past me in the doorway," I said.

Hazel's moue spoke volumes as she turned back to her keyboard. "Thanks for telling me. Trained investigators, for crying out loud."

Paul and Charlie trailed me into my office while Hazel went to work checking scars and tattoos against convicted felons.

Paul dropped into one of the client chairs opposite my desk. "We did our thing. So what do you think Jules's next move will be?"

Charlie lowered his spare frame into the other chair. "If he's smart, nothing."

We sat staring at one another, trying to get into Jules McClintock's mind, until Hazel came in.

"Here are some possibles," she said, laying three images on my desk. "Three thugs with anchor tattoos."

Paul and I both pointed to the same mug shot.

"That's him," I said.

"Definitely," Paul added.

"Henry Motts," I read aloud. "Thirty-three, two arrests, one conviction. Mugging. Spent a year in Santa Fe."

"No sex crimes?" Charlie asked.

"No indication of it," she said.

I tapped his mug shot. "Gaydar doesn't work too well on a photograph, but I'd bet this guy isn't gay. Did you get any feeling, Paul?"

"Nope. Had trouble figuring out why he was so intent on joining us to buy a round of drinks."

"Let's go ask him," I suggested. "He works at Macinas Upholstery Shop on North Fourth."

"I'll meet you at North Fourth. After that, I'm on my way home." His car was in the parking lot downstairs.

"Let's see if we can find a little more about him first. Hazel, go do your thing."

We took turns studying Motts's jacket until Hazel rejoined us. "He doesn't leave much of a footprint. Single, never been married so far as I can find out. Seems to be a loner. Worked at the upholstery shop for three years. Took the job right after he got out of prison. No trouble since then."

VERY FEW people look worse than their mug shot, but Henry Motts accomplished the deed. Not ugly exactly, but he was

Hollywood's proverbial bad-guy type. His demeanor matched his appearance.

"What the fuck do you want?" he demanded in a near shout when we entered the upholstery shop.

"Talk to you a minute," I called over the shoulder of the woman manning the front desk.

"Git outa here. Ain't got time to talk."

"You wanted to talk the other night," Paul said. "You wanted to buy me a drink. I had the feeling you were in a romantic mood."

Good old Paul. He's usually right on the mark, but sometimes he goes overboard. If there hadn't been a counter between us, I believe Motts would have charged. As it was, he swaggered right up to it, frightening the woman manning the till.

"Shut your mouth, you little fag." I guess Paul was "little" to a man of Motts's size.

"At least I know who I am," my companion continued. "I'm guessing you're hiding your lamp under a basket."

Motts didn't bother with the gate; he started scrambling straight over the counter. Paul wanted to stand his ground, but I jerked him backward as two men from the shop grabbed Motts's arms, frustrating his efforts.

The better part of valor was probably a headlong flight, but I planted myself squarely in front of Paul. "Mr. Motts, we only want to ask you some questions about the other night. We can do it here, or we can call the cops and do it down at their house."

Motts settled into a sulky mood as he eyed us with a speculative look. "I need a cigarette. I'm going out back."

Not certain what we were walking into, Paul and I pushed through the gate and followed the man's aggressively masculine stride through open back doors. The shop was a busy place. Half a dozen men ignored us as they worked on reupholstering a torn couch or refurbishing a worn chair. Motts plodded outside the building and around the corner. He turned to face us as we caught up with him.

"Just so's you know it, I ain't no queer."

"Then why'd you follow me into Roary's the other night? Why'd you try to buy us a round of drinks? Join us, even?"

"Being friendly. I'm new in town."

"You've worked here for three years," I said. "Before that you were in Santa Fe making license plates. I'm not here to cause trouble, but I do expect straight answers."

"And you didn't follow me to Roary's to be friendly."

Damn, Paul was going to jam us up again.

Motts waved some ash from his cigarette and let it go. "Okay, so somebody paid for me to harass your butt."

"Who?" both of us asked at the same time.

The big man shrugged. On him, it looked like a threat. "Dunno. Buddy of mine said he heard someone was looking for a dude with a white van to do him a favor. Willing to pay for it."

"Who was this friend?"

"Name won't do you no good. I asked him who was paying and what for. He didn't know. He was talking to somebody else who was talking to some muck on a computer. But the dude got my money to me right away."

"How much?"

"Fifty, if it's any of your business."

"How'd you get paid?"

"Half up front. Other half after I hassled you in the bar."

"How'd it come?"

"Buddy who told me about it paid me. Hell, it was easy money for me, but then I found out he got paid for lining me up."

From the glower on Motts's face, I wasn't sure the buddy got to keep his cut. We argued through two more cigarette butts, but he wouldn't give up the name of his contact.

"What were your instructions?" Paul asked. "What were you supposed to do to me?"

"Keep you occupied. Talk to you. Get you to leave with me."

"And go where?" I asked.

"Shit, I don't know. Supposed to get him to leave the bar with me. Once I done that, I was done. I figured the guy footing the bill was in the bar somewhere." Motts threw a thick thumb Paul's way. "Figured this guy had his hooks into a money bag and the guy wanted to cut him loose. If sugar daddy seen him leave with me, that'd give him an excuse."

"But he didn't leave with you, and you got paid anyway."

"So I was wrong. Maybe he didn't make it to the bar in time."

"How did you know what bar to meet Paul in?"

"Didn't. The guy give me an address, and I waited down the street. Sat on my butt for two nights before this one roared outa the drive in his black Charger. Then I tailed him."

Mrs. Wardlow wasn't up to her usual standards as neighborhood watchman if this guy waited two nights for Paul to boogie. Nonetheless, I studied Motts a minute and decided he was telling it straight… at least as he saw it.

"How did you tell the guy paying you what bar I was in?" Paul asked.

Motts shrugged. "Didn't."

"Then why did you figure he was there waiting for you to pick me up?"

"I don't know, man. You're trying to confuse me."

I stepped in to calm things down. "Now let me fill you in on something, Motts. The guy who hired you to go harass Paul is probably the cutie-pie murderer."

Motts scratched his nose. "The who?"

"The guy who's been killing young men and dumping them naked all over the place drives a white van. That's why he needed somebody with a white van. He was setting you up for one big fall. He probably asked for an ex-con for the job. There

are two APD detectives named Guerra and Hastings who are
going to want to talk to you."

"Hey, man! I didn't kill nobody."

"You know what? I believe you. But I'm not sure the
APD will. The more you can tell us, the better."

That pried his tongue from the roof of his mouth, but all he
could tell us was the name of his buddy. That led us to a slightly
more intelligent hood who led us to a geek who made his living
off a computer. I'd bet he was more successful at parting people
from their money than the other two. Even so, when we found
him, all he could do was give up a link called baldbrownguy@
innet.com. Jules was neither bald nor brown, but I was willing
to bet he was our guy.

Roy and Glenann hauled them all down to the station, but
in the end, they got no further than we did. The IPO address was
used once and then abandoned. We could spend a year trying
to pry the ID of the owner out of the carrier, but in the end the
result would likely be the same—a dead end. Even so, the two
detectives started the process. No stone left unturned.

But the episode did give me a possible answer for
something puzzling me. Jules—or at least the killer—probably
found Matt Zapata by scrolling the internet. We had Matt's laptop
computer, and both Paul and Hazel had searched for Matt's site
without success. I had them try again even though considerable
time had passed since Matt's death. But I had no idea how such
sites are paid for. By the week? Month? Year?

It didn't matter; they came up dry.

Chapter 22

TUESDAY'S DAWN painted every cloud in the sky a range of hues from the blush of a young girl's cheek to the pink bubblegum she might have chewed. Beautiful. I know because I was standing in the backyard, taking it all in. My sleep had been so restless, I was afraid of waking Paul. No use heading for another bedroom. I wouldn't catch the sandman again this morning. With nothing better to do, I wandered into the backyard and took in nature's awakening.

I had to stop this. I took all my cases seriously and experienced frustration often, but I was letting this duel between Jules McClintock and me become personal... something that violated every rule I held dear. I'd worked this case for two whole months—sixty-two days if I remembered correctly—and was standing helplessly in my backyard while Jules, a man not far removed from being physically helpless, doubtless slept peacefully in his bed, untroubled by my efforts.

For the first time, I *seriously* considered doing something illegal to break the case. Illegal how? Break into his house and find a supply of zopiclone, the drug he used on his victims. See what was in that building at the rear of his property. Better yet, find Strumph's DNA in the box freezer in Jules's garage.

That was as far as I got in my ruminations. If I lost my principles, what was next? I'd no longer be a confidential investigator, I'd be a PI, like Bogey or Robert Mitchum in the old film noir flicks: do anything to clear a case and earn a buck. Principles be damned! No, that wasn't me.

After thanking God's beautiful dawn for clearing my head, I turned back into the house to make coffee and repair

to the home office where I scoured—for the umpteenth time—
every scrap of paper, every photograph having to do with the
cutie-pie murders. The Good Lord only carried me so far. He
failed to reach out with a holy finger and indicate a detail I'd
overlooked.

By the time I heard Paul in the shower at around six thirty,
I'd determined on a face-off with my principal suspect. Hell,
my *only* suspect. I got up and fixed a passable ham-and-eggs
breakfast, nothing as fancy or as tasty as my loving companion
prepared for me, but then ham and eggs are at the upper end of
my gastronomic efforts. Tuna salad is at the other.

Looking freshly scrubbed and handsome as hell, Paul
eyed me as he tackled my pitiful breakfast, seemingly with
gusto. "Couldn't sleep?"

"Restless. Afraid I'd bother you."

His look of concern melted my heart. "Don't let Jules get
to you."

"I'm not having much luck getting to *him*."

"So what do you do next?"

"Gonna face him down."

"I'll go with you. He won't let you inside his house
without me."

"I'm glad you recognize it's you he's fixating on."

"Hard not to."

"But you can't come with me. I don't expect to get inside
the house, but he'll probably talk to me with the screen door
between us without calling his lawyer."

"What about the restraining order?"

"So far as I know, there isn't one yet. I'll go straight from
here to Colorado Street so I can claim innocence if one's been
delivered this morning."

"Wouldn't Hazel call you?"

"That's what I'll claim if I run afoul of one."

"What do you hope to accomplish?"

"Just to let him know Larry Bingman hasn't succeeded in running me off. I'm still on the case. He's still in danger."

"Seems kinda puny."

"It is, but it's what I'm reduced to at the moment." I thought for a second. "But maybe it isn't. Tim and Alan are keeping him tied down. He knows his chances of evading them long enough to pick up another victim are slim to none. The steam ought to be building up again. And my smirking in his face might help push him into something rash."

"That's about all we've got left, isn't it?"

"Sometimes I feel like I'm pushing the guy to go kill somebody so maybe I can catch him in the act. What kind of investigator does that make me? Hell, what kind of human being?"

Paul's smile turned weak. Not at all reassuring.

I BRAKED the Impala beside Alan's car and rolled down the window. "Anything happening?"

"Hasn't shown his face this morning."

"You sure he's in there?"

"Don't see how he could get out. Front door, garage door, and gate to the backyard are all clearly visible. He's in there. What are you up to?"

"Gonna beard the lion in his den."

"Thought the lawyer was getting an order."

"So far as I know, it's not come through yet. Wish me luck."

I rolled up the window and illegally parked on the left side of the street in front of the house. Mercy Hormel's side curtain flicked.

For a minute, I thought Jules wasn't going to answer my ring. But eventually he yanked the door open and rolled his chair up to the screen.

"Paul with you?"

"Afraid not."

"Then go away. You're good-looking enough, but you're too old."

"You like them young and fresh, huh?"

"Just like you do, B. J. Vinson. You and me, we're not all that different."

"Oh, there's a world of difference. Invite me in, and we can discuss those differences."

Bitterness displaced his bland look. "I used to look like you. Handsome. Trim. They all liked me in those days. I got some guys didn't even know they were gay." He gave a harsh laugh. "Probably weren't, but they went for me anyway."

I kept my voice soft, consoling. "I remember, Jules. You were one of the most spectacular young men I'd ever seen. Not many men can be called beautiful, but you were one of them. Everyone envied Burton Neville."

His mouth turned down, and his jowls jiggled. "Yeah. Was. And then I wasn't. And everybody ran the other way. Good old Burton led the pack. God, how I hated him!"

"Maybe he'd have come around. I'm sure your illness was a shock to him as well."

"Yeah, sure. Came around to another live-in lover. And then he ran away to California or somewhere."

"A man goes where his work takes him, Jules."

"Had a good job right here. Good enough to live in a fancy high-rise. Did you see that—" Jules bit his tongue.

I tried to keep the eagerness out of my voice. Damn, I hoped the digital voice recorder on my belt was doing its job. "See what?"

"That fancy front door to the place. Must cost a fortune to live there."

"When did you see the door to his new place?"

"Every time I drive up and down Central Avenue."

"Thought you didn't know he had moved from the Montgomery apartment."

"Didn't till you told me. Now I see those damned doors in my sleep. I stay off of Central whenever I can."

"Jules, I told you Neville had moved. I didn't tell you where."

"You said on East Central."

"East Central's a long street."

"You told me it was Park House," Jules insisted.

"No, I didn't. But I have my tapes. It won't be hard to look it up." I softened my tone. "Let me in, and we'll talk about the old times. Make you feel better."

He mustered a leer. "Only one way to make me feel better. Back in the day, you'd a hopped on it in a minute. How about it? You game?"

"I'm committed, Jules. And I don't violate commitments. Not then and not now."

"Yeah, I've seen your commitment. B. J. Vinson came out on top again. Eating high on the hog, like always." His demeanor turned thunderous. He rolled his chair back. "Why're you here, anyway? You're violating my lawyer's restraining order."

"So far as I know, I haven't been served."

"If you haven't been, you will be." He slammed the door in my face.

I walked back to my car feeling uneasy. Oh well, I'd intended to poke the bear, hadn't I? And it sure hadn't taken much. And that address thing might just pay off.

I ARRIVED back at the office to learn no restraining order had shown up and in time to field an irate call from Zancón Zapata. I told Hazel to decline to accept the charges but changed my mind. I'd no sooner answered the call than he unloaded on me.

"Two fucking months and you ain't delivered yet."

"I'll be happy to go off the payroll. I'll even refund what your brother's paid me already."

That brought a silence on the line. "You giving up? You ain't up to the job?"

"I don't put up with abuse from my clients. And I particularly don't put up with breaking into my office."

"You can't put that—"

"Of course I can. Lothario Stevens poured his heart out to the cops. Where the hell did you find some guy named Lothario?"

"Don't know none. And he can yak all he wants. He's got no connection to me."

"If I was interested enough, I'd find the connection, Zancón. But you know what? I don't give a damn. This is the last call I'm going to accept from you, and I only paid the charges this time to deliver a message. Don't fuck with my office or my people. Your brother's my client. Not you. I'm hanging up now, and I won't accept any more collect calls from the prison."

His voice went reasonable. "Now wait a minute. I get frustrated, that's all. Gotta vent on somebody. Leastways, that's what the shrink up here says."

"Find someone else to vent on."

"Sorry, man. Anything new?"

"I keep your brother up-to-date on the progress of the case. Get it from him."

"He tells me you know who it is. Who snuffed my nephew."

"Knowing it and proving it are two different things."

"I already told you, if you know, that's enough for me."

"I'm not about to give you a name. When this guy goes down, he goes down legally."

"Them wasn't the terms—"

"Not yours, maybe. But it's what Juan and I settled on. And like I said, he's my client."

"I hear this bozo's killed five or six young guys. Ain't doin' it my way worth it to get a crazy off the streets?"

"I hope you realize you're asking me to kill somebody over a prison line someone's probably monitoring."

"Ain't saying that at all. Just saying you might cut some corners to make the case. Offering some help in that direction if you need it."

"No, thanks. Don't call again."

I hung up hoping Zancón was jamming himself up with the prison administration. I knew the warden, and he was a no-nonsense guy. How long before a transcript of our conversation landed on his desk? This wasn't the first time the con had indicated he wanted a permanent resolution to his nephew's murder, and apparently Zancón hadn't yet paid a price.

I opened the case file and started looking through transcriptions of my recordings for the conversation I'd had about Neville's move from the Montgomery Boulevard apartment. Ten minutes later, I found it. On Paul's and my first visit to Jules on Wednesday, March 28. We were discussing Matt's murder in Neville's apartment, and Jules said he wasn't aware of a murder in the Sandalwood Apartments. I'd come back with "No, Neville's new place on East Central."

I scoured the rest of the transcription but there was nothing more specific than that. I sat back to consider how to best take advantage of Jules's slipup, but before I reached a decision, my cell phone rang. All I heard was a muffled, unintelligible voice.

"Hello! Who's there?"

"B... J, unh."

"Alan, is that you?"

"Help.... McClintock...."

"Be right there!"

I grabbed the .25 caliber semiautomatic Colt I sometimes carry from my desk drawer and bolted out the door, shouting Alan was in trouble. By the time I roared out of the parking lot, I spied Charlie making for his car. Fortunately, I didn't pick up a traffic cop in my race to the Heights.

Alan's gray Ford pickup was parked on the east side of Colorado Street, about half a block south of Jules's house. There did not appear to be anyone in it. I pulled up behind the vehicle and bailed. As soon as I reached the driver's side window, I saw him slumped across the bench seat. Charlie screeched to a halt behind my car as I raced around to the passenger's door. Between us, we got Alan out of the truck and onto a patch of grass. He didn't seem totally unconscious, but he wasn't able to communicate very well. I resorted to the question-and-answer method.

"Jules?"

"Uhnn."

"Blink once for yes, twice for no," I said. "Jules?"

One blink.

"He attack you? Drug you?"

Alan blinked once and moved his left arm. I grabbed it and spotted the puncture on his forearm.

My operative took a deep breath and made a tremendous effort. "Rolled up. Asked question. Jabbed m…."

"Did he leave the house?"

A slight shrug.

"You call for help for Alan while I check," I told Charlie.

I raced up the street with mayhem on my mind. No one responded to a good pounding on the door, so I went to the garage. I could no longer see through the little windows. Jules had covered the insides to prevent anyone from looking in. Without thinking about it twice, I poked my pistol through one of them. It was dark inside, but I could make out that Jules's new van was missing.

Charlie had Alan sitting in the passenger seat of the pickup by the time I returned and confirmed Jules was on the loose.

"S-sorry, BJ," Alan slurred.

"Not your fault. I knew I'd poked him hard this morning, but I didn't have any idea he'd do something this rash. Shoulda warned you."

Charlie rubbed his bald head. "Sure hope some kid doesn't pay the penalty for McClintock being on the loose."

"Probably should warn Roy and Glenann."

Charlie fixed me with a steely blue eye. "Probably should warn Paul first."

"Paul!" I shouted as I ran for my Impala. "My God! Warn the detectives. I'll call Paul from the car."

As soon as I got the Impala moving, I hit a couple of buttons and let my car's synced system dial Paul's cell. No answer.

Damn, why had this happened at the noon hour? Traffic clogged the streets. But I needed to get to Paul, so I broke laws left and right, including recklessly crossing into oncoming traffic whenever I could squeeze through. It seemed a lifetime before I raced north on Fourth, this time *praying* I'd pick up a traffic cop and pull him along in my wake. Despite my recklessness, I didn't break any records in reaching the house.

The hair on my neck rose as I barreled around the corner and saw McClintock's white van parked behind Paul's Charger. Oh Lord! *Am I too late?* I screeched to a halt jaywonky in the drive to block the van, bailed out of the Impala with the little Colt .25 in my hand. My Ruger was in the trunk. Vaulting the back gate, I slowed down at the rear door and sought to enter quietly. The way my heart was pounding, silence didn't seem likely. No one in the kitchen. Same for the living room and den. Then I heard a noise from one of the bedrooms. A grunt and a moan.

I eased down the hall and checked our bedroom. No one. Keeping to the wall, I made my way to the third bedroom at the far end of the hall. The door was ajar. I pushed, and the silent hinges gave way. My blood ran cold. A huge, naked figure sprawled across Paul, fat buttocks jiggling obscenely as he thrust. God!

Why wasn't Paul fighting him? Was he already dead? A moan from my lover released my paralyzed muscles.

I dashed forward and clubbed McClintock's head with the barrel of the little revolver. He merely grunted and rolled aside. Trying to see if Paul was all right, I almost didn't react to the fat man reaching for me until it was too late. I swiveled and fired three times. Flesh quivered as the bullets struck and made little reddish holes in McClintock's chest. He halted momentarily, then lurched off the bed, coming for me. His massive body sent us both to the floor. I lost my semiautomatic. McClintock's hands reached for my throat. I poked my thumbs into his eyes. He howled, and the pressure on my throat eased. Gasping for breath, I managed to roll the huge man off me and stagger to my feet.

McClintock was already upright, seemingly unaffected by three slugs in his body. I sidestepped his lunge, and he crashed into the wall, dislodging a framed landscape and sending it crashing to the floor. I planted a hard elbow into his kidney, but he merely grunted. The rage in the man's eyes seemed to drive him, give him strength, overcome his disability. He turned with arms spread wide to scoop me into them. I backed away. He lumbered forward. I was cornered unless I wanted to lead him back to the bed, back toward Paul.

I lowered my head and drove a shoulder into his bloated belly. Sour breath spilled out of him; otherwise, my effort had no effect. He clubbed me on the back of the head with a massive fist, driving me to the floor facedown. Then he was on me like a sumo wrestler, the weight of his torso pressing me into the carpet, one arm around my throat. Even in my panic, I sensed he was weakening, but that availed me little. He could have passed out completely, and the weight of his body and the pressure of his arm on my neck would kill me. I managed to get my knees beneath me and get some leverage, but it helped only a little.

My head buzzed. My sight grew blurred. In moments, I would lose consciousness.

I dimly heard three muted pops, and the full weight of McClintock's body pressed down on me, shutting off my windpipe completely. Then the pressure eased. Barely aware someone was trying to pull McClintock off me, I gathered enough strength to bow my back. That did the trick. He rolled off, and I managed to turn over and gulp lungsful of air. Needed to get to my feet. Continue the battle.

As my eyesight cleared, I saw a naked Paul standing over me, my little Colt dangling from his hand.

"V-Vince," he croaked before dropping to the floor.

Panicked, I crawled to him, forgetful of any danger McClintock represented. Cradling my lover's head in my lap, I caressed his cheek and moaned his name until I managed to see he was breathing regularly. Relieved, I figured out my struggle with McClintock had roused Paul from his drugged sleep enough to find my discarded pistol and save my life. Only then did I look at the mound of flesh that had been Jules McClintock. He lay sprawled on his back, blue eyes staring at nothing, leaking blood from the top of his head where Paul had shot him. Mateo Zapata's murderer—the cutie-pie killer—was dead, just as Zancón had wanted.

Roy and Glenann showed up almost at the same time as three patrol cars arrived to clog our little piece of Post Oak Drive. By then, I'd put an unconscious Paul on the bed in our room—I didn't want him sharing space with the corpse of his would-be killer—and covered him with a sheet. By the time I admitted the two detectives and the other responding cops, my mate was paler than usual, but his breathing was steady.

I walked the detectives through what had happened and agreed to bring Paul down to give his own statement as soon as possible. I'd already called the EMTs, who were examining my companion as we spoke.

I wasn't in a very good physical and emotional state myself, so Roy and Glenann said they'd cut it short and complete the interview tomorrow. I was about to assent when one of the attending ambulance techs said he wanted Paul for an overnight stay at the hospital to be on the safe side. I wholeheartedly agreed with safe and told him I'd help Paul get dressed.

Then I turned to the detectives and told them to do everything by the book, including having the crime scene unit come out and do their thing. They could test for gunshot residue on Paul at the hospital.

After Paul was on his way, I hung around long enough to be tested for GSR and then started for the UNM Hospital trauma center where they'd taken Paul. I didn't make it out of the driveway without having to stop and fill in Gertrude Wardlow on every detail of what had happened. I've often claimed ours is a geriatric neighborhood, with Paul and even me being the pesky teenagers in the area. As I pulled away, residents up and down the street stood on their porches, taking in all the activity. I hoped police cars and ambulances weren't too much for their aging hearts. Doubtless all were asking what the detective fellow at 5229 was up to now.

Chapter 23

THE NEXT morning, I woke feeling as if my brain were twisted into knots. Yesterday seemed like an unreal nightmare, but the bruises on my body put the lie to that. It had been real. All too real.

I showed up at APD headquarters early and gave my formal statement before heading for the hospital. Big surprise, Hazel was already there and mothering a perfectly healthy and vital Paul. Although I thought she'd probably object to Paul's release, she didn't. But I had to talk a blue streak to keep her from going home with us and tucking him into bed.

"The crime scene boys haven't turned over the premises to us yet."

"So you come home with me and put him to bed there."

Paul, now fully dressed and ambulatory, spoke up. "I don't need a bed. Heck, Hazel, I don't even have a high left from the drug he gave me."

"Tell you what," I said, "we'll come straight to the office and hang out there until they give us our house back."

That seemed acceptable so long as Paul agreed to spend an hour or two lying on the waiting-room couch. Hazel grabbed her purse and headed for the parking structure.

On the ride to the office, Paul was quieter than usual, but once he started asking questions, I figured he was on the mend.

"He was on top of me?" he asked.

"That he was."

He shivered. "Oh God! Did… did…?"

"No. You weren't violated, unless you consider having a three-hundred-pound quivering lump of flesh humping your belly as a violation. Do you remember anything? How did he get in the house?"

Paul nodded. "I remember that much. Someone knocked on the back door. When I opened the kitchen door, I saw a box sitting there. A box like something UPS would deliver. When I opened the screen and stepped outside, he stabbed me in the arm with a needle."

"Didn't you see him standing there?"

"He was at the side of the door. Didn't see him until he moved. Then it was too late. After that, everything's a blur. I can see movement inside my head, but nothing makes sense." He paused and focused on me. "I really shot him?"

"You really shot him. But if you hadn't, I'd have been a goner. You saved my life."

A glint of humor came into the eyes that always made me think of dark chocolate. "So we're even now. You saved my ass from the Brown Saints, and I saved yours from the cutie-pie killer. And are you sure he was trying to kill you, or was he just 'making love'?"

I smiled, pleased he was joking, a sign of recovery. "Either way, he deserved to be shot."

We'd settled in my office when my cell phone went off.

"BJ, how's Paul?" Roy asked.

"Recovered. He'll be in tomorrow to give his statement."

"Not what I'm calling about. You need to get over here to McClintock's place. You and Paul both, if he's up to it."

Ten minutes later, Roy admitted us through Jules's front door and Glenann led us out the back to the little building at the rear of the property. I gasped aloud as I stepped through the door. I heard Paul grunt.

"Puts to rest any question of who the cutie-pie killer was, doesn't it?" Glenann said.

"And now we know what he did with their clothes," Roy added.

The place was filled with department store mannequins arranged artfully around the room. Seven of them were dressed, three were not. A hand-printed placard was propped at the foot of each of the seven clothed mannequins. The closest one read: "Dustin Greene, September 3, 2011. You weren't as tough as you thought you were." There was no question in my mind the clothing was what the unfortunate young man wore on the day he died.

Matt's read: "Mateo Zapata, March 5, 2012. The loveliest of them all. You matched the style of the elegant apartment where we made love."

While Jules's seven cutie-pie victims each had his own epitaph, his former lover, Burton Neville, didn't rate a mannequin or a placard. But then, his was a different kind of killing.

Paul was silent for a long while as he moved from each memorial to the next, snapping photos with his phone camera. Finally, he walked over to where the rest of us stood. "This leaves so many questions unanswered."

"Like what?" Glenann asked.

"Like the blue paint on the window of the white van that picked up Petey Baca."

"Pretty much like BJ figured. We found magnetic panels in the garage. He put them over the windows, not the side panels. Also found a set of Arizona plates."

"McClintock didn't keep a diary, but he journaled something about all the cutie-pie killings," Roy said.

"It doesn't cover Neville?" Paul asked.

"Bare bones. He learned Neville was leaving for California and cajoled him into a meeting in Socorro. Why Socorro? Who knows? It's not far from Albuquerque and no one knew McClintock there. Might be as simple as that."

"Any clue as to what set him off on the boys?"

"I think it was Neville. According to the journal, it turns out Neville was the first killing, not the second. Strangling his former sugar daddy gave him a lot of pleasure. The way he put it, Neville had atoned for the way he abandoned McClintock after he got sick."

"But why the others?" Paul asked.

"McClintock picked up Dustin Greene," Roy said, "supposedly giving him a ride back downtown. On the way, they sucked on beers. When McClintock propositioned the kid, Dustin laughed in his face. Made fun of his weight. But he'd already ingested the drug. So McClintock drove to the West Mesa, did his thing with the guy, and then killed Greene because the kid had made fun of him."

He turned to my companion. "Paul, you'll be interested to know McClintock pretty well confirmed what we thought. Despite Greene's obvious horror, he firmed right up when the pervert masturbated him."

Paul looked neither pleased nor displeased. I think the word pervert bothered him. Although McClintock was perverted big-time.

"Anything about how Jules contacted the Strumph kid?" I asked.

"Guess that'll remain an unsolved mystery."

Glenann picked up the tale again. "He wrote a lot about Zapata. Matt was the only one he planned well ahead of time. Saw Matt's ad on a boy-love site and did just that… fell in love. He wrote about the kid from the time he fixated on him until he killed him. Thanked Neville several times for the key card. And you'll find this interesting. He made two prior trips to the Park House before the date with Matt. His journal said he didn't meet a soul on any of the three trips he made to the apartment building."

"Amazing," I said. "The rest of them were targets of opportunity, then."

"Right. I know I'm not supposed to say this, but I'm glad you guys killed the SOB."

I glanced at my mate. His face was a mask. But I silently agreed with Glenann—and even Zancón. Jules McClintock deserved to die. But I wished I'd done it instead of Paul. Killing another human being, no matter the circumstances, always leaves a scar.

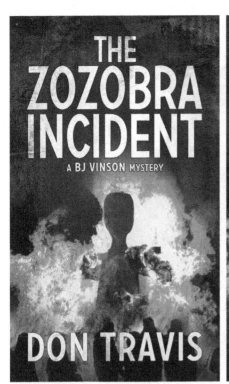

THE
ZOZOBRA
INCIDENT
A BJ VINSON MYSTERY

DON TRAVIS

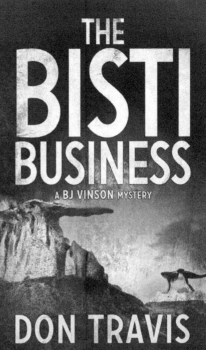

THE
BISTI
BUSINESS
A BJ VINSON MYSTERY

DON TRAVIS

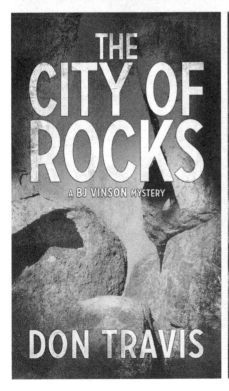

THE
CITY OF
ROCKS
A BJ VINSON MYSTERY

DON TRAVIS

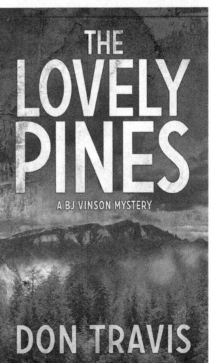

THE
LOVELY
PINES
A BJ VINSON MYSTERY

DON TRAVIS

ABADDON'S LOCUSTS

A BJ VINSON MYSTERY

DON TRAVIS

A BJ Vinson Mystery

When BJ Vinson, confidential investigator, learns his young friend, Jazz Penrod, has disappeared and has not been heard from in a month, he discovers some ominous emails. Jazz has been corresponding with a "Juan" through a dating site, and that single clue draws BJ and his significant other, Paul Barton, into the brutal but lucrative world of human trafficking.

Their trail leads to a mysterious Albuquerquean known only as Silver Wings, who protects the Bulgarian cartel that moves people—mostly the young and vulnerable—around the state to be sold into modern-day slavery, sexual and otherwise. Can BJ and Paul locate and expose Silver Wings without putting Jazz's life in jeopardy? Hell, can they do so without putting themselves at risk? People start dying as BJ, Paul, and Henry Secatero, Jazz's Navajo half-brother, get too close. To find the answer, bring down the ring, and save Jazz, they'll need to locate the place where human trafficking ties into the Navajo Nation and the gay underground.

www.dsppublications.com

THE
VOXLIGHTNER
SCANDAL

A BJ VINSON MYSTERY

DON TRAVIS